MW01153716

Advance Praise

Rose Stiffin displays uncanny insight into the human spirit. *Casino Blues* invites you to visit the characters, get to know them, see the intimacy of their tortured and varied lives. But, be careful, once there, you may not want to leave.

Michelle Howard-Vital, PhD
Blogger, Michellehowardvital-phd.com

Through exquisite narrative and intimate native knowledge of the Mississippi Delta, Stiffin takes us on a journey to terrifying places as we experience the full impact of the choices made by each member of a family as they try to pull together to face loss, sacrifice, murder, sadness, hopelessness, and the accidental if not miraculous act of a scared stranger that gave life a fighting chance. *Casino Blues* is a page turner, a tear jerker; it is a book one must read.

Alec Manzon

Stiffin delivers conflict. She presents real people, revealing the depth of their hurt and damage. She has once more created great characters in her latest novel, *Casino Blues*.

Robert McGee
Amazon best-selling author of *Justifiable Homicide*

Stiffin has marshaled all her skills as an artist and writer to present a modern-day drama of heartbreaking poignancy, exploring the redemptive power of love. This is the greatest gift Rose Stiffin offers in *Casino Blues* and her other critically acclaimed works of fiction: a compelling story with insights into our own lives and souls that entertains but also resonates in the memory long after the last page is read.

Wayne Christensen, MFA
Editor, *Imagine Magazine for Literature and the Arts*

I liked *Walk in Bethel.* I liked *Reflections* even better. Now, she's got another novel, *Casino Blues.* This woman just keeps improving.

Bobby Sherman

Author, *Am I the Only One That Signals?*

More Bull

They Don't Speak Spanish in Brasil

Casino Blues

A Novel

Rose Mary Stiffin, PhD

ISBN: 1545315116
ISBN 13: 9781545315118
Library of Congress Control Number: 2017905795
CreateSpace Independent Publishing Platform
North Charleston, South Carolina

Other Books by Rose Mary Stiffin

Walk in Bethel
(International Prize in General Fiction, 2015 and 2017)

Reflections

Groovin' on the Half Shell

A Winter Friend

Prologue

Falling in love with Angelo was probably the easiest thing Belinda Hardaway had ever done in her adult life. Meeting him four years ago was a true godsend, if you believed in kismet and that fate stuff. Belinda did not, but even she had to admit: Angelo came into her life at the right time, almost like someone—maybe God, who knew?—had directed him to her. Or her to him.

And he was so easy to love! Whoever that ex-wife was, that Gwen—she had fixed Angelo, fixed him to doubt himself, question his compassion and willingness to trust others. She loved him because he didn't know *he* could. His heart was broken, but she was determined to put it back together. Her glue would be her patience and kindness. She would help him heal, simply by listening, laughing...loving. She would tell him she understood his pain even if she did not always understand it.

He had pain. Sterility was that pain. He had told her six months ago—they were on the road to New Orleans, driving through the piney woods of Mississippi when he'd said that Gwen was pregnant again.

"Your ex-wife?" Why did she ask this? She knew very well who this woman was, who she was to him—had been to him.

"Baby number two." It was the hitch in his voice that alerted her, not the eighteen-wheeler that passed them by what seemed like millimeters on the twisting road.

"You aren't...Her being pregnant—that's important to you?"

His voice had the accent he had grown up with—flat vowels and hard consonants. In those short years of loving him, she had learned this was his "bewildered" voice. Other times, always, he spoke in the voice both were teased about—his "educated" voice, his *white* voice.

"It's not important to you?" That was the question, but his actual words that afternoon in the heat and sunshine and whir of the air cooling in the car were, "*Snot mpoi-tant* to you?" with a heavy attack on *you.*

He'd looked out the window and back at her, eyes white and black, polar opposites in color. "You c'n be with me, a man who won't ever—?"

Dropping parts of words, even saying "main" for *man.* Belinda's heart cracked.

Yet her response had nothing really to do with his anguish. "Was that a proposal?" She checked her breathing. "Because that sounded like a proposal."

She felt his large hand roam over her abdomen, to her thighs. She shifted until he could still touch her oh so thoroughly, and she could still maneuver the car.

"I won't ever be able to give you a baby." Proper speech back.

Even though the shoulder of the road was soft and the sky was darkening to a blind gray, she pulled over, cut the engine, and set the brake, all done methodically, efficiently.

"I kind of thought so." She had not, but the *idea* did come to her as they sat there, like a thunderbolt, she would think later. He was too upset over his cheating wife's motherhood. Further, they had discarded the practice of protection at *his* insistence. ("Look, we have the doctors' reports. I want to feel you feeling me.") So high schoolish, she had thought, not like the man she *knew* he was, but the more she did think…

"What?" His voice was a gunshot, an explosion, into the suddenly silent air.

"I said I figured you—there was a reason for your divorce." *Other than the fact that you both cheated left, right, and center.* She would not say those words.

She felt the smile fixed on her face. "It was the whole no-condom thing between us. And you probably never realized how much you talk about her and her kid. Her kids, I guess…And I don't know too many single men who argue *against* pregnancy-prevention methods."

For three minutes—Belinda watched the digital clock in the car—neither spoke. She leaned her head against the warmth of the window. She closed her eyes to the view: a cypress swamp, beautiful in its horror. The algae had turned the water into a silent, lumbering, green monster. They were close to Louisiana, soon to be crossing over into New Orleans.

Finally, Angelo spoke, a sliver of disbelief in his deep voice. "You think I'm in love with her?"

"I believe she hurt you, and I know you loved her." Belinda kept her voice at a neutral low.

"We've been divorced over three years." He glared ahead for a second, his brown eyes suddenly a dark umber. He looked at Belinda, and she could see the light back in his eyes, his face. "When I was married to Gwen, I wanted kids—no, that's not exactly true. I figured, if she got pregnant, it was OK...Then, she didn't. And then I discovered I'm sterile." He looked at Belinda, and she saw something in his eyes that truly startled her, a depth of love, a well of love that, if she fell in, would likely drown her. And she knew it was for her. How could she doubt what her eyes showed her, what her heart revealed to her?

"Then, I meet you, and now it's like, fuck, fuck, *fuck*."

Belinda was taken aback. Angelo was not some *boogie* man who was not in touch with his blackness. He kept his "race card" up to date. But he really was one of those men who saw cursing as a lack of a strong vocabulary.

"Excuse me?"

"I never saw my kids with Gwen."

Belinda was missing this train of Angelo's thought.

"Excuse me?" she repeated, more curious now than outraged earlier.

"My kids: what they might have looked like. You know, if we had a girl, would she have my chin and nose or Gwen's? Her hair or mine? That sort of thing."

"I—"

"But our kids, mine and yours, Bel, my daughter will have my chin and your eyes. Her hair will be coarse like mine but have your curl pattern. Her brother will be over six feet by the time he's fifteen—all legs and arms, thick brows, but not like that NBA guy Davis."

Belinda was not a sports fan, so she had no idea who this "NBA guy Davis" was, but she thought she understood: "With me, you could—can—could"—*he's sterile*, she reminded herself—"see our kids, envision them?"

His arms whipped around her like a snake from the swamp. "Every bit, without even a doubt." He began a finger walk across her face. "Your cheekbones, my mouth, but your teeth—that's the girl. And the boy, like I said, he'll be tall, skinny like I was." He sucked in his breath, said pompously, "Like I am."

By then, Belinda was laughing, happy in his arms, in his love. "Gotta be married to give me babies." She spoke as if the possibility still existed. "And just so you know, Mr. Higginbotham, I believe in that part of the vow, till death do us part.'"

"Yes?" He took her in his arms, pressed his lips over her open mouth, and breathed in her breath.

Belinda knew then that a million babies or an empty crib would never compare to this.

"Belinda Hardaway, will you marry me?"

The trip was just a getaway; they would share a room. Nothing new there. They knew each other's bodies, what pleased and provoked, what tempted and teased. Leaving Memphis, Belinda was sure neither had expected this turn of events.

"Yes!" She tried to think of more to say, but the simple affirmative was all that was really required anyway.

She wrapped a hand around his flesh, hard and welcoming. But he was more than a lover, a great lover. He was a man who had been left bereft and broken, one she had brought back to the light.

After a while—there were so many ways to pleasure each other in a car, on the side of the road, where kudzu covered an old house like an emerald monster, devouring it—Belinda started her car, heading still farther south to New Orleans. In Independence, she told Angelo about the boy who played Forrest Gump as a child.

"He was from Independence. That's how Tom Hanks got his accent down pat."

In the darkness, Belinda could imagine the sneer on Angelo's face; she clearly heard it in his voice. "Wouldn't say down *pat*, just acceptable. Anyway, so he was from Independence?"

Belinda looked into the sky at the full, fat moon, as white as marble. "He would say Tom Hanks's lines, and then Tom Hanks would repeat them."

Angelo laughed. "He didn't have a Mississippi accent; he had an Independence, Mississippi, accent!"

They laughed because they knew what Hollywood did not know: that there were eighty-two counties in Mississippi and who knew how many towns. They knew that people from the Mississippi Delta spoke nothing like the people from the eastern or the southern part of the state. Though both had left this state years ago, its roots were still in them. They knew what Hollywood did not know: that there was no homogeneity in the South. A Texan would rather die than be confused with a Virginian. And no one *not* from the Magnolia State *wanted* to be a Mississippian.

Belinda watched the road, but she watched that big moon also. She watched it until clouds swallowed it whole. What was that song? Or was it a saying? *Hang your dreams from the moon.* She was hanging hers this early evening on that big, round rock: that she and Angelo would remain as happy as they were now. She drove on, and after a while, she heard Angelo's rhythmic breathing. He was asleep. She took Interstate 12 to 190 South. She thought about their relationship, which led to his revelation, his sterility.

What cut her so deeply about his condition was not exactly that they could not—*probably* could not—become parents (*oh my God, oh my God, oh my God, we're engaged!*); it was more about Angelo himself. He was like that saying: *Some men are born great, and others have greatness thrust upon them.* Well, he, she had discovered over the few years they had been together, was born to be a father. At the park they frequented on weekends, the children were drawn to him, almost without regard to their age or their race. Teens, pants baggy and sagging, bumped knuckles with him. With a whisper, he could get them to at least tug their pants up to their slim buttocks, where they rode there, defying gravity but not dropping farther. Babies drooled all over his shoulder, and he accepted their slobber with a hearty laugh and a firm pat on their oftentimes smelly bottoms. *Yes*, she prayed (though not a praying woman), *let's be happy together.*

At the bridge, that long, famous bridge, she stopped her car. Though sleeping soundly for several minutes, the cessation of motion awakened Angelo. He sat up, alert. That was what Belinda had learned within the weeks of meeting him at that coffee shop: he slept deeply quickly. After making love, sweaty and sated, he could fall into a deep sleep and then wake up in minutes, raring to go again. Not a nap, he often told her of the dreams he had and was always surprised, when asked the time, that only minutes had passed.

She smiled softly over at him. He was not one of those men who rubbed his eyes, gathering his thoughts, clearing the wool from his brain. *There was never any wool on that brain of his*, she thought.

"I want you to drive us over." She was already opening her car door.

"Nervous?" he asked, scanning the traffic on the bridge ahead of them.

"A bit, maybe." *Not really*, thought Belinda. *I just want to watch you navigate our way over this bridge and that wide river.*

"Do you ever think about it?" She had told him of a friend from childhood whose family car had plunged into the river off this bridge. There was no saving them.

"Sometimes," she said, not lying, but the thought of the doomed family did not make her overly cautious about risk taking. She loved *him*, didn't she? Was willing and ready to marry him, wasn't she? This was her biggest emotional risk yet. "You?"

"Well, I didn't know them, Bel, but I choose not to let what happened to them affect my decision to drive across this bridge." He snapped his seat belt closed, started the car's engine. He gave her the smile that she thought was brighter than the stars. Or at least the moon hanging over them like a lamp.

"My wise man," she teased, feeling him grab her hand and bring it to the warmth of his thighs, the crux of them.

"Wise fiancé," he corrected.

Belinda settled into her seat, her hands mobile and nimble. She watched the darkness, the sky coloring the water, and the water reflecting it back. She looked out and saw only water, knew Angelo was now on the section of the twenty-four-mile-long bridge that, for several minutes, traversed only the mighty river, no land in sight. She thought their future would be like the mighty river: bright and shining. After all, her mother always said, God was still in the miracle-making business. And as her biology professor had cautioned those curious and ready girls, it takes only one sperm cell to make it to that one egg. Surely, surely, they could beat those odds?

Chapter 1

TRUDESSA "TRUDY" JENKINS got her name from her parents' combined names. It was not made up, like her friends La'Quandrelle's or Karlajia's names were. Her father was named Truman, and her dead mother was Odessa. She loved that her name was original, based on logic and love and not some idea of uniqueness that the mothers of her neighbors and friends—maybe the entire black population—thought was a way to embrace their African heritage. Hadn't her father said those silly names "marked" them as surely as their third-grade test scores gave businessmen the right to build more penitentiaries?

Trudy knew that aspect of her character alone would not gain her entry into any jail cell. But her lover could. She lay on her back and thought of her lover. She was not new to the ways of love: her mother's love, gone too soon from cancer when Trudy was ten; her father's drunken and sad love after his wife's withering away, always generous with his time and wisdom, his praise for her not too long ago, but never enough money to make their lives easy and fun even before her mom died; her brother's devoted, demanding, and delinquent love. She had loved them all. No, she still loved them all. *Still.*

This new love was what she lived for. Sometimes she felt she could die for it. Kill for it. She was six months into the relationship, this intense, mind-blowing, oh-my-*God* romance. As long as the life that shifted and pulled beneath her breasts.

Her mother was gone; her father a ghost of himself, and now Fat Boy. *They killed him like a dog in the street, Trudy. Oh Lord, my baby boy is* gone! Yet that call from his grandma didn't even stanch her feelings for this new love. Trudy could not respond to the woman's wailings, could not say, *It was because of me. And my lover.* I *may as well have killed him.*

No, she could not say that. Besides, the old lady was smart. She knew of Trudy's "case," knew of her grandson's business, and knew how dangerous the two could be. After all, her beloved grandson wasn't simply murdered—as if murder could ever be simple—but the killers had taken his "merchandise," all his cash, even that car he had taken such pride in.

"Word on the street, Trudy, is Zoe Pound is looking for you."

His granny knew about this gang, their thoroughness in the kill, the skill of it.

Trudy sat up abruptly. Her lover was calling her. And because the lover was so in tune to her needs, her emotions, there were no words spoken, no *need* for words. And unlike the people who were supposed to love her, never leave her, this new love was unconditional, understanding, and *always* there.

She knew her love affair with her lover was odd. If he were a man, she would say it was that May–December thing she'd seen in old movies. How many twenty-two-year-olds were into crack in this 'hood? Not many at all. Old men, veterans from wars before she was even a glimmer in her father's eyes, women who walked the streets, knelt in dark back alleys—those were her counterparts.

She sighed, felt the hunger that was both sweet and consuming. She had been without her love for ten hours and forty-one minutes. In the beginning, she could go days, weeks, even. Now, in these last days—her record was getting shorter, and shorter—was nine hours.

Back in Chicago, she had bragging rights with those old, broken people who shared their love for her lover on how long she could do without that love. But now she could feel its growing demands of her, her time.

She reached across the cot where her two children lay sleeping, bellies empty for the last six hours, felt under the flat, dank mattress for the coolness of the metal, the smooth wood. She cradled her lover in both her slender hands, breathed deeply, her heart already anticipating that rush it would give her.

She eased off the bed, examined her lover. At first, in those early months, he'd been made of glass. But glass could break (she recalled Fat Boy's shoe, grinding and twisting, his beautiful face contorted into hurt and rage), and heated glass could cause excruciating burns. This was made of polished metal and hardwood in a rich brown color, custom made for her by a guy she met in a head shop outside Saint Louis. It could not be crushed under the foot of a disappointed, hurting young man. And unlike that disappointed young man, that cancer-ridden woman, or the sad, lonely man, this love would never leave her.

She removed her stash from its hiding place—Matthew was too curious for his own good—and unwrapped it from the foil. She liked that word, for the aluminum foil served as a foil for her: secure, innocuous. Her own pops had no clue she was involved so deeply with her lover until he started missing money he knew he had or when an appliance that he knew worked went missing. When he knew without a doubt that she was with this lover, he forced her to watch the scene from *Jungle Fever* where the right reverend killed his older son.

I'll do the same to you, Trudy, I swear. When she had laughed at the (to her) ridiculous portrayals of crack addicts by Halle Berry and Samuel L. Jackson, when she denied that there was any danger to her, her kids, from that lover, she was exiled from his home.

"So you're telling me I can't even come visit you, bring your grandbabies?" Guilt had always worked in the past for her. For good measure, she had pushed Matthew into his arms.

Her father's voice had cracked. "I don't want to see my only daughter in a crack house, become a crack whore, performing fellatio on men for a few dollars!" He pronounced the words correctly, Trudy had noticed. He always spoke properly. And he taught her to speak the same way. BP (before the pipe), she had. AP (after the pipe), did it really matter to her connections if she said *head* or *fellatio*?

She left his house. Wouldn't say what he had to know already. *Been to the crack house, done that fellatio shtick, Daddy.*

She lit her pipe, moved into the next room, sank to the floor to enjoy the ride. The *crack-cracking* sound the drug made forced her to remember where it got its name. Her heart and mind now were in total sync. She could focus on the immediacy of her life, the sorry state of it. Fat Boy was dead. Her *baby daddy* had been killed. Both had hated that term, knowing that it did not come close to the feelings and commitment they had for each other, for their babies.

Still, in these flat towns on this flat land, she had no real job, no prospects of one, and no family she could count on.

"Trudy? You got to listen to me," his grandmother had pleaded with her. She had been so much more than a nice neighbor lady to her. She had been her grandma also, another person she had loved, still *loved.*

And Trudy had listened to the older woman because she had had her lover not an hour earlier and she could listen, even become angry, sob along with her, wail over their babies growing up fatherless, wish the gunmen into early graves, for them to suffer a fate much worse than her poor Fat Boy.

She could blame herself for her loss, their loss. She knew the dealer, knew Jean-Robert and his goons were trouble. Yet she'd left town knowing she'd stiffed him and that he would come looking for her at Fat Boy's place.

"Adrian told me about that *cousin* of yours." Trudy felt the bite of the word. "Is he still around?" The venom she spewed in that simple question could have felled an elephant. Trudy knew Adrian had talked to his granny about JW. "You have to come home. You got a job down there?"

Trudy chose not to answer.

That was three weeks ago.

After Trudy had left the doctor's office, she had taken her cell phone from her jeans' hip pocket and searched through the AroundMe app until she found TAXIS. She had learned early that in this town, there were no buses to take you here and there; you did not hail a cab.

She called the same cab company she'd used to get her to the doctor's downtown office. She gave the dispatcher her location and settled on a bench outside a clothing store. The urge to embrace her lover was so overpowering; she felt weak and unsteady. But that was one of the things confiscated during her arrest. Two days of tweaking: she could feel her blood moving through her veins; she was so desperate for that fix, that candy that would make all this—Fat Boy's death, her banishment from her father's place, her hungry babies—a foggy memory. She fingered the prescriptions.

That doctor had given her a list of contacts, *clientele*, he called them. At any rate, she would have enough bank to get her lover.

When he had asked about Matthew and Sasha, he'd gotten no response. But of course she knew their whereabouts. They were with the lady JW had found in the town—some distant relative of his who remembered him as a chubby toddler. They had not laid eyes on each other in twenty years. But family was family in the South—no matter what. He left Trudy with a few hundred bucks and had given his kin, a Mrs. Henry Anne Laster, some cash, too, to cover expenses, he said, so Trudy knew she would never see his fat ass again.

The cab came, and she climbed in, gave the driver Mrs. Laster's address. The driver had set herself out to be friendly. Trudy was still not used to this behavior: complete strangers deciding that they could talk to you about anything.

"Where you comin' from?" The woman wore her hair in unkempt braids that looked, to Trudy, like they were threaded with gold yarn.

Why not?

"Doctor's. I was caught carrying, and he and this judge worked out a deal for me." She knew not to reveal too much, but she wondered if the doctor's activities were a common secret in this town among the black people.

The driver gave her a frank look in the rearview mirror.

"You hangin' in there?"

Trudy did not think so, but she said nothing in response.

"It's aight. Least you look good, girl."

She proceeded to tell Trudy her name was Leonora and that her daughter was pregnant. Just like that.

"Yeah, I was hopin' she would be smarter than that. I'm gonna be a grandma at twenty-eight." She slammed on the brakes in frustration, throwing Trudy against the front seat. The car had only broken seat belts in the back.

"How old is your daughter?" The woman looked—what was that phrase?—*rode hard and put up wet.* She looked hard, not *old.*

"Thirteen."

Trudy said what had to be true: "A thirteen-year-old boy didn't do this to her." In Trudy's experience, that was one thing that had not changed: boys were boys until they became men.

The driver pumped the accelerator, speeding through a yellow light. "Hell if I know, but I doubt it, too."

Trudy had already done the math. "That means you had her when—"

"Yeah, when I was fourteen. Which is why I thought it would be different for her, that she would have learned somethin'."

Trudy had an image of Sasha at fourteen, belly rounded with some…rounder's baby. She couldn't really judge this woman. She herself was a teen mom. Yet she had never considered the phrases she'd heard growing up could ever apply to her: *The apple doesn't fall far from the tree. As the tree is bent, so it grows. What goes around comes around.*

She settled back in the seat and said nothing more and was relieved when the woman pulled into the driveway of Mrs. Laster's yellow, wooden-frame house. The house was a spacious, sagging building that in its day must have been the envy of the neighborhood. Mrs. Laster was much like her house, a fading beauty with plenty of charm and character.

The room Trudy rented was large enough to accommodate her and her children and their meager belongings, mostly a few outfits and worn sneakers.

They had been there a month when an old "client" of JW's, down from Detroit, had asked her to make a drop for her. Trudy couldn't resist the payoff she'd get after the delivery. She made three such drops; on the fourth, she had been arrested by an undercover cop. Two days later, she met the doctor.

When she stood before the judge, his kind voice fooled her completely.

"Why do you do this, Miss…Jenkins?" He consulted forms in his hand. "I'm sure you can get a job, a legitimate one that won't take you from your kids." He looked again at the papers and then back at her, his eyes dark with what she interpreted as southern, paternalistic kindness. She'd learned that most of the white men displayed this characteristic: the benevolent boss, *bwana.*

She thought of dismissing his question with a flippant answer: *Money. Crack. Money to buy crack. Why else?*

But she remained silent, which had saved her from prison. The judge was easily read. She pursed her lips, kept her head bowed until the last minute, and then raised her eyes to his.

He had asked her why she didn't have a job, had asked her what *jobs* she could do. In his chambers, she dealt with him, and then with that doctor in his office. She had her job.

She probably would have stayed with Mrs. Laster indefinitely had she been able to convince her that the acrid smell that permeated her backyard was from Trudy burning plastic bags from the neighborhood market.

Mrs. Laster was no fool. She gave Trudy a week to clear out, or she would call the law on her.

"I'm old, girl, but I haven't been stupid in a long time. I'm too old and too black to put up with your goings-on." Mrs. Laster was shaped like she must have been when she was courting the dead Mr. Laster. She had only widened: curvaceous hips and buxom. She planted her hands on those hips and took a stance.

"I'll keep those babies, not even a problem because what you're doing to your pitiful life has nothing to do with them. You can visit anytime."

Trudy's shock must have shown on her pretty face.

"Child, you can kill yourself on that crank"—Trudy almost burst out laughing but restrained herself, honestly believing Mrs. Laster could go up against a bear and win—"but what kind of Christian would I be to stand by and let you kill those babies right along with you?" She reached into her voluminous pockets on her not-so-voluminous, size-fourteen dress and pulled out a small wad of bills. She thrust them into Trudy's hand.

"Take it. Find you some place to stay." Then her old, pretty face became quite ugly with disgust at the sight before her. "But I know you're gonna go straight to one of those houses!"

Trudy thought of Fat Boy's granny's question from weeks ago about her having a job, her plea to return to Chicago for the funeral, return to family. Because she'd had her lover, she knew she had to see Fat Boy, gain some type of closure, see him to make this insanity make sense. Tell their babies. But, as always, her lover eventually left her, and she lied and said she did not have enough money, and could she send some—for the babies, for her great-grandchildren?

The money came the next day. Trudy pocketed the $250 from the Wells Fargo office and headed to find her lover. Even though she could probably walk the entire circumference of this town without breaking a sweat, it still surprised her that she could find her lover so easily among these people. Not exactly backward, she conceded, but they quickly deemed her, because they discovered she could figure out forms and wordy letters, that "smart girl from Chicago—the one with those cute babies, the one on *crack*."

She would not return to Chicago like her family wanted or use all the money as Mrs. Laster predicted. She would use some of her bounty to feed the babies, buy a few necessities, find a place to shelter herself and the kids for a few weeks, maybe. Mrs. Laster's brusque kindness—to her children, no longer to her—wouldn't last for too much longer.

The place she found probably wasn't the worst motel in Greenville. But, damn it, it might have come in a close second. One look at the "clientele" and she knew where she was—a place that catered to jobless alcoholics, crack addicts, whores of the worst kind, and their pimps. There was a dilapidated pool in the center of the square of rooms.

She couldn't swim, but when she and her brother were kids, her pops would drive them all the way up Maritime Drive to Lakeview Park, and they would walk along the thin strip of land, their feet hot from the dirty sand, their skin darkening to the color of chestnuts in minutes. The coolness of the water, the warmth of the sun, the happiness of those days, going waist deep in the water, shrieking at the top of her lungs as her naughty brother drenched her as soon as she dried off in the sun, she could not recreate them here.

She would not let her babies near this rusted-out pool.

"Let's get to know this little shit town." Trudy held tightly to Matthew's hand, and he, having learned the rules of being an older brother, held tightly to Sasha's as the three of them ambled along Main Street. They turned onto South Broadway, and Trudy took in the houses: some sturdy, others boarded up. She knew from being in this town these few weeks that the boarded-up ones offered many unnamed dangers. And crack.

"You got to do somethin' with those rug rats." The man might have been handsome once upon a time, Trudy thought. His skin was sucked dry, and he looked as hungry as an old wolf. "China!" He blocked the doorway until a girl appeared. Trudy saw in the dim light from the open door where the girl got the name. Her almond-shaped eyes and flat, broad cheeks spoke of Asian blood. Her coarse, straight hair and skin tone told Trudy she had black blood in her also. In fact, to Trudy, she looked like a brown Chinese woman. The clothes and missing teeth when she opened her mouth told Trudy this woman was a meth addict who relied on her exoticism to get the men to pay for her habit.

But Trudy was not there to judge looks. She handed over her children to this stranger as if she were handing over coupons at Walmart.

The house was black as night inside, windows boarded like the door, but the darkness—dense and touchable—was because someone had hung dark plastic sheeting along the walls. There were about ten people in the place. Trudy could not be sure because of that darkness. But she found the one she needed to find. He called himself LD.

Their exchange was brief.

How many?

How much?

If other businesses were conducted with such efficient alacrity, the entire economy would undergo a major paradigm shift.

She settled in a corner of one of the rooms. Someone had placed a small table lamp directly on the bare wood floor, removed the shade. The low-watt bulb gave off a hazy circle of yellow light. The shadows retreated from the weak light, which attracted the sins to it.

In another corner, a young man was lighting up, hands shaking with excitement as the small flame took hold. His features were blurred, but Trudy could see enough that he had straight, straw-colored hair, pale skin. He was dressed too neatly in a suit of indeterminate color. He smoked, crackled, and popped until there was nothing left.

Trudy thought he would leave as quietly as he had come in, but he sank to his haunches and waited. A few moments later, a burly black man, belly round and high, with a bald, bullet-shaped head, walked into the darkened room and went to occupy the space directly in front of the young white man. Trudy thought the man would stand, make some kind of monetary exchange, and leave. Instead, as if this were Christmas and he was getting the best present ever, he settled back from his haunches to his knees and unzipped the big black man's pants, took out a banana-size dick, and did what she'd seen Matthew do with the fruit. He gobbled it up to the hilt.

When she left the house, the evening sky had purpled to the color of an ugly bruise. China sat in a chair by the door. The street ran along the river, and from the abandoned house's vantage point, one could hear the barges, tugboats, and motorboats chug by.

"Warm out here," Trudy said for something to say. China, tall and rail thin, did not respond, barely acknowledged her as she stood.

"Headin' home, huh?" said LD, who probably owned this withered house, Trudy thought, as he lowered his pipe to China's full lips, and she opened her mouth, giving Trudy a flash of her ugly, terrible teeth.

"Right." Trudy extended her hands, and her children, like tiny robots, took them with no visible sign of pleasure.

China and the man closed their eyes, savoring the pull on the pipe. Both nodded to her, but it was the man who spoke. "Cool."

"Sure." Trudy swallowed hard, suddenly feeling alone in this place. In Chicago, she could control being alone, could handle it. BP, if she wanted to spend the day alone, in her own world of one, she could simply call up Fat Boy's granny, her pops, even her bratty baby brother to take the kids off her hands for the day. In this town, with JW off somewhere (she knew he was never coming back), she felt alienated, alone. She *was* alone.

She looked down at her two children, squeezed Matthew's brown hand, and he shot her a look only a child could give an adult—an adult you've learned not to trust, to suspect their true motives when receiving even the smallest overture of kindness.

She had told Matthew and Sasha nothing of Fat Boy's murder; she could not find the words. They loved him. Of course they did. They often asked his whereabouts.

Trudy knew, too, that Matthew could remember the times before, when he and Sasha sat on her father's lap, listened, enthralled, to his silly stories when he was sober, even when he was "in his cups." She knew Matthew remembered the parks, the walks, with him toddling beside her or held aloft on Fat Boy's strong shoulders, and her bumping along, cradling Sasha.

Then, she took up with this new lover. In no time at all, she overheard Matthew's advice to Sasha: *When Trudy has that pipe, stay away from her, and don't ask her anything.* Trudy refused to admit this, even to herself, but she had forced Matthew to grow up fast, his childhood filled with watching over her when she was high and watching over Sasha when she wasn't.

At the end of the corner, a tall young man stepped from the shadows, his hair a tamed state of Medusa-like snakes. Trudy had seldom been concerned about her safety back in Chicago. She knew the streets, knew the people who ran them, knew how to avoid those who meant trouble. Here in this river town, she knew no one. The kindest-seeming person could stab you in the back. The worst-looking addict could be her protector.

"I'm Shay." He extended his hand from a slim, long arm. "I've seen you 'round. People say you go by Trudy." His smile, Trudy saw, was thankfully whole, no broken, eroded stumps like the meth addicts she'd come to recognize. In fact, she considered, it was a very nice smile, going up to and crinkling his eyes.

"These your kids, too." Trudy noticed this was not a question. She supposed a single, obviously pregnant woman with two young kids trailing her like ducklings brought her a certain notoriety and definite visibility.

He said nothing more and fell into step with her. Though the stranger was silent, his lanky form hanging over her, Trudy felt no fear.

"Nice meeting you…Shay." Both said his name, she hesitantly and he as a reminder. Trudy dipped her bushy head at him, and it seemed to her that he took this as some kind of signal. *For what?*

If she were going to be killed by this person, maybe it would be now, tonight, after smoking and toking. She felt good enough to die now, with the shit the owner of the crack house had supplied. Since JW disappeared, and since meeting that doctor with his secret operations, she felt that every waking day could be ended with her cradling her children. And her lover.

Shay did not seem to be in the mood to kill anyone tonight. He started talking, rattling off names of the people who frequented that place, telling her whom to steer clear of, who was on the up-and-up, whom she should trust with her kids.

And Trudy listened, not only to this Shay's advice but to his actual voice.

"You're from Chicago, too!" She was smiling in the darkness, happy if only for the mere fact that, should she mention Washington Park, she wouldn't have to explain to those who thought they knew "Chi-town" that, no, this park is not the same one named for the late and former mayor Harold Washington.

Without warning, Shay scooped up Matthew and placed him on his shoulders, holding the boy's little legs firmly but (Trudy squinted in the darkness) gently.

"Yeah, been down here about a year. Got people here in Greenville, and I got a small place outside Leland."

Trudy had quickly learned that these two towns, small but deadly, were homes to famous people. Kermit the Frog's creator, the late Jim Henson, was from this Leland that Shay spoke of, just east of Greenville. Those two funny-looking brothers, the Winter brothers her Fat Boy listened to, had once resided in the town. She supposed that in the narrow streets, the low, ugly buildings, one could find it all: drugs, sex, and rock 'n' roll.

She gave her attention over to Shay, who seemed more interested in impressing her with his sudden southern lifestyle than taking her stash or getting sex from her.

The more they walked—he said he had no car himself but would be happy to walk them to her motel—the more comfortable Trudy became. And the sadder. She had a "job" of a sort, running the pills for the doctor and the judge. How long could that play out? She had no friends. So far, she had not had to resort to being a full-fledged skeezer. That had been the problem with Fat Boy: to him, her sucking *one* guy's stinking junk meant she was whoring for her habit.

She walked silently beside Shay, let him talk and talk while she thought and thought. They turned onto the street where the hotel was. All she had to look forward to, after putting her exhausted babies to sleep, was a long, solitary night. The television with its few channels and bad reception was hardly a companion. Even though she loved her lover, even that could be monotonous when there was no one there when the lover released her. To bring her down, to hold her up.

"Who the fuck is that?"

Trudy's eyes followed Shay's pointing finger to the guy she had seen every day since she'd moved into this hellhole.

The guy never talked to anyone, but he was always talking—to himself or rapping lyrics he listened to through his earbuds. His pants were so baggy and low that he walked like a duck. He gesticulated nonstop, wearing a vapid smile on his lips, with a gap between his teeth. His hair, thinning already, was gathered into haphazard plaits, too short and spiky to be considered braids or dreads.

She answered without thinking, without accepting or recognizing the irony. "Some crackhead."

At her door, as she struggled with the key, Shay placed Matthew on his feet. He had carried the child the whole of the way, offering more than one time to let him carry Sasha and let the boy walk, but Matthew loved his vantage point, and Sasha had cried that she did not like this man with the long hair who had what looked like little rings coming right out of his eyebrows.

"D'you want to come in, have—" If she were in a movie, on some sitcom, she would have said *drink* or *nightcap*. But she was a crack addict, and all she had to offer was either her lover, some poor-quality weed, or her body.

But she was silently stunned when Shay did not ask for a drink she did not have, a hit from her lover, or a puff from the bad weed. And not a go at her body.

He gave her son a high five, keeping his palm up, making the boy jump and giggle, giggle and jump, slapping his small hand against the long, slender-fingered paw of Shay's, who was laughing and encouraging the boy. *Jump, man; you gotta jump.* As for Sasha, he touched her hair, said it was like curly silk.

Trudy stared into his light-colored eyes, his handsomely plain brown face an open book.

His voice was clear. "You need me to walk you back there tomorrow, I'll be here by noon."

The next day, Trudy learned that he was true to his word. He stood outside her hotel room, his dreads hanging past his shoulders. He gave her a small smile and again fell into step with her. Though Sasha was still wary of this man, by then, Trudy saw, Matthew considered him as a friend, calling him "Shay" loudly and with confidence that he would be answered back.

Trudy told Shay a little of her "enterprise" for a couple of white men but never mentioned the doctor or the judge by name, yet he nodded as if in total understanding, explaining, "The white folks around here are into all sorts of illegal shit, but it's the niggas who's payin' for it."

They walked in the heat, with the children between them—almost, Trudy thought, like they were a family. She felt the weight of the baby beneath her ribs, and its movement reminded her that she had practically forgotten about Fat Boy. She had stopped thinking of him with the hunger and passion she felt back in Chicago (*BP*, Fat Boy's voice resounded in her head), but she could on occasion recall the sweetness in their lovemaking, the memories of their kisses. Over the last few weeks, her feelings for sex, for lovemaking, had become dormant, dead. Had she lost the capacity or the capability to love another man?

She looked up at Shay and tried to smile, to bolster enough feelings for him that she could use her body to thank him for his kindness. He grinned broadly at her, and when he asked her, very seriously, if she could twist her tongue (*See, like this*), she dismissed her misgivings.

At the house, Trudy did not give her children over to China. Shay informed her that, though he toked occasionally, crack just wasn't his thing.

She waited on his judgment of her, but he simply stood there, looking down at her with those unusual-colored eyes in that brown face.

"Get your candy; I got your kids, babe." At that word, Trudy stopped, confused. He had made no pass at her, had not touched her except in greeting by placing a hand on her shoulder. Was he Chester the Child Molester? Maybe he was into Adam and Steve, not Adam and Eve? Still, even with those questions weighing on her mind, she stepped right into the cave of the house and found the man who had her lover.

In the background, somewhere, Adele's "Someone Like You" was playing. The last time, Amy Winehouse's "Valerie" had been bouncing off the black walls. Wouldn't be ironic, she would have laughed to Fat Boy, if it were "Rehab" playing?

"Got no money today." She did, but she had tied it in a small pouch inside Sasha's panties. Who would think to look there?

Adele sang on about the comparisons, the cares.

"Bitch, you got somethin' better than cash. The fuck over here."

LD tasted of salted beef and smelled worse. But he was the only one she had to service, and he came in minutes, his penis hanging like a wrinkled, brown cucumber. She saw in a dim corner the same young white man, wearing a suit and looking anxious, as if his present, the one he had begged for all year long, was not among the gifts. His face lit up when a man, not the same pot-bellied man from before but a younger, thicker one, came and stood before him. Trudy was straight, but her fear was that one day, she might be tweaking, tweaking, tweaking so bad that her natural inclination toward men wouldn't matter anymore. Could she be gay for pay? But the look of sheer pleasure on the young white man's face told her: He was not getting paid to be gay. He was.

Trudy watched in the darkness as LD tossed her a square of foil. *Four rocks.* Silently, she laughed. She was that good at giving head?

She crab walked over into a corner, took out her lover, and lit up. *Damn, this is it*, she thought, sucking that pipe like she had sucked that man. She would have to space them out, smoke them *slowly*, two today, two tomorrow. Afterward, she...Well, she would think of something. She wasn't going to trade her body for her lover. She wasn't going to become that skeezer! She wasn't!

And Adele's words were true: nothing compared to this feeling!

Three hours later, Trudy emerged from the house into the sunlight, blinking like a mole. Her eyes were bulging and their pupils dilated. She was on top of the world in her happiness and wanted everyone to share her love for life!

She wrapped her arms around her children, hugging them tightly. Her sweat and stench caused her children to jerk away, Sasha with her nose actually crinkling like an old woman's. Trudy's lover had been so intense and strong, she had actually had an orgasm, the seat of her pants wet and sticky.

Shay stood by, staring into her face, smiling in a way that she instantly took exception to. She did not like his look of mockery, condescension. And he was asking her all these damn questions. What the fuck was his problem? Her being a single mom, doing a little candy, was none of his fucking business!

"What the fuck are you looking at, you punk-assed nigga!" Trudy's entire body went rigid, but to her it felt as if she were racing in place. Her mind soared; she felt as if her arms could lift her high above this place. Her heart pounded, and her hands were everywhere now, reaching, retreating to her sides, reaching. She wanted to throttle Shay. She was sure he had turned her kids against her. She saw how they looked at him—how they didn't look at *her*. In her paranoia, she thought he had taught them to despise her.

Her lips were crusted and dry from smoking crack; she smelled like fuck and suck. Matthew and Sasha were hungry, probably, because she hadn't fed them since she'd given them the leftover Happy Meal from Mickey D's over on MLK Boulevard that Shay had treated them to last night. But she convinced herself that none of this—how she looked, smelled, their hunger—had anything to do with their looks of confused disgust.

"*Det er greit*," he said soothingly, and at her angry then blank stare, he smiled down at her. "Hey, it's cool, Trudy. *We* cool." Shay draped his arm around her, but he did not draw her into an embrace.

His arms felt familiar, as if Fat Boy had returned. For the first time since she had left Fat Boy, Trudy felt a scrap of happiness. But she already knew this feeling would not last; she would choose her lover over this man, over any man.

Trudy could detect no anger from Shay at her outburst and insult. He talked almost nonstop, mostly about his theories on what the white man was doing to keep the black man down. Trudy had heard this all before, in one form or another, from one black man or another. She supposed there was some truth in his frenetic ramblings (he sounded like she did with her lover, she thought), but she knew no white man *made* her take up with her lover; no white man had *made* her suck off that man in the black house. She supposed all the white man had done was make crack available and affordable to her.

"I'll come by tomorrow, girl."

She was surprised to see they were at her door. He rummaged through her wristlet—pushing the pipe aside—until he found her key. He unlocked the rickety door, which he pointed out could be pushed in by any man with intention and a strong shoulder.

"Need to take care of *all* those babies of yours." He pointed to but did not touch her belly, distended now with neglect and lack of proper nutrition.

Once the door opened to the dark room, air like a dank cave, she thought he would ask, demand, beg. He did not touch her. At one time, she'd had no doubts of her physical beauty. Even now, she was still quite pretty, she knew without conceit. Was he so turned off by what she *did* to get her lover that he was turned off by *her*? No, her mind refused to wrap itself around such a ridiculous possibility.

He wants me, dammit. It would be just a matter of time before he played his hand.

"I'll be back tomorrow."

Trudy watched him—what would Fat Boy call the way he loped, skipped, and trotted?—*trundle* away, his dreads secured in a big ball of ropes at the back of his long neck.

"I might want tomorrow for me and my children." She knew this was not true. Her children fought too much for her to want to spend an entire day with them, alone. To her, they fought over nothing at all. They would cry, calling for

Fat Boy or her father or Fat Boy's granny. And their crying for anyone other than her, their own mother, would take her patience with them away in a snuff. She'd yell at them for their silly tears, screaming that if they kept up that—that caterwauling—she would put them out like cats on a doorstep, or she would leave them to fend for themselves, like kittens on a doorstep. But, of course, she never did. And never would.

"I can find you." He spoke decisively. Trudy told herself this was a promise, not a threat.

"All right." She raised her hand in farewell, undone. "Noon tomorrow, then."

That Friday, Shay showed up in a Mercedes. She was not an auto aficionado, but she knew the green sedan was from the E class. He told her it was a 1996 E320.

"Where'd you get it from?" Even thought it was old, it was in excellent condition. He hadn't stolen it, had he? His wide grin was amused, she saw. Was he laughing at her? Her voice thickened and hardened like cement.

He raised a conciliatory hand, silencing her curses. "Fuck no, I'm *not* laughing at you, and I did *not* steal that car. Old Jew in Greenville sold it to me for almost nothing." Trudy wondered if Shay's eyes flickered with something like a lie. But which part of his short story should she question? She did not pursue the matter.

Still, she was enchanted. His shy smile and darting eyes were all she needed to know that he had been working up to this moment. He needed something to prove to her that he…deserved her. Men were as simple as babies. Pet them, kiss their boo-boos. Feed their fragile egos.

Trudy invited him into her room, and she sat at the window, curtains pulled back to let in the rainy sunshine, and smoked the last of her lover. She looked at Shay standing at her threshold and smiled. His face was blank, she saw, so like the face her father presented to her, or like Fat Boy. But unlike them, his disapproval never left his lips, did not soar through the air like disappointed, lost blackbirds.

"Did you come down here to start a new life?" She knew so many did. The North was too small, and the South had all the space one needed to grow and spread out.

"Maybe I wanted a change of scenery." There was that odd glint in those eyes again. Was he lying? Did he have secrets that, if outed, could lead to his own downfall? She knew there was more to this story, but once more she held her tongue.

He looked across the room at the bed. It was a rickety affair whose frame bounced against the floor whenever Trudy got in or out of it.

"How're my best pals?" Shay asked, walking over to the bed.

Her children were still fighting sleep and gnawing their lips in hunger.

"I'm gonna get them some breakfast. I have to get them some food."

"No shit?" His voice dripped sarcasm. True, the children were in need of solid, healthy food. Since the time she'd taken the children from Mrs. Laster's neighbor when that old lady was on some errand, her kids had not had three squares in days.

"I'll take them to McDonald's. Maybe another Happy Meal." She had that much money to spare.

"I'm taking you all with me. Shit, I can't believe somebody hasn't been shot before this!"

He had arrived minutes before the police cruisers wailed their presence on the grounds of the hotel. A small crowd was gathering around one of the rooms, its door now a gaping black hole that seemed to spill people from it or was engulfing them.

The victim, Trudy learned from the hooker in the next room, was the tranny who went by Edwina but who was probably born Edwin, the man with the beautifully tailored pantsuits and dyed-red pageboy haircut.

"Went to check on him—her—and found her with her brains blown out." The Indian woman who ran the hotel for some obscure relative sucked on the thick wad of khat that had turned her rotting teeth red and disfigured her mouth. The prostitute puffed on a Black and Mild, her thin robe rising like a curtain, revealing an expanse of thighs and no underwear.

The presence of the police was enough for him, Shay told Trudy. The dead man whom he had seen a time or two and had assumed was a down-on-her-luck woman and this old whore simply added to his resolve for them to leave with him.

Yet Trudy balked at his high-handed behavior. "I have to get my kids together, get out stuff." She had very little "stuff" to get together, but she stood her ground. She saw his willingness to help her as a way to control her. She could not give her strength over to anyone—anyone *else*. Her lover had all her strength and power.

Shay gave the hooker a disgusted look. "Then fucking go get your stuff together." He turned his back on the hooker and the red-toothed Indian woman, on Trudy also.

Trudy inhaled, the stale air filling her lungs, reviving her. She clapped her hands, claiming the attention of her drowsy children.

I have a friend.

"Come on, Matthew, Sasha; Shay's waiting for us."

Chapter 2

WAS THERE EVER an easy way to tell a man he was sterile? That, for *some* reason (*We did a battery of tests, Mr. Higginbotham, but sometimes, there are still mysteries we can't solve*), Angelo Higginbotham had slow swimmers and dead *things* among the slow swimmers; that, yes, more than likely, he would never father a child *naturally.*

Sitting there, a bit stunned, very angry, he suddenly thought of his life. That life was his old life, as if he were looking back into a tunnel or through a glass darkly.

Gwen stood at the sink (not washing dishes: he had bought her that Whirlpool, after all). The memory expanded. She was drinking her morning coffee. There were red flowers in a pot behind her on the windowsill. *What were they?* He liked to think they were a type of daisy, but he didn't know flowers.

"I guess you're wondering where I was last night." Her eyes, that strange olive-green color that no black person should possess yet she did, held his without falter.

He admired that. Always had. What strength they reflected, what chutzpah.

What was she saying?

"What're you talking about? Wasn't your father sick?" After all, when he had called the old man, he had heard the cancer in his voice. He had talked to her, heard the grief in hers.

I'm staying with Papa-Dee. Just want to make sure he takes his meds.

"He's fine," she was saying into the vortex Angelo found himself in. "I left him as soon as he fell asleep, around ten thirty."

Angelo knew his father-in-law, Deland Teasley, was on a morphine drip for the pain, for the cancer that was eating away at his lungs. The man had smoked two packs of Camels a day for over thirty years.

But what Angelo processed was, "You left your own father, when he was sick in bed, when he could have—"

"I'm pregnant."

Angelo's lips were parted, his mouth frozen. If he had seen his reflection in the mirror, he would have thought, *What an idiot.*

His happiness at the thought of being a father immobilized his body and his brain. He stared mutely at her, the smile creeping into his lips, his unblinking eyes.

His arm shot out to embrace her. But at that tiny change in those odd green eyes, he wondered if he should strike her. There was something—

Her laughter shook him alive again. "Angelo, you oughta know by now that this *can't* be your baby I'm carrying." Her laugh, that hissing *chu-chu* through clenched teeth, told him she was *not* amused.

"For the last year, I've made sure that we make love when I'm ovulating."

Here, Angelo's memory must have self-corrected. She never said *made love* or even *had sex*. No, she would have said *sexed each other* or *fucked.*

"What're you saying, Gwendolyn?" His mind said harshly, *She's saying you're the one fucked.* His outstretched arm snaked back to his side as if on a string.

Gwendolyn drained the coffee from the mug in one long swallow. Her joke when they were dating was that it was the polite thing to do—swallow.

"You can't get me pregnant." Her voice became accusatory, as if whatever marital sin she was admitting to was his fault.

If he were in a court of law, he would have sworn there was someone else in that kitchen, on that bright Saturday morning in April, with those unidentifiable red flowers in the window. But this would have been an insane defense. Yes, temporary insanity. There was no way, even now, hearing the doctor's conclusions, to abandon his guilt. There was no manly way he could disown it. All he could remember, after hearing those words, was Gwen's hand to her cheek, crumpled to the floor on her knees, and his handprint forming like a stain against her skin.

But if one thing could be said about Angelo Higginbotham, he was as stubborn as the southern days were long. And they were long. After hearing this pronouncement, he went for a second opinion.

"If you could roll your sleeve up, please."

Dr. Cleveland adjusted his wireless spectacles as Angelo acquiesced.

"Thought you could take a person's blood pressure without rolling up your sleeves." Angelo did not know this urologist. He had been recommended by the first one because it seemed best if Angelo, who was so sure the first diagnosis was wrong, got that second opinion.

"Yes, but why put any uncertainties into the equation?" the doctor asked rhetorically.

Although his surname suggested British ancestry, ordinary Anglo-Saxon roots, his white-blond hair; sharp, wide cheekbones; and pale blue eyes gave him a definite Slavic countenance. His voice, however, placed him from across the River in Arkansas.

Dr. Cleveland wore his white lab jacket, but it hung open, revealing a light blue shirt with square tails untucked over a pair of loose-fitting navy twill trousers. His shoes, though ugly loafers in a muddy brown, were clearly expensive and made for comfort. Sitting there, his hands hanging between his thighs, ready to talk, to listen, if necessary, he looked, to Angelo, like the most relaxed of men.

"OK, you're good," said the doctor as the instrument began to deflate the tightness on Angelo's upper arm. He motioned for Angelo to adjust his sleeve.

"Doctor?" Angelo was usually a *patient* patient, pun intended, he thought, but he felt this man held his future in his hands. And was not letting go.

"BP is 128 over 76. Lab work, good also. Kidneys, electrolytes. A little—"

"Doctor, can I have kids or not?" Angelo's voice was a loud scrape on concrete.

The man had poked and prodded. Taken blood, semen, and his piss. Now he seemed intent on making idle conversation.

No, Dr. Cleveland said, *you're not what we call* sterile, *Mr. Higginbotham, but I do concur with what the previous doctor said: there is very little chance you can—or could have fathered a child in the last three years* (the length of his cheating-filled marriage to Gwendolyn).

Was a third opinion really necessary? he wondered as he went for that third opinion. The compassionate male nurse asked the same question as soon as the doctor left the room.

"I should have had such luck, man." In his youth, he told Angelo, he had sown his seeds, as he thought he should. Now three women with seven children hounded him monthly. What with child support, court-ordered deductions from his checks, judging judges, and three creatively vindictive women, he could barely take care of himself, let alone his own kids.

"How old is your oldest?" Angelo asked for something to say.

"Gosh, that boy's gotta be…twenty-nine." He straightened the tray that held Angelo's blood, his urine. The semen was already stored someplace cold. Earlier, he had been directed to a room with a cup and told there were *videos and magazines, if you need them.*

Angelo's eyes widened in disbelief. "What?" The man looked forty if he looked a day.

"Yeah, I was fourteen."

Angelo could only stare. At fourteen, he had experimented. With *his* hands, no one else's. At fourteen, girls were just tits and asses to him, to gawk at and tease. If he were lucky, a rub up against a backside. He had heard the mechanics of lovemaking being discussed by his older brother and cousins, but he suspected even they, at sixteen, seventeen, were more talk than action. Yet this man had fathered a child at that age!

"So, was this like playing around that got out of hand?" Though he couldn't imagine how impregnating a fourteen-year-old girl could be considered by his parents as *playing around.* They would still be beating his behind. But Angelo thought he understood. The nurse shook his nicely shaped head.

"No, man, that lady was thirty!" He kept talking, ignoring Angelo's eyes bulging in shock. "See, I had to help around the house, and one chore I had every Saturday was taking the clothes to the wash house"—*wash house*, Angelo wondered—"to dry 'em. That's where I met her."

His face and voice went soft. "She'd talk to me, really talk to me. Before long, she was waiting around the neighborhood for me. She took me to her place." He shook his head, in remembrance, Angelo guessed.

"I know you're thinking it was like child abuse"—*no, more like* molestation, Angelo silently corrected—"but wouldn't I feel like it?"

Angelo raised his fingers from his lap, gave a shake to his head, a gesture meant to indicate that he had no comment or opinion.

"Yeah, so, she told me what to do, and before I knew it, man, I was *inside* her." He said the word as if he were able to walk around in the woman's body, examine all the parts invisible to anyone else.

"I didn't know the fuck to do."

Both men gave bemused laughter, Angelo remembering his own initiation into that glorious world of sexual pleasure with a real woman and not his own hands.

"She kept telling me, 'Do it harder, harder!' And, man, I'm just pumping away. Lord, that first time!" He gave a resigned but satisfied sigh. "She had that baby just before I turned fifteen."

Briefly Angelo forgot his own troubles and his reason for even being in the nurse's presence. "She was *thirty*. You were *fourteen*. Didn't your parents say something, *do* something? Hell, no matter how you felt, she knew you were a kid. That's child abuse."

The man grinned sheepishly; he was having none of this.

"My pops was mad as hell, but my mama, nah, she was cool with it. You'd think it would be opposite, right?"

Angelo said yes, of course.

"He—the baby, my baby—was the first grandchild."

"But not their last?" Angelo couldn't resist the jab.

"No…Hell, she taught me too well, and, after she moved on, you could say I developed a taste for that." He leveled a look at Angelo. "Hate to say this, considering why you're here and all, but I almost don't feel sorry for you. You want a child or two, you can damn well have a couple of mine!"

Again, both men laughed, the way men who are strangers do: spectators at a game, rooting for the same team; in a bar, ogling the same woman; as brothers sharing some inside, family joke. But it was Angelo who sobered first. After all, really, there was not a damn thing funny.

By that third opinion, Angelo knew with certainty that his ex-wife Gwendolyn wasn't exactly lying when she said part of the reason—*part* of the reason, Angelo concentrated on—she had cheated on him and then left him was the fact that she wanted kids and he didn't seem capable of giving them to her.

As if they were flowers he could buy, candy he could offer, that she didn't *need* but wanted anyway.

Now he was thirty-one, newly divorced, and shattered by a fact that should never have been. He had no genes to pass on—well, he had genes, of course he did, but they weren't in those small cells that in high school he was admonished to save until marriage or at least not share with a girl's eggs. And he had made sure he never did—a virgin until he was twenty, then a condom all the time. Every single time.

Of course, except for the necessary ability to protect him from some possible *social* disease, at some point, they had become totally unnecessary. Adding to his, not exactly misery but certainly not *joy*, whatever this feeling was—Gwendolyn was heavily pregnant, her once perfect dancer's body now plump and blooming, giving those who knew them *when* an all-too-revealing look into the probable *why* of their failed marriage. She was living in Cordova, he knew, with the latest man she had cheated with. Nothing wrong with *her* machinery.

For the first time in his adult life, he wondered about his innate goodness. He was not perfect. Not by a long shot. But he was what used to be called a good guy. But he didn't want to be good. He wanted to be good *and* happy. Were those qualities mutually exclusive?

Newly single, he went to his favorite bar. But after four shots, he knew the drink would not do it. He knew the blunt the woman next to him surreptitiously offered him would not do it. He'd given that useless drug up years ago. All it did to him was leave him flaccid and paranoid. Who needed that?

Then he got to worrying. If he wasn't thinking about his blank-shooting scrotum, then he was worrying over the cause of his sterility. And if he wasn't cursing the tight jeans that must have been in fashion once upon a time, maybe the innocuous infection he ignored—who knew?—then he was bemoaning the fact that Gwendolyn had had the boy that should have been his. Which led his tortured thoughts right back to his blank-shooting scrotum, and no way the bartender, with his offerings, could help him forget.

He wasn't by nature a worrier; nor was he given to bouts of depression. Well, not before this news, at any rate. So, to ease his mind, he tried to think of his rather pathetic love life.

Her name was Tabitha, named for *that* Tabitha, she proudly announced to him on their first meeting, and he had to stifle his laugh. *Really*? And he gave up, snickered when she said her mother was named Samantha. Well, he said, that's really something. And she, too self-involved to get the snicker, said, *Wasn't it?* and rubbed his crotch to ask if he wanted to see a movie or go to the park. He said either one was OK, knowing that he would get some action.

But thinking of Tabitha, tall, raw-boned, with thighs strong enough to break in an ox, gave him no comfort. She was an easy girlfriend, mainly because, if both were perfectly honest, she was a one-night stand that had lasted for the last two months. They were each other's FBs, even though both chose to call these poorly disguised booty calls a blossoming relationship.

Lately, their being together had changed. Or maybe she had changed. She had never stated she wanted more from him. In fact, lately she was stating nothing.

Their times together lately, even he had to admit, hardly set the world afire with passion: television, a glass of wine or two. She often served or he brought, at her insistence, a red, based, he supposed, on the wines' names: *Ménage à trois, Toro Loco,* or *Freixenet.* After what had become a strained conversation between them, he would make the gentle suggestion that they go to bed. Good sex—really good sex. But after it was over, he invariably slept and she went to watch television until he awoke to do his leave taking.

He seldom spent the night, and she, likewise, seldom asked this of him. Yes, something was definitely in the air. Without evidence, he decided that Tabitha was preparing for their eventual separation. He would do with her what he had learned to do best when married to Gwen: wait and see.

Well, he waited and he eventually saw. Three months and no texts, no calls, no e-mails, nor FaceTime. And her status on Facebook told the tale: her new status was definitely *single.*

Today, he sat at a small table in his favorite coffee shop in Memphis's Midtown, Café Eclectic. Of the three chains scattered across the city, he enjoyed the Midtown locale the best. On warm, clear days, like this one, he often opted for outside seating at the small, comfortable tables with their red awnings. Facing McLean, he would eat his meal and people watch.

He liked the waitstaff also. He came so often, he was generally recognized by the hostess and waitresses. They liked him because he charmed them, not by flirting or giving them empty compliments but by remembering their names and any snippet of information he may have gleaned from previous visits.

His waitress today was a stranger to him: young enough to be pretty even when you're not pretty, a fresh-faced blond girl who gave him a hundred-watt smile as she pushed her hip out and placed her pen to paper to take his order.

"And you are?" He never consulted the menu. He ordered the same meal whenever he came. Rather than thinking himself predictable, he simply told himself that the food was perfectly prepared, perfectly seasoned, and always well presented. He ordered his favorite snack/meal, an Americano and the bacon-and-cheddar scone. Both tasted as he imagined heaven must look like, and usually he enjoyed the hell out of them, knowing that he would hit the gym that afternoon anyway to burn off the carbs and fat from the scone.

"I'm your server, today. Call me Gypsy."

He turned his smile upon her. "Call you that, or is that your name?" She certainly did not look like a gypsy, at least, not as television and his own thoughts dictated. She was blond, tallish, slim, with pale skin.

Her smile matched his, and he felt comfortable with her. No flirting—the girl was all of twenty-one and, oh, yes, *white.*

"My name." She exhaled a breath that Angelo got a whiff of: old coffee and vanilla. "My dad named me." She pointed to the badge.

"Well, Gypsy," he lied in a friendly way, "you were rightly named."

"You don't have to flatter me, Mr. Higginbotham." *She knows my name*, he thought, pleasantly surprised.

She gave him that smile.

"What?"

"Never mind."

He was intrigued. "Gypsy," he sounded like a father, her father. *You will answer me, young lady.*

"That's how I know you. By your order. They call it the *Higginbotham*...behind your back," she said apologetically.

"Because I always order it?"

She shrugged. Other patrons were staring at her, but she was ignoring them. He loved her for this.

He leaned on his elbow. "Since you have me at a disadvantage, what else do you do, Gypsy?" Certainly she couldn't be a full-time waitress. *What a waste that would be*, he thought, surprised that he meant this.

She gave him that happy-little-girl smile. "I've got two semesters before I get my master's in counseling: marriage, couples, family." She did a childish thing, crossing her fingers in hope and luck.

She glanced at his left hand, saw the faded band of skin. Her eyes sobered, and the smile disappeared.

He saw her looking and placed his hand in his lap.

"You know, Gypsy, you're going to be a great counselor." He wasn't sure if he was being sincere or not. He simply wanted that smile back.

"That's the nicest thing I've heard all day!" He was pleased that she didn't lie and say *all my life*.

"I'm serious. You've got a spirit, an aura…" He discovered he was no longer flattering her but speaking quite sincerely to her. "You're going to be great." Of course, it was too late for her to save his molded marriage to Gwen or his rusted-out thing with Tabitha.

She tapped the pencil to her empty pad. "Your food will be out soon, Mr. Higginbotham." She skipped over to the other table, and he sat there, a dim smile on his face, waiting because he did that very well.

But when his food arrived, he ate slowly, sullenly, his mind drifting back to his earlier thoughts. He could not allow himself to cry, but dammit if he didn't want to! He knew his life was not over. He had a great job at the utility plant down on Viscount. It paid very well, and when he finished his master's, he knew his salary would increase. He supposed his life was *stalled*.

Gwendolyn hadn't stayed for the "finer things" he could eventually provide. She hadn't stayed out of a sense of guilt or loyalty. Certainly not love. No, she'd left to have the life she suspected he could not give her. And her suspicions from over a year ago had been proven right three times by three different urologists in less than three months.

Angelo nibbled on the scone, sipped his coffee. He hadn't asked for a double shot of espresso, but he felt his heart thumping as if they had sneaked it in. He had to *get a grip*, as the interns at the plant said. This couldn't be the worst news he had ever received. Could it? His parents were alive, healthy. And to be black, of a *certain age*, and not diabetic, hypertensive, or cancer-riddled—they were miracles. His three younger siblings were gainfully employed, if not wealthy. (They didn't borrow money from him.) Up until today, he would have ended this litany with *he had his health.*

He supposed he did have his health; certainly, his *sterility* was asymptomatic. No stranger would look away from him, embarrassed that they had their quality of life and he did not. No friends would shake their heads and sigh. *Poor Angelo*, they would not say, because there was nothing they could see missing in him, on him.

The managers of the bistro had heeded their customers' suggestion about being able to listen to music while they drank the Cinnful Jims or Karamel Sutras or ate the delicious omelets or specialty sandwiches. They had music piped throughout the restaurant, inside and out. This afternoon, it did not surprise Angelo that country and blues music, staples of the mid-South, played alternately over the speakers as clear as if the singers were sitting on stools right before the diners, strumming their guitars or twiddling their fiddles.

The song blasting now was a favorite of his father's, an old, solid blues number by a guy with whom his maternal grandfather claimed kinship: Milton Campbell. "Casino Blues" was not his favorite song by the late bluesman. It rang too close to home. The man depicted in the song was almost at his lowest point. Despite his system of winning, he had lost the money to pay all his bills and was even considering asking for an improbable loan or, worse yet, stealing from his wife, pawning his wedding ring, and going so low as to break open his son's piggy bank! Yet the man still claimed, upon finally winning, that he had no gambling problems. He was fine. Denial: an emotion Angelo was definitely familiar with.

He swallowed the last of the scone, promising himself a vigorous workout to sweat away that coppery tang in his mouth that tasted less like coffee or bacon and more like fear mingled with sadness. Dejection.

He drained his cup just as he felt a hand on his shoulder and his name being called, hesitantly, as if the speaker were unsure if she—yes, it was a woman's voice—had the right person.

"Angelo? Angelo Higginbotham?"

He turned to stare into brightly shining, dark-brown eyes set deeply in an oval face of the richest caramel color he'd ever seen. He stood because she was standing over him and it felt odd to sit while a woman stood. He extended a large hand, shook the one that was already extended toward him.

"That's right..." He smiled down at her, having no clue who this woman was, but she did look familiar, like he'd seen her several times but never engaged her in conversation. *Where*?

"Oh, I don't expect you to remember me," the stranger said with a friendly chuckle, reading his face. "It's been a while. We went to Valley together."

Angelo felt his facial muscles move. He was smiling. *Valley*, not what people who did not attend the university called it, who were not from Mississippi called it: Mississippi Valley State University or MVSU. *Valley*. Or *Valley State*. That reference placed her, not only as a graduate of his alma mater but a Mississippian to boot. A *homegirl*.

"I'm Belinda Hardaway. We took some classes together, and I think you graduated a year before I did?" She named a year, and he found himself nodding, smiling still.

He felt that he should engage her in conversation, so he offered her a seat at his table, and they sat. He ordered another coffee and asked what she was having.

"Any flavored iced tea," she said, her pretty face wreathed in smiles. Yes, she was pretty, he decided, trying not to compare her looks to Gwen's. Before her belly swelled with that man's bastard, Gwendolyn looked exactly like what she had once aimed to be: one of *those* girls in *those* types of hip-hop videos.

"I thought you looked familiar. Yeah, psychology and sociology, right?"

The woman nodded, her eyes staying in his. He realized she was acknowledging her (great?) luck in meeting him.

"Among others. Mostly those gen. ed. courses for the core..." Her frankly appraising eyes reminded him of what he hadn't thought about in a while: that he was *attractive*—tall, well built, good-looking in the "You look like a guy who looks like..." way, and the man would be some handsome black movie star, athlete, or entertainer.

He was trying to think of things to talk about. Since they were not friends back in Itta Bena, he could not bring up "What ever happened to so-and-so" questions. He watched her full lips sip the tea; she liked flavored tea but not a lot of add-ons—no special Eastern spices. Black-cherry-passion-fruit blend, one packet of raw sugar.

He needn't have worried about "making conversation." This stranger, this Belinda Hardaway, talked breathlessly, breezily, about the weather (hot and humid, but what was newsworthy about that?), her love of Midtown versus East or North Memphis (*Oh, you, too*, he'd asked, pleased that they had this in common, for he loved the area, too), her job (something to do with STEM or education or maybe both; he wasn't sure), and wasn't it a shame about what happened to the youth slain in Whitehaven last week. (He hadn't heard about any youth being slain down in Whitehaven, but he nodded and murmured sympathetically and let her talk, liking her voice.)

As she talked, Angelo played with his ring finger, a pale band of flesh marking what once was. If this Belinda Hardaway took notice, she said nothing. Her own ring finger had a ring on it with a large green stone. (He very much doubted it could be a real emerald, but it was not an engagement ring or wedding band.) In fact, several of her slim fingers sported rings. Costume jewelry, pretty, he supposed, but probably worth very little.

Angelo had never considered himself to be a vain man. But his lack of vanity had more to do with his total dependence on Gwendolyn for her view of his attraction than his own beaten-down view. Yet, as he listened to Belinda's happy nattering, it became important to him that she did find him attractive. So Angelo arranged a smile on his face that, in his unfamiliar vanity, he hoped would keep her looking at him the way she was right now.

She took a deep breath, letting her nice bosom swell (very nice, Angelo thought in surprise), and sipped the last of her tea. Before he knew this gesture signaled a change in the thread of the monologue/conversation, her warm hand had landed on his cool wrist. "So, tell me what's happening in *your* life, Angelo?"

Chapter 3

Dr. Henry "Buck" Bowden would not demand head from the dykes anymore. Especially the nigger ones. For one thing, looking down on their heads, short hair, nappy hair, if it was a nigger one, it looked as if a man were going down on him. Since he didn't *roll* that way, he saw no need to fake it with those butch bitches. Besides, the last time (two years ago?), a lesbo had sunk to her knees, raised her work-roughened hand to him, and—well, had he closed his eyes, he never would have seen those sharp teeth, those claws.

He smiled to himself at the memory, his glacial blue eyes trained on his diplomas, certificates, and licenses that crowded one wall of his spacious office. Her good behavior for a five-year stint meant early release, which necessitated his friend Barry Calhoun's intervention. Barry was the circuit court judge in the district. She'd been referred to him by Barry for a routine physical checkup, a practice both men had established over fifteen years ago. Which necessitated her coming to *his* office. He was sure Barry had already "interviewed" her. Hell, truth be told, he suspected Barry occasionally didn't mind the homos. A mouth was a mouth and a hole—well, for Barry, a hole was a hole.

That lesbo had been in chronic pain from a debilitating fall a year earlier while working in the kitchen at the penitentiary. At least that was what the records showed once he'd written up the prescription for OxyContin.

Since he'd started practicing medicine twenty-four years ago, he'd offered his services first to Parchman and then, later, farther north, to the facility in Tutwiler. He would set broken joints, refer cancer-ridden patients who would have been in hospice anywhere else to medical care facilities, prescribe drugs to ease pain. In those early years, his services were free. He was building his reputation, after all. What he did was almost inconsequential—a boon, he thought. But times changed. *He* changed.

His smile grew malicious. His free medical services for these criminals eventually came with a price—for some of the women, at any rate.

By the time he was through with that one, she *did* need those pain pills. He'd called Barry over, who had arranged for her to be transported back to the Tallahatchie County Correctional Facility in Tutwiler. As judge, he had the power to revoke her release.

The bruises and contusions, Barry's report read, were indicative of some prison altercation and her recalcitrant behavior. No early release would be granted. She was picked up the next morning from county jail.

But not before both enjoyed her again—plentifully and, he supposed, to her, once Barry got her again (neither of whom would ever speak of it), painfully.

Now, Buck was sitting comfortably behind his desk, looking at his latest potential patient. She was a pretty thing, curly hair, not nappy or kinky, and thankfully, her bronze-tone skin, though obviously bespeaking her as a nigger wench, was not that repulsive darkness Barry had told him that he *must* loathe.

"Judge Calhoun provided me with the details of your arrest." He stared at her belly, her thin T-shirt straining against the roundness. She had to be six months pregnant. He tapped his pen against her file: arrested for dealing for some lowlife, probably out of Chicago or Detroit or New York. But where was that person? He'd (yes, Buck thought, it was always a *he* who led these women astray) left her, evading arrest himself. Buck wanted that man here now. He would beat him soundly about the head and shoulders.

Be a goddamn man, he would have screamed to him. *Don't let this pretty little girl suffer for your ignorant mistakes!* He checked himself. He was in charge, like Barry was, Barry, who never second-guessed his decisions or apologized for his thoughts or actions.

What was it he always said? "I'll try anything once and say anything twice." Buck chuckled to himself. *That Barry—what a character.*

He glanced up at the girl, almost as if he had forgotten she was there. But she *was* there, awaiting his instructions. Maybe he should talk to her, *tell* her this lifestyle was—he caught himself again.

Who the hell cares?

She was caught with pot, pills, crack, even some heroin, all for distribution, based on the amount on her person. She herself had tested positive for crack at the time of arrest.

A crack whore: he knew they would do anything to get that pipe. His eyes traveled over her. She was slim but not that emaciated gauntness that meant she had been on it for years. Probably considered herself to be a "recreational smoker," skin still pretty, clear, and smooth. She didn't have that nervous, bug-eyed twitching he'd seen over the years. Like a slow-growing parasitic infection, these crack addicts were in the Mississippi Delta, he thought. In *his* Delta.

He placed his left hand in his lap, stroked his crotch. He had not so much as touched a woman in six months. And she *was* fetching.

"You know why you're here, right?" He didn't bother to wait for an answer. "Judge Calhoun wants me to make sure you don't harm that baby anymore."

His fingers fairly hummed as their speed increased on his hardening flesh. His eyes fastened on her lips. "He said if you can promise that, he might make it easier for you."

He stood, all six feet two inches, 210 pounds of him. He was one of the few Deltans who jogged every day, across the flatlands in the country. He was fifty, but he knew he looked years younger. Except for his balding head—which he decided three months ago simply to shave, the little blond hair that was left—he could easily pass for forty-five or even younger most times. This chippie was maybe twenty, twenty-one. These niggers carried their age well, and she was no exception. He took in her skin, her head of thick, curly hair, those long legs and perky breasts, even with the protruding belly. How long would her beauty last?

Who the hell cares?

He watched her watch him, those big, dark eyes going exactly where he expected them to go. She looked frightened—and so very beautiful. Full lips, wide cheekbones: probably, if her folks came from around here, part Choctaw. Even more, she looked…intelligent, too smart to go down this bottomless pit. *How could she*—he pursed his lips. Maybe she was half spic and half nigger. What was that joke Barry told?

Why don't niggers and wetbacks marry?

Why?

Because their children would be too lazy to steal!

He smiled again. He'd convinced himself that that joke was damn funny. But she probably wasn't mixed like that. *What would Barry say*?—She was just a common nigger with common nigger blood, mixed over the generations with probably every type of race that came through.

Who the hell cares?

She had no right to look scared of anything. She had no right to make him think about her. Like she didn't know the score. Like she was a person worthy of his consideration. *Godammit, she is a crack whore.* If Barry had got the law to bring her over to his office, he'd already had this.

He sat on his desk, hands clasped loosely in his lap. "Judge Calhoun said you could do serious time, girl." He opened his hands slowly, allowing the tent they had created to uncover what was hidden.

"I…I…" Her mouth hung open, and she made gulping sounds, as if drowning.

He snickered, his good-looking face becoming truly ugly in his contempt for her: pregnant, on crack, and selling dope. Her being black did not add to his contempt of her. In truth, it had nothing to do with it at all. Any woman who could do this to herself, to her own *children*, deserved his contempt. Oh, she was not fresh out of the gate! He picked up her thin file.

"Says here you already got two children. Where are they now? And who were you selling for?" Suddenly, he was angry. Not because she was poisoning her body, not because she already had two babies she obviously was unfit to care for; no, his anger was deep-rooted and long-standing. He was a son of the South. Traditions held. And she was—oh, he could tell by her hair, her dress, her attitude—the enemy. Not (just) her color or her sex (he told himself that he loved white women, the *right* women), it was her accident of birth. She was a Northerner. It didn't matter that the records lying next to him on his pristine desk said she hailed from Chicago, which was considered, by most of America, to be in the Midwest. Like most people from the deep, *true* South, he considered any state north of that standard, the Mason-Dixon Line, to be a northern state. She was a Yankee. He sniffed. Even in this day and time, with who had been in the president's office, with his own old and deeply abiding friendships, Barry said he shouldn't—*mustn't*—let old hatreds go. Truth be told, he had no real, race-related hatreds to let go. But he was in with Barry and his kind, had been for years now. He didn't want to lose that inclusion his own family had been denied all his early life.

"Doctor—"

She stopped speaking when he held his long hand up in a purely imperial gesture, one he had mastered over the years.

He was not born with a silver spoon in his mouth like Barry. Oh no, his family was what the landed gentry called *poor white trash.* Would hire a nigger over his own father.

As a teen, he himself had worked right alongside black boys who were hired as day laborers just like he was by the white landowners. They called him *Buck*, like they accepted him, like they genuinely liked him. *Hey, it's Buckaroo!* The fact that they *did* like him filled him with an impotent fury. The supposed enemy had treated him much better than his own color. He knew as a poor boy that those landowners looked down on him and his family, knew that they accepted they were his color but rejected the very idea that they could be his *kind.*

Unlike Barry, he'd had to work like the devil, getting paid under the table at whatever job he could find while in medical school down in Jackson. Hell, if not for his...other enterprises, he'd still be that poor white trash with an MD behind his broke name.

He pushed the girl's head back, not painfully but a push nonetheless. "Let's get one thing straight: you listen. You don't talk. You do what we say, and you don't do a day in county jail or state penitentiary. You hear me?" His hand squeezed into her curls, and she nodded, her eyes wide and unblinking. His handsome smile was one of malevolent triumph.

In high school, the beautiful blond girl who would become his wife said she fell in love with his smile before she ever heard him speak, before he even courted her, before he ever touched her, before he proposed, and before she married him, before the arrival of the hungry, mewling, but loved babies, before she slowly but irrevocably turned into a nagging shrew, before her screaming and pointing accusations pushed them further and further apart, before her desertion.

Her parting words caused him to—not *abandon* medicine, its oath, just—elongate it, circumvent it, occasionally dismiss it: *first, do no harm.*

He had stood in their bedroom, hearing her words but not understanding them as she gathered her belongings, the stranger who was her lover waiting with their three children in the living room.

Buck, you're just too nice.

Into his stunned, stupid silence, she added, "I know people can wear their hearts on their sleeve, but you wear yours on top of your goddamn head, so everyone can see it, and anyone can destroy it."

"How long have you known my wife?" The three of them were in his modest living room: him, his wife, and the man who had cuckolded him. Buck had sent the children upstairs.

"You can watch a video in your mom's and my bedroom." This unusual treat might have alerted the oldest, Henry Junior, that there was something amiss, Buck thought, but the boy said nothing to his younger brother and sister.

Buck had returned to the living room, and he sat as if he were really comfortable in his favorite chair while they sat, already like a couple, next to each other, opposite him, on the floral sofa that he and his wife had picked out the week of their marriage and her parents had paid for, eight years ago.

"Off and on for two years." The man cast Buck's wife a possessive look. "I guess you mean how long we have *known* each other. Six months…It started at that teachers' conference up in Memphis."

But Buck's wife was not a teacher. The closest she came to being involved in the school district at all was when she was designated at certain PTA meetings to bring a batch of her oatmeal cookies and ginger punch. The conference the man referred to was the one her sister dragged her to for company when the tedious meetings were over and they could explore the nightlife.

Buck suddenly felt a calmness settle over him. He crossed his legs at the ankles, steepled his long fingers, looked at the man over the tepee they formed.

"So that's how long you've been screwing her?"

"Buck." His wife's sharp voice had a sharper edge to it, as if *he* had crossed some boundary in the etiquette of adultery.

He looked at his pretty wife, her mouth a thin, sullen line. He glimpsed an image of her in forty or fifty years—beauty faded to invisibility, lips lined with age, her lovely cheekbones hollow. He had imagined this look before, and it had never caused him any great concern; after all, he saw an older version of himself right beside her.

"What?" He looked at her innocently. "I'm just asking—"

He stared at the stranger, realized that the man had come to his house, announced his intentions with *his* wife, and he had no idea who he was.

"James Carl Griffith, like Andy Griffith. You know, the actor," he said unnecessarily but just as innocently.

"James."

"No, James Carl. I go by James Carl."

Buck's large hands with their long fingers, which could have belonged to a classical pianist or a skilled doctor (he was that, he thought without arrogance), clenched into fists of fury, shame, and disgust.

"What the fuck, *James Carl*? You're fucking my wife, and you're telling me in my goddamn own house to call you by the name fucking you *prefer*?"

His wife had teased him years ago that he really did not know how to swear, that he used curse words as adjectives oddly and often misplaced them.

His outburst had no effect on the man, on this James Carl Griffith.

The man stood. He was a decent-looking sort. Wearing short sleeves, creases in his pants, leather shoes shined to a glistening brown, he did not dress expensively or ostentatiously, but the clothing looked pricey.

The man was not exceedingly handsome: dark-blond (or maybe light-brown?) hair combed to one side, clean-shaven, about five feet eleven, a few inches shorter than Buck. Average—that was how Buck would have described him if he had passed him on the street, knowing that five minutes after passing him, he would have forgotten every physical characteristic he possessed.

He could have been the guy who fixed his car ("It was the carburetor, Dr. Bowden") or perhaps the honest-looking salesman who sold him the car ("Yep, Dr. Bowden, this baby'll see you and your lovely family well into the twenty-first century").

"You wanta bring your stuff down, Betts?" He ignored Buck's outburst.

Buck felt his head leave his body, float above them. It ricocheted off the walls, the ceiling, threatened to sail right out an open window.

His wife's given name was Ilsbeth, which was a misspelling of Elspeth. For reasons that were never clear to Buck, her parents had decided, since it was spelled that way on her birth certificate, to keep the incorrect moniker.

He called her Beth. And she had always answered to it, seemingly *preferring* it.

Ilsbeth looked over at him. She stood, and he stood. Three people standing and each realizing that whoever said whatever would change the others' lives forever.

"OK. We're leaving." Beth did not careen out the door, in tears of shame or proudly with a straight, defiant back. She held the front door open as James Carl made five trips back and forth, up and down those stairs, until, with a small pat to her blond hair, she nodded perfunctorily to Buck and closed the door after the man had exited, leaving him alone with his thoughts.

She had not been sentimental in her leave-taking. There were no empty picture frames, no favorite crystal or china (gifts from both sets of parents), no claiming of this favorite knick or that treasured knack.

Buck stood silent for a few seconds, trying to digest the last couple of hours. He found that he could not. So he did what he knew he could do. He went to the downstairs bathroom, lifted the toilet (unlike most women, she never complained about his leaving it up: should that have been a clue he ignored about the state of their marriage?), undid his fly, and proceeded to urinate. He flushed the toilet, adjusted his clothing, and washed his hands with warm, soapy water for twenty seconds (the time the AMA recommended to kill all germs).

He made sure the house was secured and took the stairs two at a time, anxious to check on their three small children, who would, tomorrow morning, realize they were suddenly motherless.

As he turned to his and Beth's—*his* bedroom door—he was shocked to see three small faces, with his blue eyes and her honey-blond hair staring up at him. He knew that, though they had probably been asleep or engrossed in the video Junior had picked out when this shit all started, they were awake and attentive when it all ended.

Of course, the children stayed with Buck; not so much because he wanted them—he supposed he did—but it was because she definitely did *not* want them. How could that stranger who had been in his living room, her lover, accept another man's kids? "You keep them, Buck," she'd called back as she climbed into the man's GMC Yukon.

In those early years of shy courting, she had taught him how to love, completely, wholly, holy. When she had abandoned him, cuckolded him, he was sure that, without her, he would never be able to love again, completely, wholly, holy.

He took custody of their children because his "niceness" won over his anger, his hurt. The smile that Beth had loved still came easily but, for so many people, with a price.

Now he nodded as if in answer to the silent crack whore. "Good."

He reached behind him for his prescription pad. It wouldn't be OxyContin. He avoided suspicions by being careful, by not being *greedy*. He'd been doing this for almost twenty years. That "slush fund" amounted to half a mil now—no, not enough to retire on but a cushion that did not jeopardize his livelihood, his license, the stable life he'd built for his kids.

Maybe every dozen or so patients got the opiate. And there had to be evidence for the need—an old injury that recurred, a new one that was substantiated by either another doctor or the local hospital. And the carefully chosen patients had to agree to the plan. The scheme. And to a man, or woman, they did.

For this one—on crack, pregnant, desperate enough to be selling drugs. *She has to be depressed, suffering from anxiety issues.* He scribbled *Xanax* on the pad, added a dosage, indicated the number of refills. He placed his notes inside a folder. Nothing like a paper trail to disprove any wrongdoing.

The girl would not take a single pill, of course. That was not how this worked. He had his clientele. Knew who would take the pills with alcohol, increase that high, maybe even use it as part of their boudoir games.

"What's your name, girl?" He listened, ignoring the information in the file on her, got the spelling right, shook his head at the obvious nigger name:

Trudessa. Didn't they learn anything? Didn't they know that these names, their very zip codes, were enough for them not to get that loan, move in that neighborhood, get that job?

Though he gained no pleasure from this question, he asked anyway.

"Where'd you get that name?" He expected some outlandish tale—it was Latin, Swahili, even Greek for some philosophical reason: she who laughs last, the girl everyone wanted—silly shit like that.

He listened as she spoke. Her voice gained strength and conviction as she talked. *She's smart*, he thought, angry that she could be this fucked up and smart, too.

Who the hell cares?

He wrote another; this time it was for OxyContin. It would be in her mother's name. He looked at the girl.

Did she have relatives here in Mississippi? *Their ages? Names?*

All this information he got and used. No, not her mother (she'd mumbled she was dead anyway, head down), her grandmother, he decided. Or rather, with his "contacts," he would *create* her maternal grandmother, one he could produce at will, all on paper.

He handed over the prescriptions. He would not take the time to complete the paperwork for the Pharmaceutical Assistance Program. Instead, because he knew there was a return on his investment, he would give her money to pay for her meds, and he would get his assistant to do the Medicare paperwork for the fictitious grandmother.

They stared at each other. There was no anxious question in her eyes, no eager expectation in his. Her large, Asian eyes were as old as time. He knew nothing he could say or do could surprise her. Unless he showed her true kindness.

Perhaps it was her eyes. Was she wearing colored contacts? A lot of them did these days. He decided her eyes were a regular brown but had a luminescence that shone from behind that fringe of lashes. How long would it take for crack to snuff out that brightness?

Wasn't he helping her along this perceived destructive pathway? He thought about this. She was using way before he came on the scene. Fact of the matter was, they were using each other. *What was that phrase?* Quid pro quo. *Something for something.*

Who the hell cares?

He was sure he was imagining his actions. He stared at her little belly, thought of her children. The file said a boy and a girl. Though he had struck the lesbian two years ago, he told himself he'd done what any man would do to protect his genitalia. He was not a woman beater. All the years with Beth, he'd never lifted a hand against her or his three children. He had been a strict disciplinarian; make no mistake about it, but, like his parents before him, he tempered his corrections with a willing ear and a loving heart.

This girl was a mother. She was six months older than his youngest child. He rubbed his chin, the gesture nonthreatening.

"Well," he said, his voice not exactly unkind, "we're going to have to learn to trust each other."

This was ridiculous! *She* was the crack whore; *she* was the one abusing her children. *She* was the real criminal!

His voice hardened. "I'm in fucking charge. Don't you forget it."

He opened the office door, called to the Filipino nurse to make copies of the prescriptions. He closed the door, turned to the black girl.

She did not speak, to his inner surprise. Instead, she stood, turned her back to him, raised her shirt and lowered her pants, exposing a naked ass, round as an apple, firm, caramel-hued, slightly lighter in color than her face and arms and looking as smooth as the baby's bottom she would eventually deliver.

Trudy. Tattooed on her right butt cheek. Some bold font that mimicked Old English script. He let his fingers travel over the *T*, the *r*. By the time he got to the *y*, his hands were shaking, and his breathing was that of a dying man fighting for that last breath of denied oxygen.

He left his office, did a few signatures, retrieved the prescriptions, and went back in his office. He locked the door by pressing a button on his desk. It was lunchtime anyway. And he always recommended his nurses eat healthily and undisturbed for that hour.

He smiled yet again. He had three nurses: a white woman, whom he'd known since childhood; the Filipino, even though he would not hesitate to describe her as a Chink in his snobbish friends' company, just to get that much-desired laugh (her name was Maria); and a colored woman from some place down on the coast, whom he called Tella, her given appellation some unpronounceable, made-up name. All were helluva nurses; he wouldn't have it any other way.

He could hear Barry's wife chirping, "Even the nigger one, Henry?"

He did not know how to tell her that coming up, the word *nigger* had meant nothing to him. It was more descriptive than demeaning, never meant to harm. That was *then*; that was *back there.*

Honey, my car wouldn't start today, and this old nigger happened by. Helped me get her going. His father would relay this to his mother and sit to supper, a pleased smile on his face that a stranger, who happened to be black, had helped him, and he would wonder how he could one day repay the favor. And he invariably did. *Look, boys,* he told his three sons, *my daddy told me that if you cast your bread upon the waters, in many days, it would return to you, but* (and here, he pressed his index finger into the table), *if you treat people* right, *sometimes that bread comes back with butter on it.*

So he would ask his wife to take a pot of soup up the road to old Mrs. Archie, a parchment-colored Negro woman who had to be ninety if she was a day. Or get Buck or one of his other sons to fix a hanging door on Mr. Moses's fence. Never asking anything in return.

How then could he himself ever be considered a racist when he had what he liked to call an International Office? That's what he'd learned from his redneck parents, his bourgeois medical-school classmates, and his long-gone, cheating wife: do right often enough so that when you do wrong (getting some inmates to sell a few drugs for him, having sex with a few of those who sold for him), it takes a very long time for anyone to know or believe it.

"You sell every goddamn pill; your cut is twenty percent." He felt that was fair enough. He and Barry split the 80 percent evenly. If she were dealing a thirty-milligram pill of Oxy for them, sixty per bottle, over ninety days, she could easily make over a grand in those months. But her low-dose Xanax guaranteed her less than six hundred dollars in the same time frame, but he knew she could sell both easily. He knew his clientele and would direct her to them.

He gave her one last warning. Junkies had a habit of mixing and matching, testing and taking. "Short us even one of those pills, and your cute little ass is hauled straight to jail." He sucked his teeth, almost embarrassed that he'd let her know he appreciated her body, *noticed* her.

From his earliest childhood memory, he had been surrounded by black folk. If not black, then poor. Often, the poor were the black. He had not known until first grade that his dusty pink skin and corn-silk-colored hair had the ability to differentiate himself from the many shades of brown skin and kinky hair surrounding him. Out on the place, he did not attend kindergarten, so his interactions with other whites were the same as those of the blacks. They were the workers, and the affluent whites were the landowners, the bosses. As a child, other than his parents and a few other poor white families, he assumed *those* white people did not have to work, that they never worked. In short, until the landowner told his parents he had enrolled little Bucky in the white academy outside town, he had not known he was the *same* white as those landowners. He knew his family was poor, *yes,* but this importance that his teachers paid to skin must have escaped the teachings of his parents. He recalled some of their edicts: don't eat green plums; don't play with the dog when he's eating; don't say *yeah* and *naw* to a grown person; don't accept food if offered (it reflected badly on them as providers).

For most of the lessons the teachers gave him, he paid attention. Do your math. Pronounce the *g,* and don't add that extra *r* to some words. But in the summer, his friends and fellow workers were the same black boys on the place. He forgot some of the lessons. He did eat green plums; he did drop his *g*'s, and he did *warsh* his hair. And if his friends' mamas offered him an ear of corn, a serving of berry cobbler, hell, yeah, he ate them all with relish!

His best friends, Jason and Jimmy, whose neat, small houses flanked his own small and neat abode, often stated their concern and fear: that he would go after and get the local black beauties simply because he was white. (It surprised and angered him that they had known the difference in skin color all along.)

Did he notice those colored girls on the place back then? Did he pay attention to their myriad skin tones, their hair textures? Their impossibly round buttocks and tiny waists with their heavy breasts that, despite their ripeness, defied the pull of gravity? Yes, he supposed he did. But the teachers had made one successful impact on his young psyche: race purity *must* be maintained. He assumed that this tenet was important to all races. After all, Jimmy and Jason drooled over the black girls on the place, told him of the girls at their schools.

They never even hinted at finding the redheaded girl with blue eyes pretty or the blonde with the buck teeth the slightest bit attractive. So, no, he never went after those girls. He had been a clumsy, eager virgin when he had tumbled atop pale Beth in his junior year at State.

Over the years, he bent and outright broke a few of those laws he'd learned in school. But that one, sticking to your race, remained intact.

He told himself that his…dealings were to secure a future for his children, for him. After all, the world was corrupt long before he joined the game, wasn't it? And the women whom he occasionally made use of? Hell, they were already on the slippery downside of the law, and most would as soon kill him as look at him. Like maybe this one before him.

Now, he ripped open a condom, watched her as she assumed the position. He laughed outright at that. Not hands behind the head, on her knees. No, not *that* position, the one these poor colored boys he saw on television or read about in those northern states must have imprinted in their DNA by now.

Her assumed position was to bend a little lower so that, when he plowed into her, he didn't have to stand on tiptoe. After all, she was fairly tall.

Chapter 4

ADRIAN "FAT BOY" Ricketts—so named as a youth because, unlike the nickname, he was not fat at all; rather, he had been skinny to the point of boniness as a child and since turning fifteen had seldom displayed boyish behavior at all, nor did he have the bone disease his surname suggested—stumbled to the mounted bathroom mirror and stared at the face staring back at him.

He was twenty-three, taller than the scrawny child he had been over on Colfax, still slim, but the muscles and wiry build made him lithe. Although he knew that word, *lithe*, he would never use it, never speak it. He had his rep to consider.

He looked at the scruffy hair growing in uneven patches on his chin, cheeks, and above his lip. He shaved but mainly to remove those uneven patches of hair. He would never be able to grow a full, thick beard.

His sand-brown skin was stretched taut against muscles, sinew, and bones. His curly, but not *exactly* kinky, hair was long and stood in thick tufts around his head. Not *exactly* an Afro—too curly to kink and too kinky to pull into a sleek ponytail.

He grinned, and his white teeth—the ones he had once covered with a gold-plated, removable grill—shone brightly. Nice, straight teeth, which had no reason to be: he had not been to the dentist in ten years.

"I'd like to talk to the bank manager about a loan." He chuckled. Like another visit to a dentist, he knew this little convo wouldn't happen anytime soon, either.

He bent low in the sink, rinsed his mouth with mouthwash, the whitening kind, and brushed his teeth. He'd always had good *enough* hygiene, even though his customers couldn't care less about it.

He removed his shorts and replaced them with a clean pair. He did not bathe; his granny had taught him that if he didn't bathe every day—and no one did in his family—at least change the underwear on a daily basis, a habit he clung to. He shoveled baby powder into his crotch and swiped deodorant under his arms. He took out the razor, the bone hair pick, and began his "gettin' fine" routine, as his granny used to tease him.

He looked in the mirror once more. His reflection was still that of a young man, a young *black* man, who, as he walked down the streets of Chicago, caused black and white women alike to hold their purses tighter, for white men to stare him down, and black, brown, and white boys to look up to him with envy.

He knew that if they were alone, those same white women would not shrink from him in fear but rather stare at him with longing, come-hither looks. He knew he was handsome, like he knew he was tall, knew his address, his cell number, just more facts: wide, full lips; long-lashed, black eyes; broad, open face. He flexed and posed, posed and flexed: great skin, the planes and the angles of his face giving him a look that could well be splashed across the pages of a men's magazine; washboard abs with no exercise routine to credit; tight, round runner's ass.

The white men would look at him with open anger, knowing that their self-named condition of *penis envy* was correct. After all, he was a *black* man, a young man. Those rumors were true. He was a *young, black* man. He was built like a stallion.

He went into his kitchenette and fixed a bowl of cereal with milk. As he ate, he surveyed his work space. The scales were pretty new; he'd lifted them from a chemistry lab at a college down South. He laughed aloud.

Last summer, he'd driven seven hours to Tennessee to visit cousins and to lie low for a few weeks. He was not running from the law, escaping some felonious endeavor that the Chicago cops had his name written all over.

No, he had, through no efforts of his own, attracted the attention of the girl of one of the biggest smack dealers on the South Side, a guy from some Saint Thomas mountain village, who went by the unlikely name of Bishop. When he found out that his girl had the hots for Fat Boy, he showed his decidedly unchristian side by putting a contract out on Fat Boy's handsome head. He could have hired either one of the junkies who lined up outside his brick bungalow house for that fix to do the deed. Instead, he used men so skilled with a rifle they could split a grasshopper's nuts with one shot.

The fact that Fat Boy had never touched the bitch meant nothing. So, like the advice given outlaws in his TV westerns, he got the heck out of Dodge.

There were no guards at the gate of the college, unlike the one in his Chicago neighborhood, where the guards were packing every day in every way. He'd parked his mint-condition, brown-on-brown 1975 Mercury Monarch on the small, neat campus, found his kin, and simply walked with her into the chemistry lab. Once there, he engaged a few students in conversation, asking and answering remarkably intelligent questions about the lab they were doing, and left with two of the top-loading scales.

An old Greek barber in the neighborhood had told him when he first started his *business* that stealing was more about confidence than stealth. The problem with thieves who got caught, he told Fat Boy in his thick accent, was that they got nervous or looked guilty.

Look as if it belongs *to you.*

And so Fat Boy did. He had boxed them up carefully, taped them, and walked out. He had credited his tan shirt and khaki pants as having been mistaken by faculty and students as a uniform of some sort. No one had questioned him.

Luck was on his side when he returned to Chicago. Bishop had been found in his South Springfield Avenue house with a needle between his toes on his right foot, keeled over, dead eyes open like fish eyes, dried foamy spittle on his mouth. The girl (Fat Boy never really got her real name) had disappeared into the crowd. It was rumored Bishop wasn't even a user, that she'd rigged the whole thing and absconded with his money.

Whatever. All Fat Boy knew or cared about was that he didn't have to worry about his life being snuffed out by that crazy-ass dealer.

He finished his cereal, rinsed the bowl and spoon. He had a couple of hours before he had to leave for class. He sat at his workstation and began his daily routine with the meticulousness of a watchmaker. He sorted, weighed, and bagged what his customers considered to be the best weed that was not straight from some Mexican farm or smoke shop in Amsterdam. His supplier had raved about the two strains he'd sold Fat Boy: Yellow Amnesia and Sensi Kush. He piled them in ten bags per stack.

He supposed being a drug dealer was the family *bizness* he had inherited. His paternal grandfather had joined the tail end of the migration to the North from Tennessee. He told his grandson he'd grown tired of working like a goddamn slave.

Fat Boy learned when he was a chubby toddler that, at twenty-four, his gramps had dropped his pickax, walked the five miles to town, and, with the bus fare and sixty extra dollars in his pocket, boarded the first bus north. He got off in Toledo, stayed a few days until he gambled and won enough money to go west to Chicago. He'd been there ever since, doing what he'd come to be pretty good at. When he'd established himself and found a small apartment, he sent for the girl who would become Fat Boy's grandmother. He never married her, but he had four kids with her. They'd lived comfortably on the South Side of Chicago, her working as what used to be called a nurse's aide at Provident. Not much more than a maid, really, his granny had told him, but it made her a woman with a profession, one to be respected in the old neighborhood. His grandfather was a plant worker by day and a drug dealer by night and weekend. Twenty years later, when the plant closed, his clandestine deals became his livelihood.

His undoing, Fat Boy reasoned, was that he didn't keep to his neighborhood. Oh, no, he traveled to the suburbs, sold to the *white,* bored housewives and rich, smart-mouthed *white* teens. In his defense, which he'd never had, he should have stuck to his own neighborhood. Failing that, at least to his own *kind.*

His gramps had been arrested a year ago at *sixty-seven* for possession with intent to distribute and, unless paroled, would be in federal lockup until he was a hundred, if he lived that long. His grandfather was considered to be a hero to the youngbloods, who revered him for staying true to the trade and lasting as long as he did.

Fat Boy's own father took to the streets when crack reared its ugly but very profitable head in the early eighties. Like his father before him, he never married Fat Boy's moms, but they lived together as common-law husband and wife until she got a whiff of a more profitable life as a girlfriend to a gangster who saw himself as a gangsta rapper. Fat Boy had not seen his mother since he was twelve.

The rapper made one CD before he shuffled off this mortal coil. He was not gloriously killed in a hail of gunfire, to be martyred, discussed, or his words analyzed for their profundity; he died pathetically from an undiagnosed heart condition, in bed, alone, and ironically sober. He left nothing, Fat Boy heard, to his mother or to the world that soon forgot him.

His father, as unlucky in the drug trade in later years as his father before him, had been arrested nine months ago. He'd turned forty-four in federal lock-up. Although drug laws in the state had essentially decriminalized possession of marijuana, possession of almost any amount of crack still bore stiff sentences. Fat Boy's father was caught with five grams. In his defense, his state-appointed lawyer had unsuccessfully argued to the judge, had he been white, he would have gotten a slap on the wrist, would have been given probation.

But he was *not* white. No slap on the wrist. It was *buh*, as in *buh-bye*. To the jail he went. He did not pass Go; he did not collect his two hundred dollars.

Fat Boy figured he might see both his father and grandfather, what with good behavior and parole, released before he himself was half a century in age. Or bury them beside his granny, who couldn't live forever, no matter how healthy and vital she was now.

Which was why he never dabbled in crack, that "affordable" cocaine. And crystal meth was too insane for him even to consider. Molly was good for a buck or two. Staying away from crack and that heroin shit meant he didn't have to deal with the crazies who would sell their mother for a hit. Those "designer" drugs were too unpredictable. Marijuana would always bring in the Benjamins. His shit was pure and damn good. He saw no reason to mix it with anything. Unadulterated—he liked that word, stood by that word.

As was his custom, he donned his Beats earphones and waited for the music to bathe him, wash over him as if he were in the studio or even onstage with the singer. Only a few people knew he did not listen to the bump, thump, and grind of hip-hop, pop, reggae, or rap (gangster or otherwise). He wasn't even into old school, since he could have been easily influenced by his granny or some of the old bloods still on the streets.

Fat Boy was a true oddity. Born and raised on the South Side of Chicago, he was a city-bred product of a place that gave the world blues singers, award-winning artists of any genre of modern, black music; yet he eschewed them all. For reasons even he could not articulate, he loved country-and-western music. He did not like it with amused disdain. He was a true fan.

He had surprised his woman a few years ago with a trip to Nashville. He refused to tell her why they had taken this flight. When they showed up at the Schermerhorn Symphony Center, she was stunned to see they were the only blacks at the place. Well, three if you counted the black woman who showed them to their seat.

Now, his favorite artist sang into his ear as he went about his business—Lyle Lovett, that long, tall Texan. He smiled, mouthing the words to the song.

He wondered about the champagne, the caviar, even the airplane and the car her father would buy her. Still, he left. He had to go.

He loved the *irony* of the song. The man described the perfection of the woman he had, yet she was not enough. In the end, the man had to let her go, refuse the material trappings. Fat Boy wondered if he could refuse a girl who could offer him the world. Could he recognize both the real and the imitation and choose the right one? And yet tell the girl he just had to go?

He loved country music, math, and science. But he refused to think of himself as a total oddball. He had his tats, like any youth on the street these days. He loved his tats, proudly showed them off when the opportunity arose. Too bad no one really got them. No ancient tribal symbols, Chinese characters, or a Bible verse. His muscular forearm had his favorite, the chemical structure of tetrahydrocannabinol stenciled on it. He remembered the artist who almost got the chirality wrong. *No, man! Don't fuck it up: a* wedge *on the left and a* dash *on the right.* Then, when he saw the final product in the mirror, he'd grinned and praised the artist. *Cool, man, cool.* Another tattoo was on his chest: $Ca(SH)_2$. Everyone thought it was for the money he made dealing. But it was his own private joke. Ca^{2+} bonded to two thiol (^{-}SH) groups. Maybe he was a bit nerdy, after all.

His cell rang, and he looked at the picture and name on his iPhone screen. For business, he used a throwaway. This was no customer.

The caller was cracked out and crazy: his girlfriend and baby mama. Trudessa Jenkins: *Trudy*.

He snatched off the Beats, hit the accept button. "Whatchu want?"

They'd had three babies together—well, the third one was firmly implanted in her womb, but it was still his. She had left him a month ago, hooking up with some cuz who was headed even farther south than where he'd driven to visit his middle Tennessee peeps.

"Baby, I miss you."

He shook his head and felt that other head grow and groan for her special attention. Had it been only a month, thirty days, since she'd left him? Since he'd awakened on the sofa in this very apartment, found no one else here—not her, his son, his daughter?

They had started off pretty good. Damn good. Getting her knocked up at seventeen was no big deal. Her dad was fine with it. Her old man's only pronouncement was simple: *You hit her just once, boy, and I'll fuck you up but good.*

His granny was over the moon to be a great-grandma. *You go on to college, Fat Boy; we'll take care of this baby. Then, it'll be Trudy's turn.* Matthew was born three days before Trudy's eighteenth birthday.

Even when she got pregnant again and they still had no real jobs, no marriage in sight, their extended, albeit small, family was still cool. Trudy had a baby girl, wanted to give her the name of Sasha (she was a huge fan of Beyoncé), but Damien, her younger, smart-ass brother didn't agree (he was not a fan at all of the Texas singer/beauty).

Name her Natasha, he advised, *but y'all can* call *her Sasha. That way it won't sound like such a—well, you know what* they *say about* our *names. Besides, that's BO's* (that was how he referred to the former president, always with a smirk, as if he had known him when he was a simple Chicago lawyer) *daughter's name, so she would be in good company.* So it was Matthew and two years later Natasha, who were called Matthew and Sasha.

Her turning to crack in the last few months was a very big and terrible deal. Pot here and there, toking when the mood hit, didn't seem so bad, and the two babies they had were fine. Shit, they were smarter than he was at that age; that was for damn sure! For God's sake, Matthew could read almost all of Tarpley's *I Love My Hair!* And the boy loved the fact that Tarpley's first name was the same as his sister's. As far as Fat Boy was concerned, he and Trudy had created a fucking genius in that boy!

Fat Boy and Trudy had met when she was eleven and he a year older. She had only her younger brother and father. He would learn later that they both were motherless but for vastly different reasons. He'd lost his mother to the good life that became the not-so-good life, and she'd lost hers to cancer the year before they met. She was a tomboy back then, flat-chested, angular, and as tall as he was before his growth spurt. Great for a pickup game of basketball in the park at the end of Tripp. They lived with their fathers (and he with his paternal grandmother) and siblings in narrow brick homes on opposite sides of the street.

At thirteen, he thought they would be best buddies forever. Until, as she was going for a layup, she came down, atop him, and he, to steady both, had grasped her budding breasts with one long hand and the other wrapped around her slim waist.

The sensation of her soft flesh cupped in his palm caused his skin to heat. He pulled his hand away as if her skin were fire. And to him it was. Burning him, branding him.

When she landed, sprawled atop him, long legs flung wide, both were surprised to see first a pink and then a red flowering bloom in the crotch of her cutoff white shorts. He thought he had hurt her in some way or that she'd been shot! Hadn't that kid been killed right on this very court not two weeks ago? But there was no sedan speeding by with a hail of bullets in its wake. No lone gunman, shouting obscenities and bolting away when realizing the error of his aim. She seemed fine. Except for the blood.

The blood—for he had seen blood before, oozing from the crushed teenaged girl who had lived over on Keeler—had begun to flow, sluggish like ruby-red syrup, down her legs.

He pushed her up until she was standing over him; he struggled to his feet, feeling suddenly clumsy and foolish. He noticed that she had grown taller, fuller. She might be dying, and here he was thinking of her new body.

He had to get her home, had to save her. He could not carry her, so he grabbed her hand and sprinted down the street, pulling her after him.

No one was at her home. He banged and called, but no one came to the door. Her father, he knew, was what his granny called a *weekender*. He drank himself into a sad stupor on the weekends. Her little brother could be anywhere on these streets.

His granny! He dragged Trudy behind him, terrified that the blood would not be stanched. Why didn't she feel the pain from whatever injury she'd mysteriously sustained that was surely causing the blood loss?

His granny would know what to do; she always knew what to do. And she did. She took one look at the scene before her, took Trudy firmly in hand, and led her into her bedroom first and then, minutes later, to the bathroom Fat Boy was forced to share with her.

He tried to listen but could hear only surprised whispers (Trudy's voice) and amused, patient responses (his wise granny's soft voice).

Then, Trudy was standing before him, looking suddenly secretive and superior. He didn't understand what had happened. He was just relieved that she had not been at death's door.

She skimmed across the street, changed the bloodied shorts, and they finished the one-on-one game. She won 46–39.

His granny did not tell him what the blood was all about; neither did Trudy, but eventually he figured it out. The older boys joked about it, lamented about it, "that time of the month," something that happened to girls and something to do with getting pregnant, something that stopped many of the teen boys from "hitting" that.

So he reread his health book on the chapter about reproduction and women. He thought he understood the biology of this; he understood *menses* was like monthly in its origin, that the uterus was said to *cry* for lack of a baby in it. The book, of course, never said how to understand *women*.

Two years later, she whispered to him that she was ready to be a woman. She was barely ready to be a *girl*, he meanly teased, and certainly not a woman. But her hand on his junk explained that she was and that he was a man. She would be *his* woman. He would be her man. His erection grew under her hand and pushed against her like an insistent puppy. He'd had those erections for a few years now and had used his own hands as he pumped himself into exhaustion. His body understood her actions and words more than his mind did.

The fact that she never got pregnant before she was seventeen was sheer luck. (He wore condoms that invariably came off way too soon and way too often. *Forget them,* she'd said, frustrated at his frustration.) They always wanted each other, and neither ever refused the other.

"You're the one who up and left in the middle of the night," he said now, tucking the cell into his shoulder as he continued to sort, weigh, and bag. His goal was to make about a thousand bucks today and relax a day or two. He knew the Amnesia would make him bank in no time, and he could keep below the radar. That was why he had avoided any serious interplay with the cops.

He was enrolled in college (he even had a respectable 3.23 GPA), and by selling a day or two, by stepping back every few days to admire his results, he was simply "that guy who had the hookup." No gang affiliation. No *operation* he had to guard. In fact, his "guard dog" was a fluffy rottweiler-Labrador mix puppy he called Charlie. His granny kept him at her larger house.

Fat Boy was a chemistry major, and, although he tried not to love the subject, he did. He could lose his cred if his customers knew that he read his Gen Chem textbook like they read—well, they didn't read too much of anything, did they?

He had heard the next class, organic chemistry, was the toughest class he would ever take. He'd see about that. Fuck, the only reason he had the GPA he had was because of what his gramps said once.

What do you call a black PhD? A black doctor or black dentist?

And like the adoring, idiot grandchild he was, he asked seriously, *What, Granddaddy?*

A nigger.

So he seldom cracked his other books or simply didn't buy them. But his phenomenal memory allowed him to recall equations and definitions, rules and principles, with almost perfection.

With his drug sales, he took care of Trudy and their babies, helped his granny out when he could. He was *not* a so-called thug like the cops killed and the politicians disparaged in the media. Hadn't been arrested, had no gun tucked in his waistband. Wore no colors. He just had a crack whore for the mother of his kids and a gramps and pops who were doing jail time maybe until they died down in Chester.

"You can come down here, too, you know."

He ignored that, ignored that pillow-talk voice she used on him. He thought he knew her: friends since children, lovers, parents. But the familiar-sounding stranger on the other end of the phone, who was she?

He didn't have time for her shit today. Had she forgotten their last night together? But he remained silent, knowing that if he said anything, his heart would be in his voice.

He finished with the Amnesia, started in on the Sensi. He picked out some debris using tweezers he'd lifted when he took the scales. One thing could be said about Fat Boy: you got good product from him. Always.

"You're not gonna ask about Matthew and Sasha?"

He didn't ask how they were getting by, how she was feeding and clothing their babies. He didn't ask if she was still on the pipe. She'd left him, and he had a life to live. Besides, if he knew crack hos—and he did—she was doing a fuck here, a blow job there, and earning enough money for fast food to shovel down their gullets and for her to get that hit. And he knew she always needed that hit.

He supposed it wasn't *exactly* her fault that she was cracked out. Even though no one their age was into the drug, both had tried it, just to *try* it, smoked behind her father's house. She hadn't known—or hadn't told him—she was pregnant again.

The high he experienced was so intense, so fucking *good*, that it scared the shit out of him. He had refused to go after that high again. He didn't know it then, but you never got that first high back. But you chased it. She was chasing hers.

No, he refused to ask after his kids' well-being, refused to show his weakness—for her, for their babies. After all, *she* had left *him*. "I gotta go."

He recalled their last night together, the licks he'd delivered upside her head. He could accept her growing neglect, of herself, of him and his needs, but he could never accept her neglect of their children's needs.

He'd returned from a visit with his granny, to see if she needed anything, having taken Matthew with him. Standing in the doorway of their apartment, he'd heard the unmistakable sounds a man makes when he's being given good head. He'd made those sounds so many times with her that he knew what was going on even before he *thought* it. He'd quickly deposited their son at the small dining table, went in search of the moans and pants.

He'd wailed on her for sucking a guy off right in Sasha's face. True, the toddler was asleep on their bed, but BP—he measured their life together like that, Before the Pipe and After the Pipe—Trudy was his and his only. Yes, he got the occasional pussy from a customer, but it was purely business. Trudy was his woman. AP, he was sure she was any man's hole, to let him put whatever he wanted into whatever hole he wanted.

And seeing her on her knees, almost begging for the guy's dick to choke her as it pumped into her mouth as if his hips were motorized, sent him into a rage. The guy barely made it out of their cramped studio alive. And he'd turned all his disgust and anger on the mother of his kids.

That damned glass pipe—*that* was the cause of all this drama in their lives.

He destroyed it under the heel of his size 13 Nike KD8s. He had stormed out, dismissing her blows and curses. He'd run half the block, her shouts diminishing in the dim but noisy night. The night first cooled the tears on his cheeks and then dried them. When he'd returned from the streets, emotionally spent, ready to forgive, to *talk*, he saw his babies, and he knew she had wailed on them. That was another thing he had to learn about that pipe. It could erase memories. Though both had swatted their children's hands when naughty, neither had hit them in anger. Their little legs were red with her handprints. He wondered if she had used her fists. Regardless, her punishment was severe and thorough. He could have killed her just for that alone. But of course, he couldn't. He rocked his babies to sleep and went to the couch. He would deal with all this in the morning.

Exhausted and dispirited, he'd fallen into a fitful sleep on the too short sofa, only to awaken before the sun was up. He went for a drive, just to clear his head of the waterlogged cotton from the night before. An hour later, he'd returned home to find a note on the bedside table and his babies and her nowhere to be found.

The note was like she could be at times AP, succinct, terse, and deadly. *Left with JW. You're gonna pay for this!* Next to the note, the shards of broken glass that he recognized as her pipe. JW was her cousin; he was not exactly sure how they were related. What he did know was that JW had been paroled two years ago. Was he even allowed to leave the city, let alone the state? Not just selling dope—that was time, Fat Boy was told, a man could do in his sleep. But this JW, he'd written bad checks, gotten into a bad scam with ID theft. A real fuck, he had used a broken, empty gun in a robbery gone bad. And she'd left with him. That was a month ago.

"What happened? Your cuz split, took whatever money was lyin' around?" He changed his tone; he sounded angry and jealous of JW. (He was both, but he did not want her to know this.) "You got a hustle goin' on there in the Sip?"

Why couldn't she seek a legitimate job? Even stripping had become more acceptable, what with Usher's song "I Don't Mind."

But he refused to ask the real question, *Why did you let this shit take you from me?*

She giggled, and his hard-on reminded him how she'd been BP: the gentleness of her touch, the *thoroughness* of it, their talks of a future for their babies. He would finish college; then she would go. She would study—not that ubiquitous nursing crap, no. She would do something perhaps less substantial but, to her, much more satisfying: a double major in English and history. She would become, she told him, a Nancy Grace–, Star Jones–, Johnnie Cochran–type lawyer while he would be a pharmacist. Or pharmacologist. He wasn't sure. All this planning was BP. Now…

"I got a little sum'n-sum'n lined up. Not just weed and crack down here. These white people are fucking seriously into meth, baby. Got labs all over. And Oxy is doin' real good. Shit, heroin hasn't even stopped."

He smiled. She pronounced the word oddly, *haer-rahn*. And BP, he could always make her laugh when he corrected her.

There was a knock on his door. He checked his watch: not even noon. He never sold before noon. In his logic, that was the mark of a desperate man.

"I gotta go."

"They ask about you."

Shit. She could suck all the dick she wanted, and he could kill her for that, but he knew that she *knew*, no matter how much he pretended he could go either way, he missed and loved those babies.

"Go find that dick you been livin' off, bitch. I got a customer." His gramps had told him over and over, never let the pussy be stronger than you.

"It's not like that, Fat Boy."

He ignored the knocks. "It's not?" The question was automatic, desperate, love-filled, foolish. Then, he remembered: *Don't show your weakness.*

He didn't wait for her response. He hit end and went to the door. He did not open it. The raps had intensified in rate and sound.

"Yeah?"

"Fat Boy? Open up, man. It's—"

Some French name and the deep voice had a distinctive accent, a man's timbre. Fat Boy knew then that the stranger on the other side of his threshold was Haitian. Alarms went off in his head.

"Not now, bro. On the phone." What was that phrase? "*Apremidi a.* This afternoon."

What was the man doing here? He steered clear of Haitian gangbangers. They had started in Haiti and then swelled into South Florida, moving clear up into Indiana. Now, they were here. He didn't know much about them, those Haitian thugs, into everything they were big and bad enough to do. But he knew this: Zoe Pound did not play.

Adrian felt the door cave in, as if it were forced open by a dozen murderous knights brandishing a battering ram.

The door was utterly destroyed, and he lay on his back, wind knocked out of him from the impact but still clear-thinking. He scrambled to his feet.

In part of his mind, when he saw, but before he felt, the cool touch of the SIG Pro against his cheek, he thought clearly, *What is that, an SP 2340*?

With the muzzle next to his cheek, he maintained his composure. He didn't recognize the maliciously smiling face. And it kept speaking in Creole. Was he drunk on that *clairin* crap? Nah, the shit made you happy-go-lucky, not murderous.

Why was he here? Fat Boy seldom dealt with them. They had their own territory, their own way of getting what they wanted from their clients.

"*Kisa ou vle*?"

Fat Boy had no idea what this guy wanted.

"*Kote se madanm ou*?"

Adrian didn't understand this question. He shook his head, feeling the cold metal bounce off his face as he moved.

"Your slut wife." Before Fat Boy could fully interpret the harsh accent, the Haitian punctuated the question with a punch to his solar plexus, knocking the wind out of him and threatening to bring up his breakfast.

Shit. Money. That had to be the real reason Trudy had bailed. She owed this goon money. He was her supplier, and she'd stiffed him.

"*Konben*?" He'd learned this word. But did he *really* want to know how much money Trudy owed this guy?

He thought quickly. In his possession, he had about two pounds of weed, a few thou in cash. He would freely offer him this bounty. He wouldn't beg for his life. He would not tell him where his Trudy was. He wouldn't.

Chances were, Fat Boy thought, he could take him. He was a scrapper, pretty good with his fists. Quick and light on his feet. He just needed to—

But he got no further than the thought. Two thugs stepped over the demolished door, each bigger and tougher-looking than the other. He wouldn't stand a chance against three of them. And he didn't miss the dull glint of the metal from the guns they had pointing midway between his gut and his heart.

There was no sound from other tenants, he thought. But then, hearing a door being crashed in meant they stayed *inside*, would not venture out. To get hit, shot.

He gave them the cash, his product. And they took it, cursing him, he assumed in Creole, that strange language that, to him, sounded as if they were speaking some African language in French. Cursing Trudy.

"*Desann, desann*!" The first guy screamed, and Fat Boy knew enough about the language that this sounded like *descend* in French. *Sit down.*

He sat as instructed on the sofa that faced his wide-screen television, and he watched the men. One of them seemed nervous, twitchy, which meant nothing since the other two were so cool as to be cold, dead-eyed in their mission to—*do what*?

"You got the cash and weed, man. She can't owe you that much." *But could she?* It was his fault that he let the drug overtake her, that he didn't know who her suppliers were, what they were capable of doing. But then again, it was her own fault. He had been able to put the pipe aside, step far away. Why couldn't *she* have shown that same…fortitude?

After these goons were gone, he'd call her back, give her a piece of his mind. No, on second thought, he would drive down there, *take* his kids from her. It would be up to her to come with them. He knew she'd put up a fight about his taking their babies back. But he'd let her know: the only way he'd take *her* back would be if she got off that pipe.

As he argued with himself, forgetting the men, their guns with the silencers, one of the bullets ripped part of his head off, and before he thought about dying, he felt a *whompf* as another one tore into his chest. He knew that the impact of a hollow-point bullet could shred a person. Fuck, on these streets, in this trade, he'd seen it up close and personal.

He was ten when his grandfather told him a woman had shot him with a .22 pistol. Fat Boy had been understandably intrigued, looking at his grandfather's exposed flesh for the scars and torn-apart muscles. His gramps's hairy chest was devoid of color, looking more whitish gray than any shade of brown. His nipples showed through the wispy hair. But there was no scar, no hole where the bullet would have pumped through that pale flesh.

Finally, he'd asked, as only a child could, *Why aint you dead*?

His gramps had laughed his big laugh. "Boy, being shot with a twenty-two by a woman? Hell, I wiped the blood away and kept doing what I was doing."

"What was you doin', Granddaddy?"

"Screwing her best friend." Fat Boy didn't know that word then, but he understood his grandfather's dark humor.

Now, he wished to hell that this Haitian Sensation had been a woman with a .22. He would have been able to tell his gramps all about it.

Though half of his face and brains were splattered on the white wall behind him, he was smiling. Because of the irony. He didn't carry a gun. He'd never had the need to. He was small-time, after all. The idiots probably could have panhandled on the Magnificent Mile and made more than what they took. And Fat Boy was smiling for another, totally unrelated reason.

What is the final concentration of a solution of 1.50 M HF (hydrofluoric acid) if the original volume is 0.40 L and the final volume is 1.20 L? Show all work.

$M_1V_1 = M_2V_2$; x is M_2. Solve for x.

$x = M_1V_1/V_2$; L cancels and M is left over.

Final answer: (1.50 M)(0.40 L)/1.20 L = 0.50 M.

He knew that hydrofluoric acid was not that corrosive of an acid but quite toxic; he knew that this lack of corrosiveness was due to the electronegativity of fluorine. The bond between the H and the F was polar covalent, and, in water, it didn't fully ionize like HCl or even HBr did. He understood that the pKa of

3.17 for HF versus -8 for HCl made HCl approximately a 10^{11} stronger acid than HF. He knew that HF was stored in plastic bottles because it could etch glass; the other hydrohalogenic acids did not.

He knew, too, that sodium hydroxide, when concentrated enough, could dissolve bones. He'd done this lab in his freshman bio lab: chicken bones in the lye for a week. He'd excitedly told Trudy all about the destructive power of this simple compound while she nursed Sasha and while he watched her nurse Sasha.

He got hydrates and their decomposition, that copper sulfate was a rich blue when hydrated and a bland white powder when anhydrous. He understood half-cell reactions.

He'd studied the structure of cocaine, just to see how it was related to heroin. He knew them to be alkaloids, and like most alkaloids they had good and bad properties. He knew that marijuana had more than just tetrahydrocannabinol, that these other cannabinoids were not psychoactive. He even knew that there were receptor proteins for these drugs.

He'd gained all this knowledge by inadvertently wondering in Pickett's presence how these drugs got a person high.

"Good question, Mr. Ricketts. I expect to have that paper with the answers on my desk in a week."

Fat Boy could only stare until the professor shooed him away. "And pull those pants up, mister. Nobody wants to see your drawers!" He pulled his trousers up. And made an A on that paper. Pickett was old-school. He'd fight a nigger if he had to.

Mathematics came easily and fast to Fat Boy. It made sense to him. After all, he used it daily.

If Fat Boy has a pound and a fourth of prime weed, how many eighths can he sell in one day? *NOTE: Ignore the possibility that he could be arrested, mugged, or seriously jacked up any time during that day.*

The smile on the remaining part of his face—unblemished and even sweet-looking—would remain a mystery to his granny. That was because she wouldn't know that he was not thinking of her, his pops in the pen, his gramps there, too. Not even of the sweetness he had with Trudy BP. Not his babies, little Sasha and Mr. Man Matthew. That baby he would never know.

He was thinking that he would have gotten an A in G. Chem II. He thought of Dr. Pickett. He secretly admired his stern chemistry professor and considered, because their names almost rhymed, this to be a sign that he would be not a street pharmacist who got all the ladies (read: Trudy) but a pharmacist/pharmacologist who got all the ladies (read: Trudy).

The smile was one of confidence. He didn't think that Orgo would be as tough as the other students said it was.

Chapter 5

To reach Shay's little house, Trudy knew the doctor would have to drive north on Potter Road until it played out, past Deer Creek, and take the road—little more than a path—that ended at the front steps of the house, which squatted on the farmland like a brown brick toad. He had made the trip three times, like clockwork. Pick up the cash, give her the drugs and her cut, and screw her until he was spent. Then, as if he were some benevolent uncle, he would go through Shay's house, calling to the children (Trudy made sure they were watching TV and that the room she and the doctor used was locked) as if they were playing a game, and give them a treat—a few clementines with the chicken tenders, chocolate milk with the tiny pancakes. He usually left bags of healthy food.

"For *them*," he sternly told her, his eyes cold as he took in her post-crack-smoking appearance. Often, though so fleeting that she was sure she imagined it, he would look at her with something like anger, not hatred—that is, *racial* hatred—but anger, the same look her father often had cast on her, loving her and angry that she had become something he could not bear to have in his presence. Abject disappointment.

And like so many things she had to ignore to keep her lover, she let those imagined looks go.

The area surrounding Shay's little place epitomized what Trudy thought the South would look and sound like—slow-talking white people with either a cigarette or a toothpick stuck between their thin lips; little black children who called everyone "Miss" and "Mister," said "ma'am" and "sir"; dust that layered the skin and frosted your hair.

There was running water and electricity in Shay's house but no washer or dryer. He'd explained the Laundromat was in town and that they would have to bring their damp clothes back to hang on the clothesline, something she had to get used to.

She also quickly got used to the unpredictable cell-phone service until she found a spot about six hundred yards from the house that inexplicably had perfect reception. It was there that she made arrangements with the doctor. She told Shay nothing more of her "enterprise" with the doctor than before, but he knew the man often visited, ostensibly, Trudy told him, to check on the children, on her.

Did he believe her? She didn't know, but they decided that when the doctor dropped by, it would be best if he were out, peddling his products.

Trudy and her children had been with Shay for a month now. The children grew content with the regularity of meals and the chance to balk at taking an actual bath. Trudy, still in deep with her lover, discovered that, while Shay viewed himself as her man, he was not so enraptured as to take her to get her crack nor would he allow her behind the wheel of his car so that she could.

Back in Chicago, her entire world was in a ten-block radius. Here, in this land of trees and fields, she had to walk. There was no L, no bus services, no hailing a cab. Had Fat Boy been with her, she would have had him in stitches, laughing at the fact that one must call a cab, from one's home, on the phone!

When the car pulled up next to Shay's little house, it was two forty-five, and the afternoon air was wet with humidity. The sun, like a lemon drop hanging from a string, seemed to burn away any gray cloud that could diminish its heat.

The car, an older Cadillac with a red body and a cream-colored Landau roof, was unfamiliar to Trudy but one her father would say was a nigga's car: long, shiny, meant to impress the kinfolk back home.

Like the car, the man driving was a stranger to Trudy. The car shuddered to a stop next to her. The stranger sighed and got out of the car. He was tall, indeed, taller than her Fat Boy by maybe two inches, and thickset, leaning actually, on closer look, toward flab. In his day, he probably was considered handsome by the local women: caramel-toned skin, wavy hair, all the traits that signified he was a swirl of the races: African, European, and Native American.

The doctor sat in the car, but his eyes were flashing, as if waiting to see what would happen between them, his nigger crack whore and his *what*? Who was this man to the doctor?

"Dr. Bowden here said you a mother. Where are your children?"

His accent placed him from the South, and Trudy could tell, not necessarily by his dress—he wore a wilting gray gabardine suit—that he was educated, enunciating every *r* and keeping the *d* in *children*. Another doctor? Another crooked lawyer? This place was full of them, she'd learned.

It was the smoothness of the question and the dead look in his green eyes that alerted her to the gravity of her situation. Green eyes? Yes, Trudy saw that his eyes were a surprising green. Her father had jokingly said never to trust a black person with green or blue eyes. They were the devil's spawn.

Her hands, already unsteady because of her lover earlier that day, began to shake as if she were convulsing, but only in her hands.

Fuck. The man had already unzipped his pants. In the open. He would take her in broad open daylight, outside, in the hot sun, on the gravel road, in the grassy yard. This small and, if she thought about it, expected gesture should not have surprised her. He was here to get drugs. Surely. But why *this*? Other than the pills, why else would any man be here? Hadn't he money? But fucking *her* did not pay *them*.

And that was when the tears began pouring down her cheeks. She had been with many men since the lover—so many men. The things she did with them, for them, did not embarrass her, make her rethink her life. No, she had come to realize this would be part and parcel to keep her lover near. But for this man, for any *black* man, to know what she did, with the enemy, with that white man, *any* white man, crooked or no, could not be borne.

She cried the entire time. Though she had been with many men, AP, they had not been particularly cruel. This man relished in it. If there was a way to inflict pain, he would: a hard slap here, a wrenching jerk there. She cried when he stood behind her, a fistful of her hair pulled so tight, she thought he would rip it from her scalp. His breath smelled of some deli meat and sour mustard. He forced his fingers deep within her rectum, deliberately using his sharp fingernails. She cried when he, finished with her, thrust himself away from her, stood to one side, looking with casual interest at the doctor, who must have stepped out of the car sometime during the rape. Trudy just knew he was standing close to them, his face a blank. Her face was swollen from the blows and her tears. She was bleeding. He had even bitten her, leaving his sharp teeth imprints on her shoulders, her breasts.

"You said she was a good fuck, but damn, you didn't tell me she was *this* good! My dick won't be able to get hard for a month!" The man was grinning, a sheen of sweat on his smooth brow.

Trudy did not adjust her jeans. She waited, kneeling now because the doctor liked it that way. Her eyes were streaming, and, because she made absolutely no sound, her grief, pain, and shame were all the more terrible.

Perhaps it was her humiliation, her absent lover, or simply her time. There was a silent *popping* sound that she heard inside her and then a rush of wetness. Her tears dried, transferred to a tributary that traveled down her thighs, bathing her legs, sliding over her sandaled feet.

There was another strangely muffled pop as the black man sank to the ground, clutching his shoulder. Trudy, still on her knees, mutely clutching her belly, stared at the blood blooming like a rose on his shirt front.

What happened?

Unlike Fat Boy, who did not own a gun but knew all about them, Trudy had no idea the type of pistol the doctor was holding that had been at chest level with the man. In pain and now dreaded fear, she saw that the man was equally stunned by the blood pulsing from his body and the water soaking the ground around her feet.

Both stared at the doctor. The man croaked out a shocked accusation and announcement. "You shot me?" Then, ridiculously, considering his own wound, he added, "Christ, her water broke."

Trudy was struggling to her feet, struggling to make sense of this turn of events.

The doctor raised the small weapon once more. Fired. For an instant, Trudy thought he'd shot *her*, but the man fell at her feet, facedown, more blood, dark, foamy, pooling red near his torso.

"You're going to be their message, McDaniel."

He advanced to stand before Trudy. His voice spewed venom for the dead man. "He was an animal—a goddamn sadistic *rapist.* He deserved this."

Trudy blinked rapidly, trying to think. She didn't know this dead man, whose DNA surely had traveled down her legs with her own birthing fluids.

She stood now, holding her belly protectively. She hurt all over.

The doctor did not even look her way. He nudged the body, being careful, Trudy saw, not to get any blood on his expensive loafers.

He stared at Trudy, the gun still in an offensive hold. Then he smiled, plainly. Trudy would even think later that it was the first friendly smile directed at her she'd ever seen from him.

She watched as the doctor, still saying nothing to her, opened the trunk of the luxury car. Inside, lying faceup on large plastic sheeting, was a small, dark man. His straight black hair and olive skin, those high, wide cheekbones and broad nose, said he was Asian. Trudy had heard of the influx of Asians into Mississippi, not the Chinese grocers, never Japanese, but Laotians, Vietnamese, Cambodians, those Hmong people.

The doctor hauled him easily from the trunk. The floppy way the man moved told Trudy—once an avid *CSI* fan back in Chicago—that the man had been dead less than an hour. She saw no wounds at first. When the doctor laid the dead man near the black man, also most definitely dead, Trudy saw the wound: a small hole in his shirt front. The bullet had gone straight through his heart.

Then the doctor did the most curious thing. As hard as he could, he hit himself in the abdomen. He took up a sturdy stick and pummeled himself about the neck and shoulders, even managing to bring blood on his shoulder and neck.

He stooped and scratched the man's skin, which drew a little blood. Trudy knew from movies and television that corpses didn't bleed. Maybe because he had just died, the blood trickled. The doctor punched the man in the gut, kicked his shins.

He reached into his pocket and extracted what was familiar to Trudy: the pills she was supposed to sell. He stuffed them into one of the coat pockets on the dead black man.

Trudy's mind was racing, but she still could make no sense of these senseless actions.

The doctor took the plastic from the car, the sound like crackling fire, and bundled it in his arms. He jerked his smooth bald head toward Shay's little house. Trudy saw that he was not sweating, not in this heat, not after what he'd just done, not a bead of sweat. His cool calmness terrified her more than what she had just witnessed, more than her own plight.

"Whose place is this again?"

She had told him before, but it couldn't have registered with him.

"My—Shay lives here. I'm with—we're with Shay." Her breath was heavy, as if the very air she used to speak could sink, heavy and foul, to the ground.

"Where're your babies?" The same question the dead man had asked. In his voice, she'd detected a threat. But in the doctor's baritone voice, there was the barest hint of caring, concern.

"Watching TV. Asleep." In truth, she had no idea exactly where they were and what they were doing. It was Shay who had given them a slice of raisin toast, scrambled eggs, half a banana, and a small glass of milk that morning before he went on his drug runs. She had been sleeping off her lover. Upon waking, not checking on her kids, she had submitted to her lover again.

"Don't you move, you got me?" The look of disgust in his eyes would have shriveled a lesser woman, a caring woman.

Why was the very reason he chose me to sell these drugs so...repugnant to him now? It was as if he actually regretted his own decision. But that was ridiculous, she thought. That would mean he...cared, right? No, he hated her, but he needed her. A mule—that's all she was to him.

Trudy could only nod at his order. Her mind was a blank. No, one thought was clear. *Run.* Her feet felt cemented to the ground.

The doctor walked up the low hill to the small house. In minutes, she saw smoke billowing from a barrel that Shay used to burn trash. She herself had done the same since she'd been here.

In a few minutes, he was back at her side. He placed the gun in the Asian man's left hand. He was motionless for a few moments, chin tucked into his chest. For an insane second, Trudy thought he was praying. He looked at her, the blue of his eyes almost invisible from the bright summer sun.

"I guess that third bastard of yours is ready to meet this world."

Trudy tried to find some compassion in that blue stare. She was convinced she did not.

"Go feed your pickaninnies, and let's get out of here." He reached into the backseat and retrieved a large plastic bag that was zipped shut.

The food was still warm, if the condensation told Trudy anything. But no smell emanated from it. She understood. There would be no evidence that he had ever been in this car. Though he was not the driver, he had worn thin gloves that must have been explained to the black man because he'd made no mention of them before he was killed.

Trudy moved as if a puppeteer's hand guided her. She took the bag of food, climbed the low hill; the baby, the rape, and the beating weighed her down with each step. The doctor was strolling—yes, strolling—behind her. She opened the front door, went to Matthew and Sasha, who were awake, their large eyes dark with curiosity, and maybe fear, for there was the smell of bleach, not overwhelming, but it was there, hanging in the still air of the small house. She watched the doctor go through each room, opening windows.

Again, her agile brain was piecing things together. Bleach, she knew, could easily destroy forensic evidence. The doctor must have washed his hands with bleach, maybe the plastic sheet before setting it afire in the barrel.

She served her children the small burgers, complete with apple slices and milk. She nibbled on a French fry, all the while praying that the doctor would not cut this baby from her. But why would he? Unless this food was laced with poison, he was doing even more than she was for her own children. She had not reached the point—yet—of giving her children small tokes on the pipe to stave off hunger. She knew women back in Chicago who did; even here, she'd met a few who sacrificed everything for their lover.

The doctor, she saw, was stuffing things—their belongings—into a large garbage bag. How were those dead men going to be explained? What would be the doctor's role in the explanation? Hers? The police would think the obvious: she was a crack whore. Like others, she stole. Like them, she lied. She knew she was screwed.

"Let's go." The doctor was at the door, holding the bag. Like tiny soldiers following the general into battle, Matthew and Sasha were behind him, each one clutching a paper bag of food.

"My baby's coming! Where're we going? Where're you taking me—us?"

The doctor raised his hand as if to give her a backhanded slap and then thought better of it. "I'm taking you to town to the hospital." He went through the door, the children goose-stepping behind him.

She knew the baby was coming soon. Matthew and Sasha had come so fast, by the time Fat Boy got her to Mercy, the babies were pushing their way free of her.

Trudy trundled behind them, the labor pains, though minutes apart, were sharp and searing. She saw the pickup parked in the small clearing a few hundred feet from Shay's house. When had he driven it there? Probably that morning, when Shay left on his runs and while she was getting her day started (read: smoking crack on the side of the house).

Of course, she thought, he would have his lies straight for the cops.

I drove out to check on Miss...Jenkins (she imagined that he would not recall her surname immediately) *and her kids...I was worried about her—you know, her past drug use. When I got there, I saw this man raping her. I stopped it before he could do more damage, fought him off her. That was when I saw that the Asian man was...watching. While I was trying to help her—her water had broken—I heard what I thought was a firecracker or something. There were shots fired, two, maybe three. Lord, I don't know. I turn around, and I see the bodies. No, she couldn't have killed them; I was helping her, remember? Maybe they came here to...*meet *her. I heard them arguing. That altercation must've resulted in each killing the other. She said she doesn't even know them.*

She would be tested for gunshot residue, and of course there would be none. Seminal fluid would corroborate the rape. Her scars and bruises, the beating.

The children had scrambled into the backseat of the truck and sat like stunned mice as they watched Trudy waddle up. The doctor did not help her in, but he did close the door for her before climbing in himself.

"When you have this bastard baby, you better leave town."

Trudy struggled to be comfortable. He drove around the parked car, the slain bodies, as if they were so much gravel.

Once more, Trudy thought she understood. *Why didn't you stay*, the police would later ask him, *wait for us?* He would have waited, he would say, but the woman was in labor; there were her two kids. She could hear the terse answer: *I'm a doctor. Nothing I could do for those poor bastards, but I could help her and her children.*

"You killed that Vietnamese man, too." Her voice was a raspy whisper, not because she did not want the children to hear but because she was too terrified to give her voice the air it needed to be heard above the rattle and rumble of the truck. She clutched her belly, stared at the man's profile, like pale granite.

"Not Vietnamese, OK? Cambodian."

Trudy waited for more, but the man simply looked in both directions (they were at the intersection between 82 and the road that led from Shay's house) and crossed the highway to a paved road, heading into the heart of the town.

She looked back at her babies. They were both napping, Matthew looking so like Fat Boy's baby pictures his granny had shown her that her heart melted. Then it froze in fear as she looked again at the killer beside her. He'd killed as easily as the Haitian dealer must have killed her Fat Boy.

"Please don't hurt us. Don't kill my baby." She wondered where the feisty girl she was had gone. She could stand toe-to-toe with Fat Boy, his granny, her father, but not anymore. Her lover, to sustain his existence in her life, had weakened her: give in and get.

She took her lover out of her front pocket, nervously caressed it in her trembling hands. The pains had started to come in a rhythmic pattern. This baby was coming, and she needed her lover. Now. She took out the lighter, warm from her body, took out the foil.

The doctor snarled at her. "You don't deserve those kids or the one in that belly of yours!" Before she could guess or counter his move, he had snatched her lover—the crack pipe—from her hands, tossed it out the window.

She stared uncomprehendingly for a second; then the tigress in her came to the fore. She hit, scratched, yelled.

And the doctor, trying to steer, hit back and pushed. Trudy screamed, and the fray caused the sleeping children to stir, awaken fully, to see their mother—who sometimes clothed them, sometimes fed them, and sometimes hurt them—being manhandled by the man who always fed them, never clothed them, and had never hurt them.

Loyalty if not love must have been the deciding factor.

Trudy saw a flurry of small fists—Matthew pounding the doctor's broad shoulders. He was screaming something, but Sasha's screeches obliterated any understanding.

The doctor cursed, pulled over on the quiet road, and cut the engine. Trudy watched as he hauled first a flailing Matthew from the truck and a wailing Sasha next. Trudy fumbled out, the coming baby making it difficult to maneuver her way to her children. She gathered them close, kneeling down, staring up at the heaving, red-faced killer.

He dumped the bags next to them from the back of the truck, spit on them, and got back in the truck.

Was that thunder she heard? No, it was the engine of a powerful truck—his truck. He was turning back. He would do what she feared. He would kill her, like he'd killed that slimy black man lying just a few hundred yards from her, kill her and Fat Boy's babies. She tried calling out for help, but her voice was a stream of tears.

She wondered how he would do this deed—kill four more people (for she knew her unborn baby would be counted as a person) and get away. She thought only a true monster could do this dastardly deed. She thought a lot as the truck got closer and closer, of Fat Boy, of this baby, of her mother, of—

Her last thought as pain and darkness claimed her was that her lover had to be found.

Chapter 6

Buck looked in his rearview mirror. He couldn't believe his eyes. The woman—that nigger *girl*—was on her knees, groveling in the grass, looking for that damn crack pipe. She deserved to die, just like Don McDaniel and that slant-eyed Atith Lim. *What the hell kind of name was* that? Well, he knew, of course: Cambodian.

He'd had enough of the threats from Lim. How the man had discovered his "extracurricular" activities Buck did not know. And it really didn't matter. He could not—*would* not—risk exposure. The threats were mainly to get Buck to turn over his clients to Lim, to have that nigger McDaniel to "handle them." Or he, Lim said in his perfect English, would be only too happy to "talk to some people." Of course, Lim hadn't considered that McDaniel was a snake in the grass.

Buck had never killed a *human* before, and it surprised him how easily he could pull the trigger. He was way too young for Vietnam, and those other wars—he thought of them as sand and oil wars—did not require conscription. And there was no way in hell he could volunteer when the Persian Gulf War started. He was in med school down in Jackson. With the overlapping of the wars with Afghanistan and Iraq, he had started his practice; he was, by then, raising his kids alone.

No wars to train him to kill the enemy, but he was a hunter. He'd killed many game in his years of hunting. When he'd shot McDaniel, he likened it to bringing down a buck, a wild boar—an animal. One shot to get his attention, the other with deadly accuracy to end his life.

He had lured McDaniel to accompany him to the country with the promise of letting him screw that girl Trudy and "to come to a mutual understanding."

He had been shocked to learn when he arrived at McDaniel's office that the Cambodian was there also.

"Dr. Bowden, I understand you're going to give my man here a good time?"

Buck nodded. "Maybe he deserves it. I understand you work him pretty hard." He understood nothing. He and McDaniel had barely spoken. He had heard from one of his old contacts that the man was into kinky sex. That was enough to start his plan.

Of course, Buck's offer to drive the man in one of the cars from the small fleet the Cambodian owned and leased in his car rental business gave the impression of his humility, his giving in to them. But McDaniel took it upon himself to drive one of the fleet of cars.

Lim gave a smile that looked to Buck purely reptilian. Maybe it was the small teeth, the flat, wide lips. "Dr. Bowden, how would I know about how hard a black man works? You were the slave owners."

Buck stared at the man. Where had that come from? He was simply making loose conversation. And Lim was so wrong about one thing.

"My people never owned slaves. We were always just people who worked the land. And I don't see how that has anything to do with anything."

Lim looked at McDaniel, raised his sharp, black brows. "So you were never his nigger? Because you're *mine*."

Buck wasn't sure who was the more surprised by this comment, him or McDaniel.

"What?" Such a simple word, Buck thought, looking at McDaniel. It carried the weight of his betrayal by Lim. He must have been loyal to the Asian, Buck considered, and only just now realized that, with that ugly statement, he was less than an ant in the man's eyes.

"They don't read. They can barely do simple math. Maybe arithmetic, right, McDaniel? Maybe to count the food stamps, WIC, or whatever you all get from this government. And you're always saying how the government owes you! For what? Wearing your pants below your butt, dressing like prostitutes? We come here and we take over—all of us, no matter what country. Asians are ruling. Same chance you had, but you're too stupid to—"

McDaniel's arm rose quickly, and Buck caught the glint of metal in McDaniel's hand. He shot once, and Lim slid from the chair he was reclining in to the carpeted floor, his flat eyelids fluttering crazily, his gaze confused and panicked.

"I've been waiting to do that for four years. Didn't think it was going to be like this, though."

Buck stayed still; McDaniel still had the gun.

"Help me get him in the car." And because McDaniel *did* have that gun, Buck felt obliged to help. When McDaniel went outside to make sure the coast was clear, Buck took the Asian man's gun, lying casually but fully loaded in a drawer.

That was that until he raped that girl, Trudy.

The two shots he took to kill McDaniel weren't necessary. The first one was just to get the man's attention, to let him know he was serious about the threats and would not yield to their tactics. But his intent all along was to kill the man. He was smart enough to know that Lim was not the top man. There might be others soon enough.

He smiled grimly into the mirror, already knowing that he had to turn around, go back, and get the woman and her kids. In fact, as he slowed the truck, cut the engine, he realized his returning was more to save those babies than their addict whore of a mother. But he remembered the assault and grimaced. McDaniel deserved what he got; no matter what she had done, she didn't deserve that horrific treatment.

With something akin to fondness, he thought of those two children clamoring after him—mostly because, like Pavlovian pups, they had learned that, invariably, if he was there, they had hot food to eat. The boy was already handsome, the little girl too thin to be considered a beauty, but proper food would take care of that. He—he refused to admit any *emotional* connection to them—took them in *stride* (so much better than saying he cared about their health and well-being).

He was within a few feet of the trio now. The woman was crying, crawling, the children standing close to each other, whimpering like lost kittens, pups and kittens. A flash of a memory appeared in his head: his own three, huddled next to him after their mother had ridden off into the sunset with her boyfriend. Though he made a good home and living for them, and though they loved him unequivocally, that scene stayed with them. Abandonment was abandonment.

Against his will, Buck smiled as he stopped before them. They were cute little critters.

"Come on, you pitiful ticks." He scooped the little girl—*she* is *a cutie,* he decided—into his arms and placed her back in the backseat of his big truck. The boy, Buck saw, was not so easily swayed, but he clamored in after his sister and stared out at Buck with huge, wary eyes.

He actually thought about it: leave her here, let her have that crack-addicted baby, and maybe even die, both of them. The baby would be collateral damage.

He stood over her, silent and judging, finding her terribly lacking in every aspect of what he deemed motherhood. Then, wordlessly, roughly, he hauled her up, and this time he did slap her, but not that pained, tear-streaked face. He slapped her hands, hard and fast, over and over again. Her hands were dirt-smeared, grass-stained, from her searching for that damn pipe!

His teeth were clenched so tightly his jaw hurt. "If it was up to me, you'd have this baby like the bitch you are!" He cut his blue eyes at her but did not see a pretty, young black girl, face swollen and bruised. He saw a white face, pretty, with blond hair styled in what was called an updo back then. He shut his eyes and when he opened them, it was the colored girl. It was Trudy. Not his cheating wife.

She was saying something, harsh and ugly, he supposed, but he wasn't listening.

"You've already had two bastards; hell, act like it so I can get you to the hospital. Like hell I'm going to deliver a nigger, bastard baby in the woods!" Though, of course, he had delivered many a black baby in the hospital over the years. In the back of his mind, with every single one, knowing what the future held for some of them, maybe for most of them, he'd wanted to do what the Egyptians had done to the Hebrews, but he would do it with compassion: sling them against a wall, bash their little pointy heads in, end their misery before it could begin.

He drove hunched over the steering wheel. She whimpered. The children cried sullenly and quietly. He turned the radio up as loud as he could to drown out everything that tried to form thoughts in his brain.

Chapter 7

TRUDY AWOKE TO a brown face peering at her with dark-brown eyes. The face had brown hair framing it, and the body wore something in brown. Had she lost her vision, was losing it, could see only shades of brown? The body took shape, came into focus: a woman.

"You're awake," the brown woman said in a brown voice.

Trudy touched her face, then her chest, going lower, and felt a small, soft mound of flesh beneath the sheets.

"My baby, where's my baby?" She pulled herself up and was immediately and painfully pulled back down. She felt a tug against her wrist and looked at her left hand. It was secured to the bedpost with a plastic restraint.

She was handcuffed to a bed?

The woman made sounds, not soothing but not angry either.

"You had a boy; he's in NICU. Tested positive for crack." The look of malevolence she leveled at Trudy actually caused the girl to shrink back into the pillows.

"Matthew and Sasha..." Not a question, rather a raspy plea.

"Your other babies?" The woman snorted and walked out of the room.

Trudy tried to think and could not. She wanted Fat Boy. She wanted her mother. The gray mist was lifting. Fat Boy was dead. Her mother was long dead.

She wanted her father, Fat Boy's granny. Her babies. She wanted her baby boy!

She wanted her shit, so she could get it together. She whimpered and was still whimpering when a white coat filled her vision, and she looked up into glacial blue eyes.

"I see you're awake," the killer doctor cordially said.

"I won't say anything—"

The brown-faced nurse appeared, and the doctor clamped a hand on Trudy's head, as if feeling for a fever, but the pressure was familiar to her. She clamped her mouth shut in terror.

He had the capacity, the *ability*, to kill: her, the babies.

"How's my baby, my boy?"

The nurse glared at her. "She *ought* to be grateful. Right now," she said in that flat, brown voice, "he's fine. For a full-term baby, he's kinda small, but other than that, he's fine. The neonatologist will release him from NICU tomorrow; he doesn't foresee any problems."

Trudy sighed. The nurse was not even going to speak to her.

"He's feeding?" The nurse nodded and left the room. The doctor settled on the girl's bed. "The police have already been here. You're in the clear—as long as you remember what I said."

"P-police?" How many hours, or days, had passed? She barely remembered the ride into Greenville. Could not even remember the birth of her son.

The doctor pinched his forehead with a thumb and middle finger, bringing his blond brows together. Trudy thought he looked…not scared, but he lacked that arrogant swagger from before. What had changed him?

"Yes, your *Shay* came home, found the car, the two bodies." He smiled as his blue eyes frosted over. "His alibi was airtight, and there was no connection between him and McDaniel or Lim." He stroked the back of his bald head, said flatly, "I told them about what he did to you, how I had to fight him."

I was right, Trudy thought in triumph.

"Wasn't too hard to prove that McDaniel had been with…a woman, and your *Shay* broke down and said the woman might have been you. His story corroborated mine: I came to check on you, and you lived with him."

She hadn't thought of Shay until the doctor mentioned him. After all he had done for her, she could dismiss him from her mind so easily. She didn't think she could feel any lower.

Trudy was spent, as tired as she had ever been. All she wanted was sleep, but she had to know. "Those men—you killed them."

The doctor smiled, shrugged. "Sometimes, there are unavoidable…circumstances, collateral damage, let's say. Lim and McDaniel wanted my *operation*, if you will, and were threatening me. That squint nigger, that Cambodian, came in with a way to move the merchandise faster. He recruited McDaniel. On the school board, believe it or not.

"The police think they had heard of your…*talents* and were there to sample them, that they got into an argument after McDaniel *spent time* with you, after I stopped that nigger McDaniel's vicious attack on you." Trudy saw his mouth turn down at its corners in disgust. "The authorities think they had some business deal that went sour, and one thing led to the other, which resulted in their killing each other. They found evidence of correspondence between them in McDaniel's XTS. But I didn't kill Lim."

Trudy frowned, trying to keep her head clear. She noticed the way the doctor used the word *nigger*. It was almost the same as the blacks who still found a use for the horrible word: to describe a friend (*that's my nigger*), to describe a black person who had shamed the race (*that low-life nigger*), and even descriptive (*that nigger there*).

"Then, who—"

"I guess sometimes you have to stand up for your beliefs." He shook his head at some memory. "McDaniel killed him. See, black lives *do* matter." This pronouncement baffled Trudy, but she said nothing.

What about her and the babies? She was under arrest for endangering a newborn, she guessed, not for possession, not for distribution.

Would the state take her babies, put her in jail?

The doctor seemed to have read her mind as he crossed one leg over the other, still sitting casually on her bed. "I talked to the judge, not Barry. He's not touching this. Anyway, this judge has a program—he's going to place you in a home with a woman in Greenville; she'll take care of those pickaninnies of yours and see to it that you don't do crack. Get a job, make enough money to show you can take care of those kids, that baby. You stay off it three months, you can leave. You're on probation, of course, and any hint of drug use and you go straight to prison. Those babies go to the state, and you never see them again."

Three months? She could barely go without her lover for three hours, and he was saying months? But to be without Matthew, Sasha, the baby—she had to think of a name for him. Fat Boy would want a junior—would have wanted a junior. Adrian.

"When can I leave? See Matthew and Sasha, take Adrian." She tested the name. Yes, Adrian, her baby, who was born with crack in his system, who might be retarded or...damaged in some other, *worse* way.

"We'll keep you both here until the weekend." It was Tuesday. "Then, see how it goes."

The doctor ran a hand over his smooth head. He grinned at her, and she was sure his eyes glinted like a spark about to be set ablaze. "Of course, it would be very nice to get this whenever I want." He ran a hand liberally over her breasts, full of crack-tainted milk, useless for her baby, her still swollen but flatter belly, and down to the crux at her thighs. He kneaded and pushed.

"And I wish I could have this in *some manner* by the weekend." He sighed, looked at her deeply, and Trudy, feeling almost hypnotized, could not look away. His voice became harsh. "But I have to steer clear of you, too, bitch. You're getting too dangerous to be around."

He smiled affably as the brown nurse came in, and he left the room. While the woman clucked over Trudy's irresponsibility to her children, to herself, Trudy thought hard, but only one word reverberated around in her head: *escape, escape.*

But how? She had no idea where her babies were. She was tethered to the bed, and the condemning nurse was urging her to drink, *drink*. But Trudy could not drink. The nurse was more than likely working for the doctor. The drink was poisoned. She had to leave before they killed her. But she was *so* hungry, *so* thirsty.

No, don't drink or eat anything. Poison. Everything is a deadly poison.

With her right hand, she slapped the drink away. "You fucking bitch, get away from me! Get *out*." She strained against the handcuff, felt the pliable but hard plastic dig unrelentingly into the skin. There was a smear of blood.

She had to leave. She had to talk to Fat Boy about the baby. She had a baby, right? A girl? Sasha...No, Sasha was three. Matthew, older. She—yes, she had a baby. A boy. A boy she would call...She fell into an exhausted sleep, her body awash with her own foul-smelling, terror-fueled sweat.

Chapter 8

Matthew liked the baby; his name was Adrian. Trudy had said that was Fat Boy's *real name*. Until he was introduced to the baby, he had simply thought Fat Boy's name was Fat Boy. He knew Trudy and Fat Boy were *his parents*. That they were his *mother and father*. But he really did not know what that meant.

He had always known that Sasha was his sister, and he knew now that the baby was his brother. He wasn't sure exactly what that meant, either, but since he knew he was older than both, he felt...happy that he would one day help take care of them. That is what an older brother did, he decided.

Anyway, he liked the baby. And Sasha, who tried to do everything he did, liked the baby, too. Matthew had heard that Adrian might be born *with problems*. He had examined the baby several times when Old Miss Carrolton changed or fed him. He cried, he peed, and he pooped. He acted like any baby Matthew saw on television.

Old Miss Carrolton was nice enough. She talked to them a lot; Trudy talked now, too. In a small, shaky voice. Old Miss Carrolton was always asking her if she was ailing, if she needed anything, to *speak up when someone is talking to you, girl*.

Matthew thought of Fat Boy sometimes; he missed him, his big smile, his silly voices he used to make him and Sasha laugh, his sloppy kisses and strong hugs. He missed Granny, who was Fat Boy's grandmother. He missed Poppa, the man Trudy called *Daddy* sometimes. He figured Poppa was their grandfather.

But he didn't miss Trudy. Ever. He saw her enough not to miss her and when he did see her, she was either sleeping—she slept a lot—or she was leaving with that white man who said he was a doctor or another white man who said he was a judge. Or, when she talked to him and Sasha, she was usually telling them to be quiet, that she couldn't hear herself think. She was always threatening to hit them, to teach them a thing or two if they continued to "look at her in that tone of voice." And she would swat at them, mostly hitting air as they dodged her licks. She never seemed to have the energy to come after them.

She never hit the baby, but Matthew thought, using Old Miss Carrolton's words, it was just a matter of time. She acted like her nerves were on fire, Old Miss Carrolton said, and he knew enough to know that it was because she didn't have that pipe. He was glad about that, at least. He knew doctors made people feel better. He wondered why the doctor couldn't make Trudy better, like she was before that pipe.

Granny used to say, *It's that pipe, Fat Boy, I'm tellin' ya.* Or Poppa: *Trudy, thank God your mama isn't alive to see you sucking on that damn pipe.* And then he would cry, holding Trudy like he was trying to break her.

Matthew didn't know what judges did, but he watched television with Old Miss Carrolton, and sometimes there were judges who talked to a lot of people.

He remembered one; she reminded Matthew of Old Miss Carrolton, whiter looking but the same short hair and thin face. She had a big black man with her who never said much, and he looked mean. But when he smiled or the thin-faced white woman in the black robe laughed or smiled, he liked them. Old Miss Carrolton said she couldn't miss her judge shows.

When the doctor or that judge came to take Trudy away with them, Old Miss Carrolton told him not to worry. *Just be patient, boy. God is working on that girl.*

Matthew did not know God. He had heard of him but had never met him. Old Miss Carrolton told him God's son was there, too, working on Trudy. God and his boy named Jesus were even in their hearts. That scared Matthew because a whole person could be inside him and Sasha and the baby. Maybe that wasn't good, because Adrian the baby might have these *problems* that Trudy gave him. And maybe God and his son Jesus inside his heart were making those problems worse.

The old woman took him and Sasha and Adrian the baby to a church to meet God. Afterward, when they were alone, he asked Sasha, *Did you meet God?* But she didn't because, he supposed, she was too little.

He wondered which boy he saw was Jesus, but whenever he would ask Old Miss Carrolton, "Is that Jesus?" pointing, she would laugh and tell him, "Hush, boy. That's DeShawn," or some other name, never Jesus.

Old Miss Carrolton showed him a painting on a fan she used in church that had a brown man with long, curly hair, like maybe a woman he'd seen on TV. *That's Jesus, boy.* Matthew looked and looked, trying to find any resemblance between this brown woman with a beard and the people at that church. No, he'd never seen Jesus.

They had been with Old Miss Carrolton for almost three months. He knew this because Old Miss Carrolton would say, *Oh, y'all been here a whole month, and Trudy's doing so fine.* Then, another time: *Y'all done been here two whole months. How you feelin', girl?* And this would be for Trudy, who answered with almost the same smile she had before that pipe, like when Fat Boy was there, making everyone laugh and giving them hugs and kisses.

Old Miss Carrolton told Matthew to pray to God that this thorn in Trudy's side be taken away. He wondered about that. He didn't know what a thorn was, but he thought that was bad. A thorn and crack! So he prayed for both. *God and Jesus, I don't want Trudy smoking that damn pipe, and I want Fat Boy to come and get us.* (He wondered about that woman with the beard. He wasn't sure which was worse—a woman with a beard or that he had to pray to God and his boy when he'd never met them.)

Matthew liked to sit and talk to Old Miss Carrolton when Sasha or Adrian slept. He should sleep, too, she would say, but ever since Trudy had started smoking that crack pipe—that he knew and knew well—he tried to sleep when she slept, and sometimes she could go a long time without sleep, all twitchy and running around, like a chicken with its head cut off. Granny had said that one time back in Chicago. He remembered that he was from Chicago, he and Sasha. Their baby Adrian would be from *Missippi.* That was what Old Miss Carrolton said: *Y'all in Missippi now, boy; things diff'ent.*

This morning, Trudy came to the kitchen and sat with them while Old Miss Carrolton stirred butter into grits. She made the best grits, Matthew thought, happy that she would add bacon and eggs to his plate. He felt like he hadn't had eggs in a long time.

"Well, well, well!" Old Miss Carrolton was smiling at Trudy. "You look like you could do with a nice plate of food, girl! Breakfast is goin' to be ready in five minutes. Why don't you pour up some juice and milk for those chaps there? You fed that baby?" Matthew wondered why she always asked Trudy that, like she might forget to do that. He looked at Trudy, and their eyes met. Her eyes were bright and sunny. He didn't like that. Like she never forgot to feed anybody, and she knew she often forgot to feed them! So when her smile started to shake and he saw how weak it was, he felt better. He knew Trudy, and if that look had reached her mouth, he would have been looking into a stranger's eyes.

"He took the bottle…I just…" Her voice got crackly, and she put her hand to her mouth.

Old Miss Carrolton, still working on those grits, said, "Yeah, girl, I know. But what's done is done. You got to—" She went through a coughing spell, and when it was over, she looked like she had forgotten that she was talking to Trudy.

There was a knock at the back door, and she called for whoever it was to just come on in; it was open.

It was the doctor. "Morning, Miss Lola."

Matthew had seen the doctor kiss Old Miss Carrolton before, like he was doing now, always with a pat on her shoulder as he leaned in and planted his lips on the cheek she raised to his mouth.

He was dressed in his work clothes—at least, that's how he explained the suit and tie and his shiny shoes to Old Miss Carrolton when she asked, *Where are you goin' all spiffed up, Buck?*

He took a seat between Matthew and Sasha. He was sitting on the other side of Trudy, who mumbled something Matthew couldn't understand. It was Sasha who waved her spoon and said, *Hey!* She was always glad to see him. Matthew blinked his eyes. He supposed *he* was glad to see the doctor, too.

"Something smells good, Miss Lola!" The doctor's face got all pink and white with his smile and teeth showing as she placed a plate full of food in front of him. Then, in minutes, all of them were sitting at the table, eating her grits, eggs, bacon, and biscuits, with the doctor talking to Old Miss Carrolton and telling what Matthew thought were not jokes, but whatever they were, Old Miss

Carrolton was laughing and coughing, coughing and laughing, like laughing at what the doctor was saying just took her breath away.

"Miss Lola, you OK?" The doctor gave her a look that told Matthew he was worried about her, that he *cared* about her. "You know you can come see me anytime." That she was his *friend.*

"Boy, a body can't cough in front of you before you go actin' all doctor like. Remember, I knew you when you couldn't even *spell doctor*!" They laughed, and the doctor said that was true. But Old Miss Carrolton didn't say she would come see the doctor, and the doctor didn't make her.

Sasha struggled to feed herself without making a mess (she usually made a mess, Matthew conceded, with brotherly arrogance), and he dug deep into the grits and bacon and eggs. Oh, and the gooey cheese and hot biscuits! His stomach might not be able to hold all he saw before him, but his eyes could.

"He's got a good appetite, that one, Buck. Probably could eat you under the table."

"Now maybe, Miss Lola, but not when I was his age, though." More laughter as they watched him eat.

Matthew didn't know what was funny, but he figured he shouldn't eat another biscuit, so he concentrated on the juice instead. It was just as good, and he emptied the glass.

Old Miss Carrolton—the doctor kept calling her "Miss Lola"—nodded and poured more coffee into the doctor's cup.

Soon, the doctor reared back from the table and looked at Trudy. "Well, guess we better head off." He stood, bent to Old Miss Carrolton, and kissed her cheek again. "We'll be back by five. You ready?" Matthew noticed he never called her "Miss Trudy" or "Trudy." And she never really spoke to him. She stood also but did not kiss Old Miss Carrolton. She did stroke Sasha's bushy hair and nodded to him, mouthing his name, *Matthew.* Then, they were gone, and Old Miss Carrolton was humming and putting away the leftover bacon and biscuits. She told him through a coughing spell to take Sasha into the living room, and she would come in later with the baby Adrian.

He had watched her lay the sleeping baby in the middle of her bed in her bedroom. So he wouldn't roll out of the bed, she always told him when he asked.

Together he and Sasha walked into the living room to watch Old Miss Carrolton's television. She scrambled up on the couch beside him, and in a few minutes, Old Miss Carrolton was squeezing herself between them (they liked that she pretended she was a big elephant and trying to get between two giraffes, when she was just normal size, as far as Matthew could tell) and yelling at the television. *See, I knew he was the father! I knew it. Look at that baby, looks just like him!*

He didn't ask where the baby was, but it was like Old Miss Carrolton read his mind. "The baby's napping. I'll get him up soon enough."

Sasha tucked the finger next to her thumb into her mouth. Just as he was going to tell her *Take it out*, Old Miss Carrolton made some type of sound and fell asleep, just like that. He touched her, shook her, but she stayed asleep. So he settled back against the couch and thought of the breakfast they'd eaten and wondered what would be for lunch. He remembered yesterday that it had been fried chicken and green beans and little potatoes, iced tea with lemon slices floating in the glass, and then something she called teacakes that looked like her biscuits but tasted like cake.

After a while, he got off the couch, went to the bathroom that was in the bedroom he and Sasha slept in with Trudy, and used it. His stomach would be nice and empty, ready for the lunch Old Miss Carrolton would make. When he was washing his hands, Sasha came in to do the same thing. She placed her little behind on the toilet, and in a few seconds, he heard her poop plopping into the commode.

He gave her a wad of tissue paper, told her to wipe three times, and put the paper in the commode. He always said that to her because he was sure if he didn't, she wouldn't. He flushed the toilet. They both stood on the little stand by the faucet, and he gave her some soap, let her wash her hands while he washed his.

Then, both returned to the living room. Old Miss Carrolton was still sleeping. She must be tired from all the cooking she did this morning, he decided, and climbed on the couch. Sasha sat on her right side, and he sat on the old lady's left, and they watched the television.

The same man from before said another man was *not* the father. And this man—he reminded Matthew a little of Fat Boy—danced around and pointed fingers at a woman who did not remind him of Trudy, who sat there crying and yelling at the people who were shouting at her. She pointed at the people yelling at her. *You don't know me; don't judge me!* Then she ran away, and the white man followed her.

They watched television a long time, and Matthew wondered why Old Miss Carrolton was so quiet, still sleeping. He knew enough about the remote control to change the channel, and since the old woman slept on, he changed channels until he found a cartoon with Dora the Explorer on it. That made Sasha happy, and he liked Dora, too.

After a while, he got hungry and got a banana for him and Sasha—she liked those, and he checked on the baby Adrian. He was awake and throwing his arms and legs about. Matthew climbed in bed with the baby but had no idea what to do, so he grabbed it by the waist and hauled it to the living room for Old Miss Carrolton to take over, but she was still sleeping, so he laid the baby in her lap and climbed back on the sofa.

The baby had started crying in earnest now, so Matthew went to the kitchen and looked in the refrigerator and saw a bottle of milk. He ran back in the room, stuffed the nipple in the baby's mouth, and watched it gurgle and choke, but eventually the bottle was empty, and the baby was quiet but stinky, his eyes on the television, too.

Matthew still wondered about the soundness of Old Miss Carrolton's sleep, but he forgot when he found a channel with *The Simpsons* theme music starting. He sat back on the sofa. Soon he got sleepy. Sasha was already curled against Old Miss Carrolton, sleeping. The baby was asleep, too, so Matthew picked it up, again by the waist, and hauled him back to the old lady's bedroom. He stood there, studying the situation. He was too small to climb in bed holding the baby, so he laid the baby on the floor. Adrian whimpered but didn't cry; Matthew climbed in and pulled the baby up by the shoulders until he was in the center of the bed like Old Miss Carrolton had done. He arranged the quilt around and over the baby—he was gurgling, but Matthew could tell by now that he was gearing up for another nap. Matthew went back to the living room.

He frowned as he settled himself next to the old lady. Usually, she was like a soft quilt, cozy and warm, making rumblings in her chest. Not now. She was kind of cold and sleeping without making a sound. He lay against her and watched television until, soon, he slept, too.

Chapter 9

TRUDY MANAGED TO stay in the house for two months after the funeral. The only reason she was not arrested, her kids taken from her, was because Mrs. Luella "Lola" Carrolton had died of natural causes, cardiac arrest. She was about eighty, eighty-five, after all. She had been fine that morning when Trudy left the house; she was the designated caregiver of the children, and most importantly, Trudy tested negative for drugs.

Mrs. Carrolton's family came—from as far away as York, England, and as close as around the corner on a side street. Family members swept through the house like locusts through wheat, taking whatever trinket or keepsake of the old woman's not padlocked or nailed down.

Trudy's father came, sad that he couldn't bring Fat Boy with him, glad that he would see his three grandkids. Fat Boy's granny came with him, equally sad and happy. She brought Fat Boy's puppy Charlie, who was all head and feet now. The children fell in love with him all over again. A bittersweet reunion was the phrase that Fat Boy would have used, who liked to use *bittersweet* for its *oppositeness.*

Go back to Chicago; come back to Chicago, they all said.

Mrs. Carrolton's family did not say this, but Trudy could feel it: *You don't have to go to Chicago, but you and those three chil'ren got to get the hell out of here.* And to ensure their swift departure, their belongings were neatly stacked in cardboard boxes and placed on the edge of the front yard at the end of those two months.

The heartless gesture incensed her father, who used their shitty tactic to drive home their point: *Come home. Be with family.*

"I'm staying here in Greenville. I have a job." She did, in fact, have a job; indeed, she had two: one was the BJs she gave the judge for pocket money, and the other was working for the nurses in the doctor's office as file clerk, getting paid two dollars above minimum wage. "And it's quieter here—safer." It was not; per capita, Greenville was as bad as Chicago in terms of shootings and drug use, but she knew her "city" people would think otherwise.

The visit precipitated the dreaded responsibility Trudy had been avoiding for the last five months. Matthew and Sasha associated Poppa and Granny with Fat Boy. *Where was Fat Boy? Where's our daddy?*

So Trudy sat the children down in the Hampton Inn her father and Fat Boy's granny were staying in—in separate but *adjoining* rooms. In a corner of Trudy's quick mind, she considered the possibilities.

"Fat Boy is...he went to...Fat Boy isn't coming. He can't." She looked to her father for help, but the man was sitting there, wringing his hands between his legs, eyes glassy with tears. If she didn't know better, Trudy would think he was deep in his cups again, but she knew he was stone-cold sober. *Grieving looks a lot like drunk,* she thought.

"He sick?" This from Sasha, who understood on some level that sometimes sick people could not travel well.

But Matthew got it. Trudy did not know how, but his gruff "It's because he's dead, isn't it?" told her he knew. He sounded like his grandfather.

"Yes...Some very bad men did it—killed him." Granny hugged Sasha to her when she said this, her voice thick with emotion.

But Trudy was not sure if it was grief or anger that made her voice shake. Trudy read her thoughts clearly, even though she knew it tore the woman apart to think this: *My grandson's dead because of* your *habit.*

"He liked me and Sasha, though." Matthew's voice dared anyone to counter that statement.

"Oh, baby, he loved you all! Loved you!" The older woman was in tears now.

"And he would love our baby Adrian, wouldn't he?" Again, that miniature adult voice of challenge.

"Yes," Trudy asserted, answering her son, holding the baby, bumping him on her knee; she refused to let the tears break from her eyes.

Matthew pulled his lips back, considering. Then, in a decisive voice that eerily echoed Fat Boy's deep timber, "Then I guess it's all right, isn't it?"

Mr. Jenkins sprang from his seat by the window and fled into the bathroom. They could all hear him sobbing through the closed door, even though the faucet was on full blast.

Trudy blinked her eyes, and the tears washed down her face in a river. All this was her fault. But no one said this. And for that small favor, she was grateful.

When Truman joined the others, his smile—*Oh, I forgot how handsome my pops is*, thought Trudy complacently—was sad but loving.

Then, let us take the babies. You know I'm not drinking, Trudy.

Her father's big hands no longer shook, but she couldn't trust that he might slip back into his habit. (Like she knew she *could*—eventually, inevitably. Her lover was getting lonely. And she was getting hungry.)

"No, I'll be fine. And I'm glad you came down. Matthew and Sasha are happy, and you got the chance to meet your new grand, Daddy!" For her brother had yet to impregnate a girl. Not necessarily *marry* before getting a child.

That morning, Fat Boy's granny had slipped Trudy three one-hundred-dollar bills. This kind gesture was unknown to her father, who had placed some fifties into her palm. She had almost seven hundred dollars, and her children, between them, had almost fifty dollars from their surreptitious generosity.

"Where are you going to stay?" Fat Boy's granny asked. In her sixties, she looked easily ten years younger.

And because of her father's past (so he said) drinking, he looked ten years older. So, both looked about fifty. Trudy smiled to herself, her old spunk back.

"You two should get together. Daddy, Granny, how about it? I know Fat Boy would like it."

And they all laughed. Fat Boy's grandmother reminded her of her very much alive man who was in Chester. And what would she do with a man young enough to be her son?

Trudy indelicately pointed out that her "man" was incarcerated and would be incarcerated for many long, cold nights. And what was twenty years when she looked so hot in that pink tracksuit?

Her father simply sat there, crushing his grandkids in a hug and blushing furiously.

This question seemed to get him thinking, though, for when they left, her father telling her they would head toward Memphis on Highway 49 to 61, then connect to I-55 and switch over to I-57 in Arkansas, to her, he was much more attentive to his neighbor of over a decade.

And Trudy was alone with her three babies and her erstwhile crack habit. She really had been clean for those critical three months, but now they were homeless once more.

Shay!

She hadn't seen him since the morning of that awful day, the day Adrian was born and those two men left dead. On *his* property.

He'd had to clear himself of any involvement in their deaths. Of course, the doctor's testimony had helped. A black man in the South, how bad was it for him? Would he accept her back in his life after all this time, after all that had happened?

From the grave, she heard a voice that she thought was lost forever in her memory, her mother saying to her brother, when he thought of trying out for little league baseball at seven. Was he good enough? Should he?

Nothing beats a failure but a try.

She was too afraid to FaceTime him or simply call him. Instead, she texted. The other social media communication outlets would not work for this request. It required words of explanation. Forgiveness.

Hey.

Trudy???

Yeah. My pops and Fat Boy's granny were just here. They brought the dog, Fat Boy's dog Charlie w/them.

You not goin back to Chi-town w/them?

I had the baby, member?

Nope. But I figured you would by now. You not a fucking elephant!

He was joking with her, a sign that maybe they could get back to their old footing: not passionate lovers like she and Fat Boy had been but decent, close friends who had good sex when it suited them.

You got jokes.

Her cell phone jangled. Shay.

"Trudy, you need anything, just say the word. I'm here."

You. I need you, she thought, recalling the tender way he held her after making love, cradling her close, his long fingers, fingers that belonged to a basketball player, a pianist, or surgeon, trailing the swell of her breasts, around her navel, down to the warmth, the heat of the treasure he coveted. Lying together, it felt as if they lived off each other's breaths.

No, her memory clogged and then cleared. That was her Fat Boy. She could barely remember how Shay fucked her.

"Can I come back?"

"Babe, as far as I'm concerned, you never left. How do I get there?"

Chapter 10

"Casino Blues" was the song playing as Belinda Hardaway Higginbotham sped up the highway, heading back to Memphis from Greenville, Mississippi, on Highway 61 N. She hadn't really been listening to the radio before, but when this song came on, her attention shifted to the words being sung by Milton Campbell. *Casino Blues…Casino Blues…*

Angelo had told her this song was playing the day they met at the little café in Midtown. Hearing it now, with recent events weighing heavily on her mind, this seemed *symmetrical.*

Perhaps it was because her background was the hard sciences, she tended to shift her thoughts to factoids that meant little to others but something to her. Milton Campbell had been called Little Milton years ago. He was born near Inverness, Mississippi. Another singer, also named Milton Campbell, who sang gospel music, was from a small town about eleven miles northeast of Inverness, called Moorhead. Because their singing careers overlapped, someone had been clever enough to distinguish them. The gospel singer was called Big Milton. And for good reason, as Belinda understood from her mother: he was a rotund fellow.

Well, certainly, she could not say she had the blues. Her mother's operation had been a success; she'd stayed two weeks in her hometown of Indianola nursing her back to a reasonable state of health. She knew she could rely on the neighbors in the old, close-knit neighborhood to help her mother with any chores she could not master yet, and she'd given her cellular and home numbers in Memphis to everyone on the block. They'd call, if necessary. She had felt a little uneasy when she was packing her car two days ago, on her way first to Greenville for shopping and then on to Memphis.

Her mother, her voice forcibly strong, had mockingly scolded her, saying through the screen door as Belinda had reluctantly backed the 2015 Camry out of the driveway, *Honey, you'd better hurry home to that nice boy. Mama'll be just fine!* Her smile, bright and sunny, was what finally convinced Belinda to leave, head home and back to that *nice boy.* Hardly a boy. She herself was as close to thirty-four as a body could get, and he was a full year older.

But the song was apropos; just yesterday, she'd spent two hours going from casino to casino in Greenville with a friend from high school. She wasn't as desperate as the man in the song, but she'd gambled (blackjack was her game of choice if she *had* to gamble), and like the jubilant man sang at the end of the song, she had actually won a little stack of money!

Belinda turned the volume up as the deejay on WDIA out of Memphis announced that the next hour was dedicated to the "late, great Johnnie Taylor." "Cheaper to Keep Her" was followed by "Drown in My Own Tears," "Disco Lady," and "Last Two Dollars."

Belinda smiled to herself. Johnnie Taylor had always been a favorite of her late father's, and just hearing his soft voice made her nostalgic for her own father's reckless renditions of the bluesman's songs.

The medley of hits lasted the full hour, and it was as the last song was played, "For Your Precious Love," that she heard the faint noise in the car. She turned the knob, lowering the music, and the noise, slight but certainly present, ceased almost immediately. She breathed a small sigh of relief. She did not need any trouble, not now. Besides, she knew that the real trouble had already come and that there was even more to come as soon as she got home to Angelo.

She'd called him last night, ready to try to tell him something about this new *wrinkle,* but he wasn't home, and she couldn't leave *that* message on their machine! She'd simply texted him a message that, content wise, said almost nothing. *Mama's fine.* Then another message, before he could respond: *We'll talk about this later; no need to call. See u soon.* Several emojis of faces with hearts for eyes, kissing lips, and smiles followed. No explanation as to what *this* was. How could she text him this, tell him this news over the phone? *Face-to-face is better,* she thought, *face-to-face.* She knew he would ignore this and text her, call her. She pushed the off button. He would have no way to contact her now. She had bought a reprieve.

At some point, her sanity had returned; the fear had subsided. Still, she drove northward, onward to a new destiny.

In Walls, Mississippi, she stopped to use the bathroom. She had always liked this tiny town, essentially a village. The people were friendly; the bathrooms at this highway service station, spotless. Good fried chicken. Even the white people spoke, engaged her in light, friendly conversation. Country white people were just like country black people, she had always considered. Same language, same food.

Nowadays people were trying to stir up the long dormant displays of racism in the state. Those nonsoutherners never understood the South!

Yes, bigotry was real, even racism, but these days, it was like their views on homosexuality or mental illness. Those prejudices or acceptances were there, but, by and large, good, bad, or indifferent, among southerners, they simply were *not to be discussed.*

Now she apologized to the short line of three women whom she went ahead of, breaking the line. *Emergency*, she breathed, with a little exasperation. The trio of women looked so much alike that Belinda guessed they were a mother and two teenaged daughters: same fine brown hair and white skin with the palest yellow tint to it, suggesting they tanned badly. They nodded in unison, seemingly in complete understanding.

She stayed in the bathroom a full ten minutes. First one, then the other. She did her business last. She said, "Turn around, turn around," in the crowded stall, but the two pairs of dark eyes stayed on her.

Hands, please, let's clean our hands. The water was hot; there was liquid soap and a neat stack of paper towels.

As she emerged from the bathroom, she smiled patiently as the woman and the girls made a fuss, cooing and *aah*ing. She answered their questions as vaguely as she could. *Yes...Oh, no...Yes, I know...Oh?*

She purchased the fried chicken (there was no baked, which she considered healthier) and two cartons of milk, got the straws, and watched the wings and breast (she had broken the large breast into bite-size chunks of white meat) disappear. The service station even had fruit, bananas: spotted brown but edible.

Back in the car, now. Let me…These things are trickier than I thought. But she got everything sorted, got behind the wheel, and slowly pulled back onto the highway, heading north, heading home to Angelo.

She had accepted on some level that she was experiencing some type of madness. But her insanity was atypical. Atypical because, once her mind *did* return to her (and she admitted that somewhere during that time, it had taken flight), it brought with it a unique sense of logic, of planning—very methodical. Yes, somewhere in some book must be her type of madness, temporary but calculating at the same time.

Her first sign of possible trouble came as she crossed the state line into Tennessee. There was suddenly a line of cars ahead of her and three state trooper cars. One of the officers eventually made his way to her car. She lowered the window cautiously, glancing back to see—but everything looked perfectly normal.

Car seats properly secured. Seat belt in place. No texting. Doors locked. Good.

Don't panic.

"Officer, is there a problem?" She didn't bother to say she was not speeding. Every car ahead of her had stopped, and those behind her were slowing to a speed of less than fifteen miles per hour.

The officer—he looked more like a friendly-faced boy—grinned widely at her and pushed his hat back from his ginger-colored forehead.

"No, ma'am, just a routine inspection." As if in afterthought, he asked to see her license and registration. He gave them a very close scrutiny, looking from her to the license and back again, fingering the registration while looking at the license plate of her car. Her hands in her lap were crushed together, the fingers on both hands intertwined in tight fists.

Simple nerves, she told herself. Everyone got nervous when stopped by the police, especially these days, no matter the offense or color of the officer.

He returned the documents to her and then spoke to her in a calm but lowered voice. He leaned closer to her. "I don't want to frighten them. But there was an escape from an Arkansas prison last night—two pretty dangerous fellas." He motioned to Belinda, pushing his hands down.

She interpreted this gesture as, *It's OK. No need to worry.*

Then he wiggled his fingers and laughed softly. "Hello in there!"

Belinda turned her head, looked at the faces staring at the officer from sleep-filled, owllike eyes. They had dozed off between Walls and entering Tennessee.

"She is a doll! Hey, cutie. And he is a smart little man, too! Give me five, my man!" The state trooper leaned inside the lowered window, had his outstretched hand shyly slapped.

"I can see she takes after her mama." The officer looked at Belinda rather sheepishly; she realized that he was flirting with her.

She accepted the compliment and smiled back at him. *Really*, she thought, *he must think I'm a—what was that acronym? A MILF!* But it was nice to know that he found her attractive and even nicer to hear someone, a complete stranger, say that the *doll* looked like her *mama*.

The little girl leaned forward, straining in the seat. "She's not…I'm not…I'm not her mama."

The officer laughed heartily, winked at Belinda. "Boy, children really do say the darnedest things, don't they? OK, sweetie, whatever you say!"

"Well, I hope you all catch those men." *What a strange thing to say*, she thought. But the officer nodded, solemnly assured her that they would, and waved her on her way.

The little boy gave a small sigh as Belinda nosed the car forward, increasing the speed incrementally as the bottleneck traffic jam dissipated. Belinda dared to think that he was as nervous as she was, that the officer might—no, she would not finish the thought. Too much ahead, too much to say soon enough.

Her progress to Midtown was slow. So when she reached the intersection of Third Street and Shelby Drive, she decided to do a little shopping in Whitehaven. But her favorite haunt, The Easy Way, had closed permanently. Another place then, she decided, heading farther north.

She looked in the rearview mirror. "I'm going to the farmer's market, to get some fruit. Do y'all like—want some strawberries?" She'd made sure they ate breakfast, and the chicken, fruit, and milk in Walls would serve as a light lunch.

Last night, in Greenville, had been difficult: crying, screams, and more crying until, exhausted, they'd greedily eaten the food given them and slept like logs through the night in the hotel.

At the store that specialized in fresh fruits and vegetables, she got a basket and placed the two children in it, even though both were old enough to walk with her. But the fear overwhelmed her that they would—again, she pushed the thoughts away. She made her way around the store, picking up various fruits and vegetables. Angelo loved fresh corn, and the store had a good sale.

She stocked up for a few days on the corn, strawberries, peaches, and greens. Her husband could use more greens in his diet. And the peaches would make a very nice cobbler or even fresh, homemade ice cream—something to sweeten the pot.

She bought bagged pecans. She knew from past purchases that they tasted almost as good as the freshly fallen autumn nuts. She added walnuts.

Did they have nut allergies? So many kids these days did…Of course, she would know this if—*no, no thoughts.*

She packed her purchases carefully in the car, secured her passengers once more in their car seats. No one spoke to her, even though she made light, pleasant conversation. She was glad, immensely glad, however, that they did not reject her efforts at…at what? *No, don't go there, Belinda, my girl,* she cautioned herself.

She pulled into traffic and headed north on Elvis Presley Boulevard, Highway 51, deciding to take the so-called scenic route up to Union Avenue and then east to Evergreen.

Their house on North Evergreen was like a giant dollhouse. Not that the house was a mansion, far from it, but perfect in their eyes: upstairs, three bedrooms with en suite bathrooms and a small room that served as a small guest room with a small bathroom opposite it; downstairs, a den, a spacious, window-filled, living-dining area, and a half bath off the large, airy kitchen—their dream house. Belinda and Angelo had been married less than seven months when they'd found the house. It was a drive for him south to work, but he loved the place as much as she did, if not more so. He enjoyed fixing it up, hiring people—mostly friends who knew the craft but were willing to work cheaper than usual alongside him because it was he who had asked.

She planted perennials that grew like pieces of the rainbow, etching color into the front lawn. Angelo "threatened" to start a vegetable garden in the small backyard, which would have suited her fine. She secretly laughed at his stern lectures on *organic* and *hormone-free*, how they should avoid GMOs and the dangers of using chemical fertilizer. If there was one thing she knew, it was gardening. Her parents had a garden her entire childhood outside Indianola. Planting, weeding, harvesting—she and her siblings could give lessons on those!

As she turned north onto Evergreen from Union Avenue, she thought about how right Angelo was for her and that he often told her he couldn't imagine his life without her. *But what about now?*

Angelo was a painter. Not an artist, he was quick to assert in a self-effacing manner that, at first, irritated Belinda.

Don't put yourself down.

He assured her that he was not, but he had to teach her that what he did versus what someone like Wiley or Kendricks did was like a four-year-old up against Einstein doing complex math. He showed her his prints the two artists had done, showed the detail and imagination Wiley had and the realism of Kendricks's work.

"They have that *umph* that I'm still struggling with." Which, he said, was why he stuck to sketches and drawings. If he painted, using acrylic as his sole medium, invariably they were landscapes, seascapes, or very beautifully rendered still lifes.

He took her to Dixon Gallery and Gardens, showed her the portrait of a young black couple in a tight embrace, enveloped in a swirling red wrap that formed what appeared to be a valentine, with the top part obscured by the embracing couple. Their eyes were closed, and they were not kissing, but the passion was obvious in the way the man encircled the woman's neat waist and how she pulled him down to her.

Belinda had leaned against him, appreciating the work of art. "I still think you're pretty good."

His answering smile was beatific.

It was in his bedroom in his apartment on McLean that she discovered the eyes: pages and pages of sketches, canvases of paintings, all of eyes, no other features. They were almond-shaped, tea-colored, and thickly lashed eyes. She decided the faceless eyes belonged to a woman, using the length of lash and arch of brow to reach that conclusion.

The eyes stared out at her, the iris of the right eye slightly toward the inner corner, giving them a focused, determined stare. Still, they were arrestingly enticing.

"Are you ever going to finish her?"

They were curled against each other in his king-size bed, drinking a merlot and going through, what seemed to her, dozens of variations of those eyes.

Belinda noticed how he'd captured the woman's emotions with only her eyes. The raised right brow suggested speculation or skepticism. The squint in the left eye meant suppressed anger or exasperation, maybe even disappointment. Both brows lifted, eyes wide: amusement. Love (or sexual passion) was easy, she thought: lids at half mast, brows relaxed into a flat, black line.

The eyes really are the window to the soul.

Angelo looked at her so long and hard she thought she had something on her face, in her nose, peeking out!

"They *are* finished, Bel." He removed the wineglass from her hand, placed it next to his own empty one on his bedside table. His movement sent the pages flying, scattering like butterflies before floating down to the floor.

Angelo pulled Belinda down in his bed until she was reclining, legs straight and arms above her head, relaxed and languid. He began undressing her. Oh, how she loved to feel his eager tug at her panties, the push and pull of her bra. When she was naked, he would touch the backs of her knees, and her legs would unfurl like petals opening on an exotic flower.

She seldom undressed him. She liked the way he unbuttoned his shirt, undid his pants, painfully slowly, his eyes never leaving hers.

Eventually both were naked. He straddled her, his knees by her caramel-hued shoulders. She should have been one of those women who balked at the *implication* of this position. After all, *he* was bobbing merely inches from her nose, her mouth, her parted lips.

"Those eyes are *your* eyes, Bel."

"Mine?" She was in no position, literally, to verify this, but she cast an image into her mind. He had captured every look she seemed capable of making in those eyes. She looked up at him, hovering over her. Her lips grazed the warmth and smoothness of him.

"Yeah, I might be at lunch, and I'll find myself thinking of you, and next thing, I'm sketching you—your eyes," he added as if in explanation, clarification. "At home, relaxing, and next thing I know, pen or pencil in hand, the brush, and the eyes are there." He settled himself lower on his bent legs, bringing himself closer to Belinda.

"But just the eyes?" Was there some gross imperfection in her face he could see that was invisible to her, to others?

He thought, his face squeezed into a little boy's face. "Because they *are* you. In your eyes, I see all of you."

He actually gasped with delight as she held him, parted her lips farther, and welcomed him into her.

When both were sated, he curled against her, his head at her breast, and slept. She stroked his thick hair and nape, even in slumber. He breathed warmly against her skin as contented as a well-fed baby, all the night long.

Yes, their love was strong. *But what about now?*

"I gotta use it," the clipped voice said from the backseat. Belinda never considered herself any type of linguistics expert, but she had traveled a little over the years; she, like most southerners, had relatives in the northern or midwestern states. *Not from the South*, she once more thought. *They are not from around here...New York? Chicago? Maybe some other midwestern state like Kansas, Indiana?*

Belinda looked in the rearview mirror. "We'll be home in a minute. Just hold on."

It was approaching dusk, and many of the houses along North Evergreen were ablaze with lights. There were a few people taking their evening constitutional: couples, children, and mothers with strollers. Somewhere a dog barked; a woman's firm command followed: *Quiet, Milo.*

She turned into their driveway. *What about now?*

Chapter 11

ANGELO WAS STANDING in the yard, looking in the opposite direction of his wife's approaching car. He turned when he heard her Camry. His heart actually lurched against his ribs at the sight of her. It still amazed him that he could love her so intensely.

Though he seldom thought of Gwendolyn, when he did, it was to remember the end, not the beginning, when everything was new and beautiful and perfect. He remembered how their marriage crumbled like sunbaked dirt. At one point, in those last, horrifyingly empty days together, he told her that their cheating was what stood like a stone wall between them. When the cheating ended, that is, when both stopped lying about it, when she told him of her pregnancy by another man, after he had hurt her, he told her there was nothing standing between them. They separated the next day.

He had failed at his marriage to Gwen. Reeling over his self-perceived failure, he took his best friend Dave's advice: *Dude, the best way to get over a woman is to get between two!*

But he knew he was better than that. He had never been that guy to get women simply because he could. When he was married to Gwendolyn, it was as if the ring became a challenge to women. *How married are you?*

My wife's married, he'd respond, because he thought it was expected of him.

Belinda helped him see how broken he was, how he had the strength to make himself whole again.

He wondered, never aloud and never to her, if he would ever tire of her. He knew it could happen. But he soon realized Belinda completed him. He knew he was not *nothing* without her. That would be too pathetic to contemplate. But he did admit, freely, if not frequently, that she was the *something* that he liked having in his life. Not just their lovemaking—though, by God, that was enough in itself. Her professional reserve was nonexistent when they were alone. In bed, she was like a wildcat. But their ability to talk to each other, listen to each other, laugh with each other—he never wanted to lose that.

He remembered their first kiss. She had invited him out for drinks at a bar out in Germantown. The place was trendy, loud, and full of what he called the Stepford crowd—women who wore full makeup just to go to the market and men who made sure everyone around them knew their six-figure salaries and their daily five-mile run, or how much they could bench press on any given day at the gym.

Angelo had to yell to be heard over the crowd. This place was not his thing. He didn't mind bars, liked a good whiskey, but this raucous, artificial crowd was nothing like the quiet (*and dignified*, he thought) set in Midtown.

To be heard and to hear Belinda, he'd had to lean in close to her ear or feel her warm breath on his cheek.

"I can tie a cherry stem with my tongue."

Angelo had sputtered over his Scotch. That line was as cheesy as a scene from some porn movie. But when she bit off the plump, pitted cherry, chewed, and swallowed, she placed the leftover stem in her mouth.

To Angelo, it looked as if she were rearranging a wad of gum in her mouth, but in less than a minute, she stuck her tongue out. Resting on it, as if she were presenting him with a gift, was the cherry stem, a thin, woody knot.

In a move he had not used since Tabitha, he finished off his drink, plucked the stem from her tongue, and swooped in, kissing her on her soft, pillowy lips. He was happy when Belinda kissed him back. He had not expected her expertise with that kiss. (She had told him she wore suits every day and sensible flats or low-heeled shoes, and tonight she wore a black skirt suit, black-and-tan, leather flats.)

"I can teach you how to use that tongue of yours to tie knots, too."

His breath caught. She looked like a librarian and spoke like a porn queen. She leaned away from him, grinning. He saw that glint of defiance, challenge in her eyes. Those eyes.

She used her slim fingers to dance the stem across his cheek, down to his chin and throat. He promptly kissed her again. And again. Such heat. Such promise.

Standing in the driveway now, his mind drifted back to the night they had first made love. Admittedly, he did not think either of them was in love. He wondered, despite the cherry-stem-tying trick, if she might be a prudish lover, maybe even a bit dull in her imagination. After all, she had confessed with no expected pity or projected piety that she had been celibate for fourteen months *and three days*, she'd added parenthetically, as if the big deal were the three days and not the fourteen months.

It was rather sweet, he thought, ready to teach her a thing or two. She had not been *out there*, as Gwen had, as he had.

Her prodigious sexual knowledge staggered him. She had no reticence in administering orders: *Here, on top; no, like this.* He realized it was perhaps not *knowledge* that spurred her on, just her nature to love him fully and thoroughly.

She bit, clawed, screamed, and whimpered. Their bodies melded together until they actually were the beast with two backs. The sweat that poured from their heaving and thrusting bodies could be wrung from the sheets afterward.

It was the next night, their second night together, that he told her, solemnly, bemused, "You know I love you." They had not been apart since.

They were friends first, quite briefly, to be honest, before they quickly became lovers, and now they were a happily married couple. So Lifetime movie, his friends teased. So *in love*.

He would retort, *So what*? They *were* in love. Even when he—no, he did not want to go there. He could only question her so many times—*Babe, are you sure?* But she was. She'd married him, hadn't she? She had proudly become Mrs. Belinda Hardaway Higginbotham. Because she *loved* him. Regardless. In spite of. *Despite.*

Now, he was all smiles as she pulled the car onto the gravel square he had created for their vehicles and cut the engine.

His voice was playfully angry. "What did you mean, woman, staying in Greenville for an extra day, shopping, spending all our hard-earned money!"

She was getting out of the car as he was saying this. They hugged, and he kissed her, briefly putting his hand possessively on her backside.

"Your mama called last night after we talked, told me you wanted to do some shopping for the house. We were going to use our week off to do that together! Let me see what you've bought!" He pinched her fleshy bottom, leaned in for another kiss. He was already seeing them stripped down, bodies slick with love sweat.

"And I really didn't like that you said by *text* that we would talk. Then you cut your phone off. You're gonna have to explain that one!" He was angry, and he wanted her to know this. She knew he preferred calling over texting, even though that seemed the preferred way so many people communicated these days. He had so much to tell her. And having no way to contact her really frosted his nuts. He would settle this later…after they made love.

He smiled as she guided him to the trunk. He lifted it and saw that it was literally stuffed with bags.

"Tyson came by yesterday—drunk *again*. Liza left him—*again*. He'll be coming back by, I guarantee." He shook his head and watched her laugh at their friends' miserable but sustained marriage.

That their friend Tyson's wife periodically left him and he, in response, became morose and drunk just as periodically because of her leave taking seemed to be how the marriage worked. Within two weeks, Liza was back, contrite and loving, and he was sober and forgiving. He and Belinda knew she was five weeks pregnant, and both wondered if this development in their relationship would end this unpredictable but almost yearly act. They both hoped so.

"Did Sarah call you?"

Angelo frowned slightly as he pulled the bags from the trunk. He sighed. Her job at the local branch of the Department of Education paid very well; plus, with her degrees, she taught a few science classes at the University of Memphis. She had what they called a few "discretionary dollars." But sometimes she tended to overspend—like now. *What was in these bags?*

He answered her in a chiding voice even though his light-brown eyes were still teasing her. "See, if we had actually *talked* last night, like a normal husband and wife, instead of your sending me that cryptic text message, you'd know that she got into the University of Alabama with a full ride!"

They were proud of their teenage neighbor, who made pocket change by coming once a month to help Angelo and Belinda clean their house. That they did not need her at all was irrelevant to the boisterous girl. She had attached herself to them and viewed them, not so much in the role of *loco parentis* but something like a doting youngish uncle and aunt.

"But she didn't take it, right? Thought she had her heart set on going to A&M?"

Angelo leaned in and gave her a kiss, breathing in her smell. She wore a cologne but had no signature scent like most women seemed to. Whatever caught her fancy she wore until another one did.

"Mm, yeah, she got a full ride there, too, and her folks convinced her that an HBCU was still the place to go."

His wife made sounds of approval for the girl as Angelo pulled the last bag from the trunk—he counted eight.

Belinda, Belinda, he silently chastised her spending.

"Baby, does one of these bags contain a bag of money? What did you *buy*?"

Then, laughing at the look on her face—he could not actually decipher it but it was a look he would playfully mock later—he started hauling the bags in. On the second trip, he saw movement in the backseat. Was that a dog? No, Belinda had a healthy respect for any sized dog, so no to that thought. More curious than concerned, he poked his head in the back of the car and jerked back immediately.

"Bel, what—"

Chapter 12

Shay often drove over to nearby Indianola to do his business. He always took Trudy and her kids, who viewed the twenty-minute drive as an adventure. They were desperate for a change of scenery, even though there was in actual fact very little difference between the two towns. But they grew restless in Shay's isolated little house, so the drive did them all a world of good. He usually treated them to lunch and a small shopping spree at Walmart on Highway 82 on the way back to Leland.

Trudy's favorite restaurant was Betty's Place on Main Street, just off Depot. The place, seating no more than thirty inside and a few outside under the shade tree, specialized in soul food, like fried fish and chicken and rice.

"Mississippi is full of black-owned businesses." Trudy had expressed her surprise at this the first time she'd entered the town and saw all the places with what appeared to be black proprietors behind counters.

Shay gave her a look she quickly came to recognize: contempt and irritation. She usually ignored the former and laughed at the latter.

"Why?" He was arranging *her* children around the small table, getting *her* children the many napkins and utensils they would invariably drop on the concrete floor. And she was letting him do so quite complacently.

He smacked his lips at her. "You listened to the wrong folks back home. Mississippi's not like they want us to believe."

She noticed he did not share what that belief they should have was.

"Shay, you're the one who's always saying how the white man is responsible for this or is destroying that. I'm just saying that I agree with you."

Trudy found their exchange already boring. Shay had promised on this run he would get her lover. Plenty of it. She was ready for it.

Shay looked…nonplussed (her father's favorite word). Then he gave her a guilty smile. "Mississippi's not all bad is all I'm saying."

He slapped the table lightly, stood, and left her. She knew he preferred another place a couple of blocks over, more for how they did their chicken and okra—both fried and spicy—than anything else. She also knew he would come back and take care of the bill.

Despite her opinion or Shay's defense, she really was surprised at the black businesses. Not in Mississippi itself. She expected the so-called cities like Greenville (hardly a city; the whole of it could fit inside just *part* of Chicago) to have a few—auto shops, eateries, and hair salons—but these hamlets did also.

The woman whose name the restaurant bore came over and made much of Adrian and Sasha. The first time they had eaten there, she'd told them she had lived "all over," but her heart was here. It had pulled her back years ago.

"What about you, Trudy," she asked now, her pretty, chubby face friendly and inviting. "You staying here?"

"What? *Here*?" Too late, Trudy realized her questions could have been heard as a vague insult.

"Girl, nothing's wrong with *here*. You probably thinking Chicago's better, less *crazy*." She shook her head. "Just a different kind of crazy."

She got up and went to the back, returning a few moments later with two sodas. She handed one to Trudy.

"I'm old enough to be your mama, so I'm gonna tell you like she would: this is the best place a person could call home."

Trudy sipped the soda: ice cold, strong, sweet. It took the edge off. "Are you some kind of ambassador for Mississippi, Indianola?" She took up a piece of fish, seasoned and fried to perfection, and popped it into her mouth.

Betty's eyes dimmed slightly. "I wouldn't say that." She shifted her shapely heft in the seat, seared Trudy with her look. "You not going to go bat crazy in here, are you?" There was no misunderstanding her.

"I'm fine," Trudy said, settling her fluttering hands beneath her thighs.

"Yeah, I can see that."

"Look—" Trudy stopped at the look in this older woman's face. In a brawl, one Betty looked comfortable engaging in, she would beat Trudy to a pulp. The coming slur stayed at the back of her throat. "You don't know me."

"Sure I do. What I can't figure is why you would be one. That shit's for people twice your age, girl."

And in that simple statement, Trudy's life was emptied right on the table.

The women watched the children and finished their sodas in silence.

The café door opened, and in walked Shay. Trudy's face brightened, just like Sasha's and Matthew's but for vastly different reasons.

He looked smug and proud, so Trudy knew all his "merchandise" had been bought or exchanged. He would surely have her lover.

As he slid into his chair at the table, Betty slid out and returned to the register at the counter. Did her gaze linger on Shay's dreads, his broad smile?

Trudy wanted this Betty to know the power she had over her man. (He was not her man in the sense Fat Boy had been, but Betty wouldn't know that.) She reached over, took his large hands in hers, and pulled him close. She gave him a lingering kiss, much to the delight of Matthew and Sasha, who could be heard giggling at this unexpected gesture of affection from Trudy.

She ran her hands along his sides and felt a bulge in his pants, but not the bulge of sexual excitement. It was in his pants pocket—cash. And she knew her lover was in there, too. She felt giddy, but she couldn't smoke here. She settled back in her seat, ready to wait out her hunger. She glanced over at Betty, saw the envy in her eyes for Shay. *Good.*

Betty had to be forty if she was a day, but obviously she was attracted to younger men.

Shay ordered dessert for all of them, a whole sweet-potato pie.

"Coffee, too, Betty, and milk for these bugaboos." Trudy watched the glint in Shay's eyes. She made him happy; her kids made him happy. And because he had her lover, she supposed that, tonight, she could make them both happy.

The coffee was strong, and Trudy had to make it extra sweet. God, she wanted to scream. Her body ached for the lump in Shay's pocket. She considered how irresponsible that was. He could be stopped by any cop in this town or on the highway back to Leland, but he seemed calm, as if his pockets were filled with cotton instead of wads of cash and crack.

The pie came, cut into generous slices and topped with whipped cream. As soon as Shay served the kids, they dug in, practically inhaling the pie down their throats.

Shay took a bite and called out to Betty, "Girl, this pie's addictive! I'm ordering *two* to go. I'm surprised there isn't some Negro out back shooting this shit up!"

Trudy watched the woman, laughing all flirty, like she was a twenty-two-year-old. She walked over to take the empty cups of milk from the table and waited until Trudy met her eyes. Trudy read the other woman's obvious look. *See, I don't need crack to fuck him.*

When the two pies came, boxed up and smelling like heaven (gushed Shay), Trudy hustled them out, anxious to leave Betty and her place. (*How apropos*, she thought, again, a la her father's vernacular.)

Later that night, they pushed the two stuffed children into the small room at the back of his small house and closed the door, and Trudy laid the sleeping baby in his makeshift crib, a deep drawer lined with soft blankets and a small pillow.

Trudy sat on the bed, wearing her customary bed attire: a thin T-shirt and skimpy panties. Shay was nude, his erection jutting out cockily at a sixty-degree angle from his groin. He knelt before her, kissed each finger, and then raised himself up and kissed her as she had kissed him in the café back in Indianola.

She lay back on the bed, let him undress her. He kissed her eyelids closed. Then, his tongue traveled over her nose to her lips and settled there, his hot tongue probing her mouth deeply, as if searching for part of her soul, Trudy thought.

She opened up to him, ready to accept his desire. He used his fingers first. She remained dry. He used his mouth, and the only moisture was from his own saliva. He tried not to show his frustration as he attempted to enter her. It was like hitting a brick wall.

"I'm gonna go get us a beer," she said. She knew Shay liked his Corona. They had smoked a joint between them after the children had been put down.

Trudy left for the beer and came back twenty-three minutes later. She was sweating, her heart was pounding, and her loopy smile was a mile wide. Her nipples were pointing like dark missiles from her pert breasts. When Shay took the beer, she pushed his hand lower to her crotch. His fingers came back slick and warm. She was wet with desire for him. The stench of the crack hung on her skin, in her breath as she plied him with open-mouth kisses.

She wanted to prove to that bitch Betty that she could fuck Shay without crack.

She could not.

Chapter 13

TRUDY DIDN'T KNOW if the blows to the tattooed white man's head killed him. All she knew was that there was blood, and the hammer connecting to the head, to the bones in the head, the cranium (she recalled from her tenth-grade biology class), sounded the same as an egg cracking against the hard side of a bowl or the bending before the breaking of a green twig. Soft. Could a sound of such a deadly act be described as gentle? Because that was what she was thinking as she sped from the house, her arm unlawfully around her baby boy Adrian, with Sasha and Matthew illegally in the backseat of the stolen F-150. Of course, the man would have no need for car seats for small children. She would have taken no time in securing them, anyway.

The tattooed white man was supposed to be Shay's friend. He had been excited for Trudy to meet him.

"He's got a plan for us to make bank, babe." Trudy remembered his excitement as he held her in close embrace, telling her how quickly they could get rich. Shay talked of him every day, practically, until, when he finally did come, barrel-chested and bald, Trudy was rather disappointed in him, after Shay had built him up to her. He looked as out of place in this flat, humid land as she did.

He told them they could make crystal meth, or *pookie*, as he called it, and in doing so make *beaucoup* money.

Trudy had taken chemistry in her South Side Chicago high school, and, to her, the steps he described were a lot like some used in making acetylsalicylic acid (common aspirin) or acetaminophen: filtration, crystallization, drying.

And that knowledge surely had to have saved their lives. The lithium catalyst and the sodium hydroxide, she knew of their dangers from, not the teacher Mr.

Stamps adding lithium metal to water, but from a silly boy named Melvin who added the largest piece he could find to the lab sink. She recalled the fiery explosion that ensued.

Sodium hydroxide was lye, plain and simple, a corrosive that ate flesh. She knew that much from Fat Boy's granny, who talked about using the lye to make something called hominy as a child down South.

"Friend of mine drank some by accident when she was a little girl," the lady had said. "Ate through her tongue and throat…Bad shit."

She knew meth would be easy money, the steps to make it straightforward. But the unending danger—the flammables used, the caustics needed, the noxious, tell-tale fumes generated—she would not chance it, too many risks just to get her lover. She figured tricking or stripping had its own dangers, but she would rather have explored those activities than probably being burned alive.

Because she backed out, giving Shay a lecture on horrendous burns and permanently scarred flesh, he did also. (She showed him terrifying videos from YouTube.) *Selling* the shit was one thing; making it, an entirely different matter.

The tattooed white man said he was cool with their decision, which Trudy knew he was not. Shay, whom she suspected—behind his easygoing manner, despite his unending questions and suppositions—was rather a dullard, that he might have trouble leading a dead cat to milk. Shay did not seem to know that because they *knew* this white man (who surely had equally dangerous white friends), *that* knowledge alone would be a ready bullet with their names on it anytime he decided to pull the trigger.

The tattooed white man was affable in his racism. He called Shay *my nig, my nig* and smoked pot with him. He laughed heartily at Trudy's *crack antics*, as he called them—her endless walking and haphazard talking. In her ramblings, he discovered she had an active brain, was in actual fact bright and intelligent. He told Shay he should be happy. *She's smart, my nig, real smart and* fucking *pretty.*

Trudy knew it would only be a matter of time before he would demand what Shay freely got from her. Just like Shay, the white man had what she needed, or at least easy access to it. *Would it be so bad?* They liked the BJs, she knew, and she could oblige him to get her lover for free. Couldn't she?

He never spoke of himself, though both Trudy and Shay suspected he had done serious time. He was neither old nor young. Trudy, a relative stranger to aging white skin, could not determine if he was thirty or forty. He looked older than both her and Shay.

His lexicon identified him. He was from the North—no, he corrected her, he was from the *East* Coast, had never been to a northern state. He said *oi* for *i*, and he was fixated on hot dogs and beer. But again Trudy did not know. Was this truly eastern or simply white?

He joked about her monkey mouth. She was offended (was this a racist slur?) until she figured out this was lingo for her endless, crack-induced monologues.

The slang he used, those neck tattoos—one was of a heart, red and pulpy, with *Mom* stenciled through it—told the story. He had done time. Hard time? Absolutely.

As the days Trudy and her children siphoned food and shelter from Shay migrated into weeks, the tattooed white man began to look at her with more than curious lust, a jealousy she recognized. His eyes revealed the truth: that idiot Shay could have all this whenever he wanted it.

So he came when Shay was on his runs and plied her with crack that cost her only her body, which she had very little use of, since her heart was certainly not in it. There was no seduction. She gave to get, and this was fine by her.

Until he started looking at Sasha. Until today, coming out of her crack fog, she saw this white man, with his many tattoos visible on his exposed chest and beefy fingers hovering over Sasha's small panties, her round, doll-size butt poking out in hunger-engendered slumber.

In the last few weeks, Trudy had forgotten what it meant to be a mother even peripherally. Shay took it upon himself to feed her children, even giving the baby Adrian his many bottles. He didn't bathe them daily, but he encouraged them to wear the clean underwear he brought them (stolen from three different dollar stores around the Delta, he gleefully told Trudy, giving her his little-boy smile, when she approved of his selections). When Shay was gone, the children had to forage for food like rats.

No, she was unquestionably an embarrassment to motherhood, but seeing this…*beast* about to violate this *child*—*her* child—she remembered her love: for

Fat Boy; for Matthew; for this little girl, her Sasha; for the baby Adrian. She remembered it all.

The hammer appeared in her hand. She would never know where she'd gotten it. All she knew was that she managed to land two solid blows against the side of his bald head and that he looked at her in mild curiosity, as if he were saying, "Oh, you're home," or "Oh, you wanted this piece of chicken?"—as if what he was doing could be of only minimal concern to her.

Then, his eyes rolled back in his head, and he rolled back on the bed, and the blood came, the moaning and groaning. Trudy was scooping up her dozing daughter, grabbing her baby, and yelling Matthew awake. She hustled them into the tattooed man's truck (the keys were never removed, as no one visited to steal anything), and she was driving west, her subconscious directing her—the hunting blind, the hunting blind.

Had he touched Sasha before? She would have to get some place and check her daughter for...what? Bruising, signs of *penetration*? The thought made her sick—literally. She had to pull to the side of the two-lane road and vomit. She heaved and hacked, coughed and sputtered, until nothing came up but bitterness and shame.

As she was getting back in the truck, she spied a small bag under the seat. Without looking, she knew what this was—the white man's stash. She knew he smoked more than marijuana but was not sure what his habit was. She'd seen him drink dark liquor and smoke weed, but a man of his surely sordid past had other, deeper vices. She was convinced of this.

That he wanted them to make meth did not mean he necessarily used. Heroin? She'd never seen a needle, but she knew people smoked and snorted practically anything narcotic.

She drove an hour, the blacktop of the road becoming labeled state roads, 3 to 49W. Then she was speeding north, heading up the highway, the trees turning to wooden houses and flat-fronted stores, then brick buildings and row houses with thin lawns and thick trees, turning right, less businesses and homes, more fields and trees.

A turn and a twist, the trees, the low hill, the gravel road, the hunting blind appeared before her. But there would be no refuge for her or her children. The late summer sun beamed down on the doctor's hat-covered, bald head. He relaxed in a lawn chair on the lawn of the hunting blind among the tall trees, drinking beer and laughing his head off. The two men sitting across from him, in lawn chairs also, were drinking beer and laughing, too.

Trudy cut the engine, and the truck shuddered to a halt. She did not alight from the truck as much as she spilled out, struggling not to sink to her knees, still holding Adrian.

The doctor was there; those men were staring and pointing—firing questions like arrows at the doctor. Trudy clutched the truck's door. She watched the doctor extend his white hand, tanned by the later summer sun, and Sasha scrambled out, with one of the men giving a questioning laugh as he helped Matthew out.

She gathered her senses and looked in shock at the two men with the doctor, not the judge, not another Asian, and not a dumpy black man in a wilting suit. But they *were* black. Her heart beat like a motorized hammer in her chest. Her brain was expanding, shrinking. There was no place, no place to rest, to gather her thoughts, to think. And then, her thoughts shriveling like dry grass in the blazing sun, she fainted, the baby spilling from her arms to the carpet of grass at her feet.

Chapter 14

"Honey, help him with that—Angelo, the bag is too heavy for him."

The boy was struggling with a bag of clothes. He fell backward on the ground under the bag's weight.

Angelo didn't move, just stood there, staring at the boy. When he'd looked in the backseat of Belinda's car, saw the two children, he'd practically fainted. Something he knew he'd never done in his life. But seeing the children, ensconced in their car seats (*Where had they come from?* part of his brain questioned), staring at him as he most assuredly was staring at them—as if neither had seen the likes of the other before now—he felt as if his head had lifted itself above his body and was freely floating high into the air.

He managed to squeeze his wife's name again from his fast-closing throat, but she was shepherding the little girl into the house, her own arms now filled with various bags. He watched Belinda take a bag inside, plant the little girl in the open door, and tell her, "Stay put." She went back to Angelo and the boy, who still had a death grip on the bag.

"Angelo, the bag is too heavy for him. Sweetie, let Angelo help."

Angelo grabbed Belinda's hand and pulled her to him with a small but forceful jerk. She snaked her arms around his neck, kissed him for a long moment, felt his mouth working against hers, trying to speak. She put her lips to his ear, told him: only three short, haltingly said sentences. When she finished, she turned toward the house.

"Come on, you guys; let's get these bags in before…before it gets dark."

Angelo ranted and raved for a solid hour, barely letting Belinda have a word in edgewise, which was just as well. She offered no excuses, but she was adamant in her refusal to listen to reason.

Somehow, in his ravings, Angelo thought to place the boy and little girl on the sofa in the den, turn on the television, and quickly find a cartoon channel. Now Angelo and Belinda were in the privacy of their kitchen so that he could get the answers to his unending questions. Which he did not.

Who are they? How did you get them? Bel, baby, what *did you* do? The same questions, said over and over, in so many permutations. His strength and voice waned. Some part of him wanted to sit quietly in a corner and let this nightmare sort itself out without him. The other part, the part of himself he clung to, would not let this go.

Finally, he stalked to their bedroom, slammed the door. He went over possible scenarios, other than what she had told him: *I found them; there were* three*; I didn't know how to tell you.* There had to be another, logical reason. But he could think of none. The children were strangers to him. And as far as he knew, to his wife also. He sank to the bed, covered his face with his large, shaking hands. *Belinda, what did you do?*

For about an hour, it was quiet, and he thought she'd come to her senses, done what he'd demanded, what he'd begged her to do. But then, outside the door, he heard voices and then tears as a child (the girl?) began to cry. Loudly, without taking a breath, it seemed.

Angelo opened the bedroom door, went down the stairs, following the sound to the kitchen. He took in the scene before him.

The three of them, Belinda, the boy, and the little girl, were at the kitchen table. Belinda had rigged a baby chair for the children by placing a stack of pillows beneath them. She was trying to get the girl to eat a few beans and a small piece of chicken. The boy was eating heartily, taking very little notice of the girl's yelps or Belinda's beleaguered pleas.

When the girl caught sight of Angelo, she clamped her lips down and vigorously shook her head.

Angelo sat at the table, looked at his wife as the child started yelling again. "Why don't you fix you a plate, baby, and I'll eat this?" He didn't wait for an answer but took the plate with the little food on it and brought a forkful to his open mouth.

The little girl stopped her yowling and looked skeptically at him.

He stopped, looked at her pointedly. "What? Oh, were you eating this? It's so good. If you don't want it, I'll eat it." He made sounds of pleasure, rolling his eyes back and rubbing his stomach. The girl giggled, and when he pointed the fork toward her, she obediently opened her mouth.

He watched Belinda turn her attention to the boy. She made sure that he had enough milk to drink. Angelo settled in the chair and was doing a good job feeding the girl.

Eventually, he looked at Belinda. "What did you say their names were again?" He had asked during his hour of screaming and cajoling, pleading and demanding. Now he had no memory of her response.

Belinda did not smile. "Sweetie, tell Angelo your name."

"Sasha." She grinned at Angelo, accepting another bite of food.

Angelo shook his head. He suspected the girl was capable of eating on her own but at least she was not crying bloody murder any longer. Angelo nodded, repeated it, and looked at the boy. "And you, little brother?"

"Maph-phew," he said through a gap.

Angelo looked at him critically. The boy couldn't be seven, yet he'd already lost a front tooth. But Angelo had noticed that the tooth beside the missing tooth was broken. Obviously, the boy hadn't lost them naturally. "Sasha and Matthew...Matthew and Sasha." Angelo sang their names, causing the girl to giggle even harder.

Matthew, obviously more discriminating than the little girl, only shrugged. He pushed back from the table in a satisfied manner. "Are you taking us back to Shay's house?" The boy looked at Angelo, but it was Belinda who answered, also looking at her husband.

"We...We don't know Shay...We thought you and Sasha could stay here tonight. It's so late and...and I'm sure you're both tired."

As if to prove Belinda's theory, Angelo watched as Sasha yawned widely, her tiny mouth stretched wide. Angelo did not look at Belinda, the girl, or the boy. He looked beyond them, into the rest of the house. He spoke without thinking. "Too late for a bath, too, but, son, tomorrow, first thing, in the tub you both go."

So Belinda picked up Sasha, and Angelo took Matthew by the hand. The quartet stood there for a moment as if undecided on what the next step was.

Angelo looked at Belinda. "My twin bed, in the guest room: the bed is made up, and they can both sleep in it fine. Come on."

They went up the stairs, the children before them, not holding their hands, but Angelo saw the boy cup the girl's hand in his. Protective. Brotherly.

His heart jumped seeing this gesture. He could not, would not, ask again tonight what his wife had done, too afraid to hear the answer.

They undressed the children; Angelo barely contained his shock when he saw the scars, but Belinda whispered that she had already seen this and for him to say nothing.

Angelo took a tiny pair of pajamas Belinda offered him with Disney characters all over them. To Angelo, for some reason, she sounded compelled to defend the purchase.

"I got them at Walmart in Greenville. A lot cheaper than Target and he needed something to sleep in." For Sasha, he watched as she shook out a little pink gown. It had tiny roses all along the neckline, Angelo saw; he was working in automatic mode, buttoning the boy's pajama top, keeping his mind deliberately blank, in the present.

After both children were dressed, Angelo and Belinda picked them up, gently stuffed them beneath the sheet and thin coverlet. It was early fall, and the nights were still warm.

Angelo stared hard at the children, his face in a ferocious-looking frown, but his voice was surprisingly gentle as he asked if they wanted to hear a bedtime story. He saw that even Belinda was surprised at this generous overture.

Matthew shrugged uncertainly. Angelo's deep voice was kind, but he knew he was still frowning.

The girl nodded eagerly. "Yay, a story!"

So Angelo began a rambling story about a boy who, as he created the adventures his hero was having, apparently lived in a cave and used a talking, fire-breathing wolf to aid in his quests. He ended it just when he saw Sasha's eyes beginning to droop.

But just before she fell asleep, her eyes flew open. "Trudy gone bye-bye?"

Angelo and Belinda looked at her in confusion. "Trudy?" Angelo looked from the children to Belinda, who shook her head, shrugged.

The little girl gave no clarity to her own question, already turning into the soft warmth of her brother. Matthew turned on his side also, placed his hands under his head, and said angrily in that clipped voice that Angelo guessed, like Belinda had, was definitely not southern, "Trudy's not nice—not at all." He said no more, and in seconds, both children were sleeping, making the gentlest of rumbling sounds.

Chapter 15

Buck cursed to himself. He thought he had rid himself of this girl. He'd managed to get her in that program mainly to protect himself. Then Lola Carrolton had died. He hadn't seen that coming, even though he supposed he should have. But he'd known Lola since he was a towheaded boy in the country. To him, she was ageless.

He'd heard that the girl had moved out—been forced out of the home, more than likely, by Lola's kin. He'd presumed she'd returned to…wherever she was from with those three bastards of hers. But here she was on his property, obviously in bad shape.

He and his friends—the same black boys who had befriended him all those years ago, who ignored their mutual poverty and his skin color, as he was forced to accept theirs, who had shown up for Luella Carrolton's funeral, and again this morning from California—were witnesses to her unexpected return.

"Lord, Buck, who is she?" Jimmy Harris, light-skinned, freckled, with red, nappy hair, helped Buck settle the unconscious girl into one of the lawn chairs.

Buck remained silent as he surveyed her appearance. Since he'd last seen her, she'd lost weight, had acquired, in fact, that gauntness that was attributed to heavy drug users. She was unkempt, smelled of sweat, old sex, and urine. Her thick, dark hair was like a frizzed halo around her head. Her once very nicely rounded hips were just bones covered by minimal flesh. He figured crack was back in her life in a big-time way.

"She was a patient of mine. She was picked up for possession several months ago with intent to sell and…and the judge found a way for her not to…to do jail time. And—" He stopped at the look on his old friends' faces.

Jason Beams, once thickset and solemn as a youth, who was now tall, broad as a barn, and as charming as a black-skinned Romeo, pursed his full lips. Buck knew of the man's dogged curiosity—he was a lawman in Yuba City—and Buck knew he wasn't fully buying any of this. The reason, of course, was the way the two children threw themselves on the doctor, hugging his legs and talking in their high voices, pleading, accusing, actions a stranger would never take with a fellow stranger.

"Buck, boy, what did you do?" Jimmy asked as he watched the doctor gently extricate himself from the children's desperate clutches.

Jason stooped and was checking out the children for any injuries. After all, the young woman had tumbled out carrying the baby in her arms. But the baby—diaper full and smelly—seemed unharmed. The older children were fine, too. Neglected, all could see, what with the girl's ratty hair and the boy's overgrown knots, their ill-fitting clothes. The boy's shirt was misbuttoned, and the girl's sweater was inside out. Their faces were dirty and smudged with tears. But as far as the men could tell, there were no injuries from the ride. But when Jimmy raised the boy's dirty shirt, he let out an expletive, beckoned for the other men to look, and they all did with mute curiosity.

Jason vomited on the spot. Trying to laugh it off, he said it was the unseasonal heat, too much beer, but the other men knew. Someone had used this boy's back as an ashtray, recently if not often. None of the half dozen or so scars were old. No one ventured to check out Sasha for fear of what they might find on her small body.

Of course, Buck said nothing. He was as shocked as his friends, but he remained silent so as not to incriminate himself. He'd killed a man—and thus far, gotten away with it. True, he could possibly argue self-defense. The only person who stood between him and total freedom was lying unconscious in his chair.

"Let's get some food in these kids and wake her up." Jason looked at the F-150. "Man, Buck, I think this here girl stole that truck."

"Probably running from whoever did that shit to that boy," Jimmy asserted, his voice like gravel over rocks.

Buck thought so, too, but said nothing. He had to get her awake, get her as sober as he could, and get her and her children away from here—from him.

Jimmy smiled in a fatherly way at the boy. "That your big ol' truck?"

Matthew answered in a watery voice, and Buck almost rushed to him. He told himself it was the irresponsible, trifling *adults* he couldn't stomach, black or white, nigger or peckerwood, but the chaps, those pickaninnies, *these* pickaninnies—he had a soft spot for them.

"Nu-uh. That white man's."

Jason and Jimmy looked at Buck.

He shook his head, said forcefully to the men, "You know that's not *my* truck. He's talking about another white man."

"Do y'all live with the white man?" This from Jason.

"No, we live with Shay. But he's not there now." The boy gave a sniffle.

Again, both men looked at Buck. He shrugged, pretending to be clueless. He had never met this Shay fellow, but he'd heard of him from Trudy, from these children, had seen his face on her cell phone too many times to think their relationship was innocent.

He spoke in a rushed, harsh whisper to the men. "She's a crack whore. They found drugs in her system, even when that baby you're holding, Jimmy, was born." He gave a synopsis of her initial arrest, his "finding" her in labor, even about the two men found dead, apparently killing each other over some drug deal gone bad, even implying that maybe, just maybe, she was involved in the double murders, even if peripherally.

Jason was piling nuts, chips, and dip—the only edible snack there—onto plates and handing them to the children.

Buck cursed himself that they had brought no milk or juice. But their day was meant to be spent drinking and shooting the breeze. His friends' wives were in Memphis, he was told, shopping and sightseeing.

For the baby, Jimmy could only cradle. No bottle, no diapers. He found a towel, relatively fresh, and cleaned the baby. Then, he wrapped him up in another discarded towel, secured it the best he could.

When both men complimented him on his expertise, he reminded them that he had four kids. He'd done this thousands of times.

He took a cup of the melted ice from the cooler of beers the men were drinking and unceremoniously dumped it on top of the young woman's chest, rousing her immediately.

She awoke screaming. “Sasha, Sasha!” The little girl, mouth grubby with dip and chip crumbs, scampered over to her, but Buck saw that she did not come close to Trudy, did not rush into the woman’s scrawny arms.

Buck took Matthew by the shoulders, guided the child to his mother. He could feel the boy hang back. Their hunger, their neglect, the boy physically abused, he knew then that the few weeks he’d been shot of the woman weren’t good for her children.

“Your kids’re right here, gal.” He nodded to Jimmy, and the man came to stand in the line of the woman’s vision.

A plate of food was placed in her lap, and the men watched as she seemingly suctioned the food from the paper plate and guzzled the melted ice in the cup.

“How’d you get that truck?”

Buck allowed Jason to ask this question. The more he stayed in the background, so to speak, the less chance this girl could expose him for the murderer he was.

But Trudy was struggling to gather her children back to her, shaking her shaggy head as if to clear it. Her voice sounded as if rain had permeated her vocal cords. “Fuck all of you. I’m going,” she said, herding first Matthew and then Sasha back to the truck.

Jimmy handed over the baby, his reluctance to do so obvious.

“Buck, I think we need to take her in.”

Jason nodded at the other man’s words. Jimmy was a high-school track coach in Sacramento, and Buck knew he sometimes acted more like a father-confessor than coach and that he still believed in the goodness of people. And that misdeeds should not go unpunished.

Buck clamped his lips shut. If they knew what he’d done…Gaining a voice that didn’t sound like his in the least, he shook his head, said, “No, *no*, I don’t want any more trouble from her…with her.” He failed to keep the desperation from his voice. He tried again. “Look, that truck, her *dope* habit, those kids—no! She’s trouble with a capital *T*.”

Trudy was in the truck, turning the wheel, and her children were once more like statues in the backseat, now with Matthew holding the baby tightly, his face a blank slate that made Buck think of an old man, made him want to cry, wrench the children from the truck. His feet felt encased in cement, rooting him to his spot.

Jason advanced toward the truck, and Buck could see the girl's once-pretty face pale, and he remembered stupidly thinking, as a child, *Nigras blush and blanch just like whites.*

"You do that to that boy's back?"

At the question, the girl, Trudy, actually gagged, but she did not vomit. She stared at him as if his words were gibberish. "Wha-at?" The men watched her twist, look at her son, and they saw the knowledge seep in. She quaked. Buck thought there was no other word for it. As if the truck were a bucking stallion, but it was not. It was her, trembling, a maelstrom in a teacup.

Before Buck could even think of what he was doing, he was rushing to the cab of the truck, thrusting what bills he had in his wallet onto the front seat. He knew most of this money would go toward crack, but she was on the run; that was obvious. Eventually, she would have to stop running long enough to feed, clean, and clothe those kids.

The men watched her disappear down the road, the large wheels of the large truck kicking up rocks. Jason and Jimmy stood close to Buck, shaking their heads at him.

"What?"

"Come on, you're screwing that girl, Buck."

"Without a doubt." Jason backed up Jimmy's assertion.

Buck wanted to use his excuses that had gotten him through his years of envying Barry and his ilk, of his awkwardly practiced racism, his illegal activities that helped him gain that social status so important to his wife, and him, back then, so long ago. The girl was a whore. She was a kid. She was a nigger. She was a *northerner.*

But these men knew him, ignored and even excused his superior, racist thoughts and actions. He could say none of those statements he held as truths.

The men had been reminiscing about their years together as poorly paid farm laborers before the girl came and interrupted them. Now they reclaimed their seats, quiet and contemplative.

Buck sighed, a thin sound, as if the air through his nostrils, out his mouth, had lost most of the oxygen. His friends waited for an explanation. His deep voice had returned to its normal timbre. "Not for a while, y'all." He grabbed a beer, twisted the cap off, and downed half of it. "And not anymore."

He wasn't even conscious of making this decision, but he decided somewhere in his subconscious, his unconscious, that his dealings with that girl would stop today. He settled back in his chair, ready to take up the walk down memory lane once more with these two men, black men, but closer to him in many ways than any brother could ever be.

As a scrawny kid in the fields, on the farm, he had admired their strength, their athleticism, thinking that it was just part of their being what they were—nigras who got these physical traits from their African, slave ancestors. But their strength of character, their innate fairness and goodness, society had neither given to nor stolen these qualities from them.

"You know I got that license plate." Jason was typing something into his iPhone. "If it wasn't already stolen, I'll know who it belongs to."

"Yeah, we shouldn't've let her leave with those kids, y'all. I felt like we were giving baby rabbits back to a starving bobcat."

"Why're you worrying, Jimmy? Hell, if she doesn't care, why should you?" Buck knew he was being obstructive, but he had no wish to get his friends involved in the girl's messed-up life.

"Why aren't *you*?" Jason asked, still searching through his iPhone. "OK, she's messed up—hell, she's f*ucked* up. But someone hurt that child, and I'd think you'd want him to pay."

"What if it was her?" He knew she was neglectful. Abuse could easily follow. And he simply couldn't let himself get embroiled in her life and risk losing his own.

"Yeah, could have been," Jimmy conceded. He then added, shaking his head, "Nah, y'all saw her; she didn't know that."

"Probably has been high on that crack shit; don't know nothin' goin' on 'round her!" Buck exploded, his speech pattern reverting to when he'd eaten dinner at these men's houses almost as often as he ate at his own. He was angry that they'd let her go, relieved that they did not stop her.

"Ha!" Buck and Jimmy looked at Jason, who was holding his iPhone as if it were a prize. "Truck belongs to a Christian Slack." He read more from the small screen. "Did time back in New Jersey. Says here he was in for drugs but beat a guy near to death while incarcerated." He showed the men the device. A man of maybe thirty-five was staring back unsmiling at them. There were visible tattoos on his neck. His gray eyes were pale as early frost. His head was as smooth and white as a billiard ball.

Buck actually shivered. The man had the look of a sociopath. But there was another reason for his feeling of disquiet. Was that device powerful enough to discover *his* secrets?

"Y'ask me," Jason asserted, "it was him who did that to that boy. That's the white man that boy mentioned."

"Matthew," Buck supplied before he knew he would. The two men were silent for a few moments, each digesting what was unsaid.

"She's about your Sylvie's age, right?" Jimmy looked closely at his old friend.

Buck's youngest child. His oldest son, Henry Junior, was in graduate school in Louisiana, and his younger son, Elliott, was a senior in college up in Tennessee. Sylvie was doing a crazy internship in, of all places, some village in Suriname! He would see them all this Christmas.

"*Buck.*" Jimmy had once entertained the idea of being a minister. But when he'd lost his virginity at nineteen, he'd also lost that fervor. But he still believed in the goodness of man—of this man.

Buck bristled. "Hey, now! Just 'cause I know that scrap of a girl don't mean I'm doin' anything *else* with her or her for me!" His childhood speech pattern once more betrayed him.

He wanted to rail against them. He had *made* it. He was a *doctor.* He was friends with rich lawyers, other doctors, all *white*, he could remind them. He thought of Barry, a *judge.*

I'm best friends with a rich judge. You're just people I once knew in my old life!

He recalled a dinner last month with Barry and his crew. Barry, as always, had held forth, keeping the crowd in stitches.

Hey, you know how dumb nigra dykes are?

No, came the collective response, each person's face open and expectant.

They fuck men!

Laughter. Buck had laughed the loudest and longest. *That Barry!*

"Are…you…going…to…*quit*?" Jason said now, biting off each word.

Both men stared Buck down. Though he held their penetrating gaze for several seconds, eventually, his blue eyes shuttered and lowered.

He thought again of Barry, his jokes. Just like Barry used other people in his jokes—Chinese, Mexicans, or colored folk—he could have used poor white trash and gotten the same laughter from those upper-crust whites. Why had he not thought of this before? Because he had been so determined to be in with that crowd. The poor white boy, the *trash*, had made it.

So if he'd made it, why was he here, with these men? How would he explain their presence if suddenly Barry or the others showed up, out of the blue, like they had? Would he be overjoyed like he was earlier at their unexpected arrival? Would he grab them in a grip strong enough to break a bone, clap them on the shoulders, ask, *How the heck have y'all been?* And want to hear every detail? Would he tell them about his kids, listen as they told about theirs, eight between the two of them?

He looked at his friends. That was how he had always thought of them—friends. With Barry, he simply wanted to be *in* his circle of friends. If Barry or any of the others showed up now, they would look at him as if he had crapped his pants at a backyard barbecue. Maybe Barry would pull him aside, ask, almost laughing, almost condescending (*almost*), definitely disbelieving, *What the* fuck *are you doing with these niggers?*

That theoretical but highly plausible question cemented his decision.

Yes, he could stop; he *would* stop. He counted these two black men as family. He would have to distance himself from Barry and his dealings, from his ilk. But he would not return the half-million dollars he had purloined over the years, nor would he confess to the crime of murder. No.

He could be brave. He could be noble, and he could be good, but he knew himself well enough to know that he would never be that brave, that noble, or that good.

Chapter 16

In the kitchen, as Belinda put away the dinner dishes, Angelo started in on her again, but before he could make any headway, she impatiently held up a hand. "Quiet! Do you want to wake the children?"

He stared, incredulous, wondering who this stranger was who looked and sounded so like his wife, the woman he loved, whom he knew. Thought he knew. *The children*, as if those strangers who had eaten their food, wore the clothes she'd bought, who were now asleep in *his* bed, had a connection to them.

So he left her, showered, dressed for bed. But he could not resist what proved that maybe he was as insane as his crazy wife. He checked on *the children*, and as Belinda had asserted, they were sleeping, their small, slim bodies curled around each other like intertwined worms. He felt something on his cheeks and decided that there was a leak in the ceiling of this room and that he would have to have the roof repaired. He pointedly ignored that, even with a leak, there had been no rainfall for four days.

Back in their bedroom, he pretended to be asleep himself when Belinda crawled into bed beside him an hour later. She smelled as she always did after a shower—of mint and roses. He had tried to come up with a scenario where a wife comes home from visiting her sick mother and has two children in tow. Kittens, dogs, even a goddamned bird he could make sense of. But children weren't dumped alongside a road or left in an abandoned house or tossed out of a nest. *Were they?*

He felt her legs brush against him, and he pulled away, escaping her touch as if it were fiery acid. Seconds later, her hands were on his back, rubbing, gently rubbing. Try as he might, he could not ignore her touch, resist her love for him or his for her. He turned to her, already opening his arms to her embrace.

They made slow, quiet love. When he entered her, he felt as he always did—what he had tried to feel with Gwen but realized he never did—instead of him filling her, she filled him. What was that word, he thought, as she moved beneath him, in perfect rhythm with his thrusts? Replete. Their lovemaking was never one act. No, he could and often did make love to her several times in one night. Tonight was no different. But he knew he was using his body to ask questions he had no words for, and her body—the body he could sketch blindfolded—answered every one of them. He just had to figure out the translation into words.

Afterward, entwined, Belinda whispered in Angelo's ear, "This state trooper thought I was her mother...their mother."

A piece of the puzzle? "When?" Angelo placed his arm around her waist and pulled her back to his front.

"Today." And she told him. He knew she would have related this story about the escaped prisoners, the flirtatious young state trooper—under normal circumstances, if only to know that he would have been sick with worry or tease her about the man. But these were not normal circumstances.

Of course, there was no resemblance between Belinda and the child—*the children.* Similar coloring and hair texture, possibly, but using those superficial characteristics, hell, he and Belinda could be brother and sister!

"What did you say?"

When Belinda related what the little girl had said—that she was not Belinda's mother—he'd chuckled. He did not laugh, but he admitted he, too, found the statement humorous. Their shared laughter lifted but did not totally remove the concrete slab on his chest. He could breathe. Maybe his wife was not crazy after all, and with this thought, he pulled her closer, burying his face in the curve of her shoulder, his favorite position, and slept.

Angelo dreamed. He tossed something in the air—a ball that got bigger the farther it soared away from him. A voice came out of the blue sky, and the ball landed at his feet. A little girl's voice—her face was unclear, but she had a head of curly hair exactly the color of Belinda's. He could actually think this clearly in his dream.

The little girl, her voice clear and crisp, one of those Disney show voices, called to him, "Again, again!" He threw the ball, and it went up and up until it became the moon.

Chapter 17

LIKE MOST PEOPLE, Belinda had her list of pet peeves. She hated to see people use air quotes. When did crooking two or four fingers equate to the use of *written* quotation marks? She cringed when people said, even those whom she thought should know better, *Quote unquote.* Didn't they know that this meant *nothing* had been "quoted"? She wondered why so few people knew that there was no such thing as $\$1.^{23}$? That it was either $1.23 or $1 23/100. Her ears went numb when her boss said *criterion* for *criteria* or when complete strangers said in her presence, *Well, between you and I*...And there were idiotic words and phrases like *supposably, irregardless, conversate*, and, in describing blathering talk, *blasé, blasé, blasé* that actually caused her skin to prickle.

So in her early days of dating—and loving Angelo—she hated his habit of saying, *Nothing,* when she asked why he was so quiet, so pensive, almost secretive. A person, she asserted, could never, with a brain, think of nothing. Impossible. And she would hold his gaze, until eventually the nothing turned into something that needed airing out, discussing, clarifying. And—irony of ironies, on that New Orleans road trip—this was what he had been saying all along. There was nothing. Maybe there never would be anything other than the *nothing.* No thing. *Not any children.*

So when Belinda awakened the next morning, felt the cold sheets on Angelo's side, she flew into an upright position. Was there a one-word note—*Gone*—where her husband's head would normally lie? Would her life without him, his love, be that all-inclusive, totally exclusive *nothing*? A shadow at the window moved closer to her until it became solid, familiar in its build and profile. Angelo.

He came to her and sat on the bed. He asked her what they should cook for breakfast. (They always took the time to cook a healthy meal when there was time.) He told her that they would have to stick to the original budget they'd decided upon for the house-improvement projects.

His behavior was so like nothing (not the *nothing* he once used as a mantra or the nothing she feared upon waking) she had expected. She twisted and turned, repositioned her body until she was sitting beside him, arms and breasts bare, the bedding pooled around her.

His normal question—*eggs and bacon or pancakes?*—induced great gulping tears from her. She did not deserve this man.

Then Angelo settled his weight beside her, his arms around her. She leaned into him, and both stared silently out the window at the live oak tree, a green giant that never lost its emerald sheen from one year to the next.

"Maybe it can be some type of psychotic break."

"Yeah, that's what I think."

She had not expected some platitude from him. Honest and unadulterated—that was her husband.

What had she done?

She stood from his embrace, naked like a brown nymph. He stared up at her, and she could see the desire, as naked as she was, in his eyes.

"Are you still angry with me, Ange?" This was her pet name for him, even though he had no problem being called Angelo—a male angel was his mother's explanation.

He never answered spontaneously, which meant that the answer he gave was well considered; this trait had earned him promotions in his job and respect from his friends.

"I know there must be a reason that I…No, I'm not angry, baby." His voice was resolute.

Belinda pulled on a gown, her tattered, almost-transparent-with-wear robe. She'd had it since she was a freshman at Valley. Though she had received several replacement robes, she kept this one. It was the last thing her father had given her. She would wear it until it unraveled at her feet.

"Let's go?"

Belinda gave him a grateful smile. This was not over, no matter his answer to the contrary. "I knew there was a reason to love you."

The fact that Angelo could chuckle—not laugh—at this comment meant that they were still on solid footing. She had not screwed up to that extent.

They walked down the hall to the bedroom where the children were. The boy was curled around the little girl protectively. Through the night, they had fought the thin bed covering off them, and now they shivered slightly against the coolness from the breeze drifting in from the open, screened window.

Neither adult approached them. Belinda did not turn on a light. She could see them clearly. There were no tear tracks. They slept deeply, as if in utter exhaustion, as if their need for rest was from an exhaustion only adults could attest to.

Angelo walked deeper into the room, bent to retrieve the cover and replace it. As he placed the blanket, practically weightless, over them, the girl's large, dark eyes snapped open.

The small gasp from Belinda was loud enough to awaken the boy.

He stirred, stretched, and scratched unselfconsciously. Then, his eyes took in his surroundings. He scooted closer to his sister, a look of terror and supplication on his tiny, old man's face that tore Belinda apart. Then, he began to cry, a keening, wailing sound that was transmitted to the girl, who started to cry because he was crying.

Belinda made a rush to the children, but Angelo was closer. He sat on the bed, and without a word he scooped up the little girl, ignoring the licks delivered to him from the boy.

"Hey, it's OK. Remember us? You took my food last night?"

The girl had given up her struggle and was now clinging to Angelo, her wooly little head buried in his shoulder. The boy hiccupped a few times and stopped his caterwauling, but he remained mute.

"You two hungry yet?"

Belinda stepped closer, sat on the narrow bed, the four of them crowding it.

The boy nodded cautiously. His eyes still pleaded the silent message. *Please don't hurt us.*

"I like pancakes. What about you two?" Angelo pushed the girl away from him to see her face. She looked from him to Matthew, who nodded. The girl took the signal and nodded, too, enthusiastically.

Belinda could have kissed Angelo, and on impulse, she did, swooping over and planting a loud smack on his lips. This caused the girl to squeal in delight and for the boy, Matthew, to snicker at the gesture.

"You kissed him," Matthew accused, sotto voce. The girl (Belinda remembered she was called Sasha) giggled and mimicked the kiss, smacking her lips loudly against her open little palm.

"Yeah, I know. I have to; he's my husband." Belinda made her voice whiny, which caused Angelo to scoff and laugh out loud.

"Maybe instead of pancakes, we can do waffles, Bel. How about that?"

Before Belinda could agree—it was only a matter of using the waffle iron and not the griddle, same batter—the little girl demanded to know what a *waffuh* was.

Matthew pulled his shoulders up in big-brother superiority. "It's a crunchy pancake made like a tri-ankle."

Belinda stifled her laugh, but Angelo guffawed. He deftly whipped the covers off the children with a snap.

"So I'm going to go make those crunchy pancakes shaped like tri-ankles, while you help Belinda, OK?"

Now the children were into it. "Do what?" Matthew started to stand up in the bed, but something, some unpleasant memory, perhaps, caused him to sit back down, his eyes wide in apologetic fear.

"Get dressed. We have to take a trip today."

"Where? Chicago?" Matthew's brows drew together, looking like an intelligent small person.

A piece of the puzzle, thought Belinda, who was pleased to have guessed this as a likely place they had once lived.

"Who lives there?" Angelo asked. They were all standing now, and he had the little girl's hand firmly in his. She was holding his so tightly, it actually hurt.

"Fat Boy is dead. Poppa and Granny told us."

This non sequitur from Matthew only confused Belinda and Angelo.

"I'm sorry...Was he your—?" Belinda stopped. There could be any number of possibilities: this Fat Boy could have been a dog, a kitten, a destroyed favorite stuffed toy, a...

"Daddy. Fat Boy is our daddy. Granny said he was shot down like a dog in the street." This commentary was parroted by the boy.

"Well, who is Shay?" Belinda was afraid of the answer she would receive. They had mentioned him last night, but he was hardly a lead.

Matthew swallowed his lips, and Sasha's answer made no sense. "That white man said Shay is a piece of shit." She shook her head vehemently in angry denial. "But Shay not a piece of shit. Is he, Matthew?"

Angelo was apoplectic with stifled laughter. But he sobered as he looked at Belinda. Their eyes read the other's face. *Another piece of the puzzle.*

"I think you two should help Belinda while I cook."

Belinda herded the children to the bathroom. She used the opportunity to examine the girl a little closer. She saw no bruising, and the child splashed around in the water like any other child. Matthew was more reserved, but he, too, soon was playing in the tub and giggling.

When his back was turned to her, Belinda counted the burn marks on his back: six, and in some pattern. *What was that shape?* she wondered. If she used an invisible line to connect them, they formed a perfect rhombus. Not only had the person been a monster, he (*or she*, she conceded) had played a cruel, *intelligent* game.

She dressed Matthew first; he was easy: undies, socks, gym shoes, and jeans with a shirt. Though his hair was overgrown and thick as carpet, she could pack it down to a reasonable facsimile of an afro.

Sasha was another matter altogether. She accepted the clothing easily enough, but getting her hair into a semblance of a style caused the child to emit murderous screams that assured anyone who could hear them that Belinda was using a butter knife to cut her arms from her torso.

Belinda was almost in tears herself when Angelo appeared in the doorway, wearing an apron that said *I'm not afraid of you. I have a wife.* She gave a tearful laugh when she saw him. She had bought him the apron last year as a gag gift for one of his many birthday presents.

"Problem, babe?"

Belinda felt helpless. It was easier than this; she knew it. She had nieces, nephews. She had babysat over the years and done a damn good job. Why was she such a…fuckup with this child?

"What?" Angelo had already hoisted the child up in his arms and was playfully scrutinizing her attire—a pair of pink pants and a bunny-covered pink shirt.

"It's OK." Belinda felt the water sloshing in her voice.

"Just pull it up on top of her head and tie a ribbon; that's what I did with my little sister when I had to help my mother."

Belinda shook her head. Angelo was the oldest; she was the youngest. That position in their family dynamics had influenced them differently. Because Angelo was the oldest, he had been assigned and carried out many duties that made him seem much older at times; he was dependable, a thinker and a doer, but not necessarily a great, innovative thinker. Belinda, passively ignored by older parents by the time she'd come along, was used to doing whatever she thought best for herself since her actions were seldom questioned because they were seldom noticed. She considered herself a creative, free spirit and a problem solver.

So why couldn't she comb a three-year-old's hair, for God's sake?

"Right." She took the child from his arms. Was there glue on her? She seemed *attached* to him.

Angelo went to their bedroom, came out a minute later with a bright-pink scarf that Belinda recognized as one she hadn't worn in years. Perfect for the attire and one she would not miss.

She gathered the girl's locks up, tied the ribbon, and puffed out her hair into a blackish-brown bubble on the crown of her head. "Cute as a button," she said, sighing with relief.

Angelo clapped his hands, right in front of the girl's face. "Then, let's all go downstairs and have those tri-ankles!"

"And…but…"

"Figure we should be in Greenville no later than four, and we head straight to the sheriff's office. And we call Mr. Sweeney." Andrew Sweeney was their lawyer. Angelo locked eyes with Belinda, and she remembered why she loved him. That deep thinker, that dependable man, understood her even when, sometimes, she did not.

Chapter 18

Scarfing down the waffles, Matthew decided that he liked this man, who called himself Angelo. And he liked the woman, Belinda. They scared him at first, because he had learned to fear strangers, especially adults. But this Angelo and his wife (this man Angelo had explained their relationship over breakfast) made him feel...safe he guessed was the best way to describe what he felt. At first, when Belinda ran screaming with him and Sasha, leaving their baby Adrian, he thought she was like Trudy. But later, he realized she was scared, too. He didn't think grown people could be scared.

He wondered about their baby Adrian. He had asked about him last night and even this morning over breakfast, but they had not answered, saying a lot of *uh*s and *hmm*s, like they were trying to think of something to tell him he could understand.

He wondered when Shay would come and get them, why Trudy hadn't come to take them back. She had left him to take care of the baby and Sasha while she went to buy food, she said. But Matthew knew Trudy well enough. She was getting more crack from the money the doctor had given her and from the stuff—the *drugs*—she must have sold that belonged to the white man.

Matthew didn't like that white man. There were two white people, both men, more or less in his life now. The white man with the tattoos and bald head, and the doctor, with no tattoos that he could see and a bald head. He kind of liked the doctor (he never called either man by any name because he never addressed them) because he always had something for him, Sasha, or their baby Adrian. Usually, it was hot food or cold fruit. He even told Matthew himself that he didn't believe in children eating candy.

Matthew liked Shay. He tried to think of Fat Boy all the time because he didn't think he should forget him. Shay reminded him of Fat Boy sometimes, mostly when he made funny voices or faces when he made them PB and J sandwiches or sneaked small Snickers bars to him and Sasha. He had reasons to like Shay and the doctor, and reasons to hate the white man. (Old Miss Carrolton had said hate was wrong, but maybe if she met the white man and knew what he did, she would hate him, too, and *he* wouldn't feel bad hating him.)

When Shay left or the doctor didn't come, the white man was there. He would take Trudy out to his big, shiny black truck. Matthew knew Trudy's habits very well. If she went to that truck, she smoked that pipe for a long time, and then she…did things with the white man. Shay had been gone for more than two nights; that much the boy knew. No Shay, no cooked food, just bottles of milk Shay had poured up for their baby Adrian.

Of course, he could not tell time, but if he watched TV, he knew more than three cartoon shows played while Trudy was with that white man. Like that time when their baby Adrian was crying loud and long. He smelled like poop. Matthew went out to the truck, saw that there was a light on in its big cab. He climbed on back, his intention to get Trudy to come and take care of baby Adrian. Maybe fix some food for him and Sasha, too.

He saw Trudy's head in the white man's lap. He could not see her face. The white man had his pig eyes closed and had his bald head all the way back. He was breathing funny, like he was running hard, but he was sitting down. He stared at his mother's head, going up and down, like it was on a string and someone was pulling it.

The white man pushed her head down, and Matthew could hear his voice—he thought of how dogs growled. *Take it, you bitch; take this white dick.*

Matthew wasn't sure what was happening or what those words meant. He knew *bitch* and *dick* were bad words. He didn't like it that the white man called her that nasty name, and he didn't like Trudy because she didn't say anything, just kept her head in his lap.

After a while, Trudy raised her head from his lap. Matthew caught sight of the white man's wrinkled wee-wee and something snotty looking on Trudy's lips.

He scrambled down from the back of the truck and sprinted as fast as his legs could carry him. He hid in the shadows at the back of Shay's house.

He heard the white man calling him. *Hey, boy! C'mere. What're you doing spying on grown folks' business?*

Matthew crawled under the house and stayed there until the darkness and hunger drove him out. Shay was back two nights, maybe three nights later. His presence lifted Matthew's heart. Neither the white man nor his truck was there when Shay returned. Matthew had not had a bath or changed his clothes since before the night of the truck incident. He'd slept, as Old Miss Carrolton said, *ready rose*. She explained that this was to save time if you had to run. He was ready to run.

"Boy, where have you been? And look at you. Covered in dirt." But Shay was just laughing and shaking his head. His words didn't scare Matthew. "Come on, sit down. You can clean up after you eat something." Hot dogs and french fries! Green beans and something purple in a plastic cup. A cup of yogurt.

Yummy.

He slid into his chair, legs dangling happily. Then, his happiness disappeared when the white man came into the little kitchen. He slapped Shay on the shoulder, laughing and talking like he hadn't already been there earlier that day *doing things* with Trudy.

The white man accepted the hot dogs and purple stuff in a glass. He took big bites and swallowed most of the purple stuff in one swallow.

Trudy was there, sitting at the table, her eyes bugging and hands flying, talking and laughing, but nobody answered her. Nobody laughed with her.

Matthew caught occasional whiffs of the stench of that pipe.

Shay was feeding beans to Sasha, who looked as thrown away as Matthew, while the baby Adrian scrambled around in his arms.

When Trudy tried to take over with the baby, Shay said, "I got this," his eyes and voice flat. And for the first time, Matthew knew that Shay didn't like that pipe any more than he did, or Granny or Poppa. Or Fat Boy.

Matthew remembered what he'd seen in that big truck, and he hated Trudy and that ugly, tattooed white man all the more, no matter how bad Old Miss Carrolton said it was to hate.

He let his eyes travel to the white man's face. He didn't look mad. Matthew knew what that emotion looked like well enough. But there was nothing on the man's face. It was like a rock, smooth and empty, no look in those clear eyes, lips and brows flat. He was more afraid now than he had been hiding out under Shay's house.

After they had finished eating the hot dogs and yogurt, the white man said he had to leave. *You can grill a dog, my nig, as good as the ones back in Jersey.*

As he walked past Matthew, he bent down and whispered in the boy's ear, "You stick that snotty little nose in my business with that whore of a mother of yours, I'll kill you myself and feed you to the dogs."

He smiled then, his lips spreading across his face. At first, Matthew thought he had said something quite different, something that should have been nice, but it wasn't at all.

Matthew looked at the man's broad back as he walked out. He slapped Shay on the back and touched Trudy's twitching shoulder. The boy looked at the door as it closed behind the man. He looked at it so long and so hard, it blurred, and eventually he felt hot tears roll down his face.

He felt something warm and wet on his legs. He looked down and saw a small pool spreading around his feet.

He stifled an embarrassed sob when Shay noticed and said in a loud, astonished voice. "Lord, Trudy, this boy stood there and peed his pants! Come on, Matthew! What the fuck could have caused that?"

Matthew could not answer him. He hadn't done this since he was a little kid back in Chicago. He hung his head and sloshed after Shay.

He spoke only to Shay and in monosyllables for three days straight, terrified that if more than one word escaped his lips, the white man would know, and he would sic those killer dogs on him.

The day Trudy had taken the big truck, the white man had come. It was so easy for the man to corner him, remove his T-shirt, and stick that cigarette to his back. He'd screamed and cried. But Trudy never came. She was sitting on Shay's back porch, that pipe to her lips while he begged the white man not to hurt him anymore.

Chapter 19

ANGELO FLAT OUT rejected Belinda's suggestion of taking the children to the Memphis Zoo, which was nearby and had attractions that would be irresistible to their young minds.

"We'd never get down to Greenville by four."

He recommended, instead, that after breakfast they should take them to the park for a few hours to blow off steam.

"Guess we have to explain how—why—they're with us."

Angelo looked at his wife pointedly. "How and why, indeed." He did not get a response to that.

At the park, as the children gamboled about under their watchful eyes, his friend Dave and his wife, Janna, strolled over, hand in hand. Angelo smiled at their display of love. *Well*, he amended, *the baby* further *cemented their love.* He had two friends who would soon be fathers. He told himself he was happy for them, *happy*.

Dave was puffed up with pride. Angelo told himself he was not exaggerating in this observation of his best friend. He looked taller, broader.

Angelo stopped pushing Sasha in the swing. He put a smile on his face as he watched the couple approach them.

Angelo and Dave gave each other the bro hug, right hands clasped tightly, elbows touching. Then, they drew back their hands in a fast jerk and snapped their fingers at the same time. Each man kissed the other's wife, a quick peck on the lips.

"Sup, man?"

Angelo supposed Dave had adopted this pattern of speech relegated usually to so-called black and urban vernacular because he had married a black woman. Angelo knew Dave was born and raised in some community in Idaho called Atlanta. He'd won a football scholarship to play for the Tennessee Vols in Knoxville. Not only did he fall in love with the Big Orange but also with a girl from the *real* Atlanta in Georgia. He returned to Idaho yearly at Christmas with his bride to, as he jokingly told Angelo, *put some color in the place.*

Though his parents had grown used to the idea of having that *pretty black girl* as their daughter-in-law, they were generally met with mild astonishment by most of his kin and friends at Janna's continued presence in his life.

Angelo had met Dave seven years ago when he joined the plant as an IT expert. His frankness and honesty, holdovers from his conservative childhood, were the links that forged the strength of his and Angelo's friendship. The expression *brother from another mother* perfectly described their friendship.

Before Angelo could answer Dave, and what *could* he say, Janna exclaimed, "These are the cutest kids ever!" She stood before the swing set, her hands already clasped protectively against her flat belly. "Belinda, she's got your eyes. Where've you been hiding them?" She looked from Belinda to Angelo.

"Thanks." Angelo and Belinda looked at each other. Both had spoken, enthusiastically, in unison, as if the possibility of these children sharing their genes was welcomed and accepted.

Dave plucked Sasha from the swing and held her aloft like a doll. The child, Angelo saw, looked too happy to be scared and too scared to be happy about the lofty position in which she found herself.

Dave set her on his shoulder and looked down at Matthew. He addressed Belinda directly. "Unless you two have found a way to manufacture clones, you need to tell us something."

"Cloning is not that difficult a scientific process," asserted Belinda, who had a master's in molecular genetics. "I've done it hundreds of times."

Angelo smirked at his wife's words. Dave gave her a flat look but said nothing. Angelo knew the man well enough to know that he was waiting for a plausible explanation. Dave knew all of Angelo's nieces and nephews.

"We're babysitting," announced Angelo. That was a brilliant statement to make.

"Whose kids are they?" Janna tickled Matthew in the sides, causing the little boy to erupt in hysterical giggles.

"Belinda picked them up in—"

"Walls, Mississippi." Belinda gave Angelo a look. *Agree with me.*

"So, yeah, we gotta get them back to…where Bel…to their…We gotta get 'em back by four."

Angelo reached up, plucked Sasha from Dave's shoulders, and handed her over to Belinda's waiting arms.

Were his hands shaking?

Angelo was a terrible liar (which was another reason his marriage to Gwen had to fail: a cheating man must learn the art of deception), and until just this moment, he thought Belinda was also.

Angelo and Dave talked a bit, about work, whether they should get tickets to any of the Grizzlies home games next season, even about their friend Tyson's sporadic drinking.

"Well, with Liza being pregnant, this may straighten out their crazy love."

Angelo nodded, telling himself again that he was happy for them, *happy*.

Janna heard this exchange and pointed a slim finger at Belinda, said half-jokingly, "Girl, it's in the water! You're going to have to watch it if you don't want this to happen to you!" She stroked her front, as if outlining the bulge of a baby that was barely the size of a kumquat.

Angelo watched Belinda give Janna a brittle smile. She was not being unkind. She simply did not know.

"We have to stop by the library, guys, so…" Angelo herded the children together, his arm around Belinda and the children close to his side.

"Give us a kiss, then," intoned Dave, a guy who believed in always telling his friends he loved them when they parted company.

Dave hugged and kissed Belinda, slapped Angelo on the shoulder, and Angelo repeated the gestures. Dave even swiped a kiss from Sasha, who gasped and threw him a kiss. Matthew gave a shy wave of good-bye and ducked against Angelo's thigh.

Angelo wasted no time at the library on Vollintine, just off North Evergreen. He quickly went to the section of local newspapers. The tiny news article read like a blurb on page three of the three-page Metro section of the Greenville paper, the *Delta-Democrat Times*:

> The body of a black woman was found near the levy this morning. Based on the county coroner's report, the woman had been dead for approximately 24 to 48 hours. Facial contusions suggested foul play; the police are investigating this case. The woman appeared to be in her early 20s. There was no identification on the body; however, the word "Trudy" was tattooed on the woman's left ankle.
>
> As of today, no one has come forward to claim the body. According to the coroner's preliminary report, evidence suggested prolonged drug use by the deceased. Drug paraphernalia was found near the woman's body.
>
> In a possibly related case, the body of a baby boy was found near the woman. DNA tests will be done to determine if indeed they are related. Anyone with any information about the woman or baby is urged to contact the Washington County Police Department.

There was a number listed after the brief article.

Back in the car with Belinda and the children, he handed over the photocopy of the article in the paper to Belinda, let her read it. When she finished, he took her hand. "Honey, do you have any idea about this? Could the dead woman and child be related to Sasha and Matthew?" At their names being called, the children leaned forward in their car seats.

Hadn't they mentioned someone, a Trudy? And they had cried, Belinda had said, for Adrian. *Where's our baby Adrian?* Matthew had screamed.

Angelo put on a bright smile. It felt close to breaking. He turned to the children. "Hey, you little squirrels, let me do this." He produced, as if by magic, two pairs of headphones and tablets. He helped them adjust them on their smaller heads, helped to find a video for Sasha and a game for Matthew. They were engrossed in seconds. Settling back in the driver's seat, he looked almost plaintively at his wife.

Belinda nodded, looked at her husband, and, slowly, she began the story.

Chapter 20

BELINDA HAD SAID good-bye to her mother and, on an impulse, had driven the twenty-five or so miles over to Greenville, intent on picking up a few things for the house—a few sets of sheets for the guest rooms, some towels that were on sale at Walmart, and anything else that she could find that would easily fit in the Camry. She could have stopped at the one in Indianola on the same highway that would take her to Greenville, but she sped past it. She wanted to look at the shops in the mall, and Indianola had no mall.

At the checkout counter in Belk's, she'd met a friend from high school, also there on a shopping trip. The woman, Dianne Jackson, had convinced Belinda to go to one of the casinos off the Mississippi. Belinda had laughingly agreed and had actually won $150 at one of the slot machines. She even ventured to the $5 blackjack table and, when her chips were three stacks of $5 chips, she cashed this in and pocketed her winnings. She treated Dianne, who had not been as lucky, to a buffet lunch at Trop Casino and bragged for an hour about the $245 in winnings lining her purse. She and Dianne had parted company on Washington Avenue, each reiterating how much fun they'd had.

Belinda walked down the avenue, smiling to herself as she thought of the conversation she would have with Angelo that night about her *wild* gambling. She was so deep into her reverie that she did not notice the young woman, her thick, red-tinted hair wild about her head, until she had walked straight into her.

The young lady was fairly tall and slim. Abstractedly, Belinda noted that if she got any slimmer, she would be to the point of gauntness. She was dressed in dingy jeans and a long-sleeved T-shirt that had an obscene phrase on it written in fluorescent pink letters. It seemed that she'd purposely bumped into Belinda.

"Oh, excuse me, Miss High and Mighty!" The younger woman's dark eyes were very bright and wide open, darting back and forth, up and down, as if she was surprised at the sun's presence on her skin, on her face. She sneered at Belinda, who apologized softly and stepped aside. There was no need to have an altercation with this woman, who so obviously spelled trouble.

But when Belinda made an effort to go around her, the woman—Belinda caught a good look at her, barely in her twenties, maybe twenty-two, twenty-three at the most—grabbed her wrist and hissed at her hoarsely, "Look, could you let me have a few dollars, maybe ten or twenty. I just need a little candy, you know, to get my morning wake-up."

Belinda couldn't help but look at her watch. It was well after four. *What did this twitching, itching girl mean? Candy?*

Belinda, not wanting to give in to her fright, reached into her purse and handed the woman a twenty-dollar bill from her winnings, silently convincing herself she was not giving *her* money to an addict. She knew the woman was a—what was that term she'd heard of?—rock star. (Was that term still used?)

She'd seen them increase in number over the last ten years in the small Delta towns in Mississippi. Many were from up North or out East, coming back home to family and, sometimes, even escaping the law. Many were also Mississippians, from Indianola, Moorhead, and here in Greenville. She idly thought that the girl had been a beauty at one point in her life. The drugs were sucking away what remained of her looks.

Wasn't she too young to be this deep into drugs? Belinda, for all her scientific acumen in the workforce, was rather naïve about the drug culture. She could speak with intelligence about the neurological effects of many drugs, their properties, both physical and biochemical, but had never used a single illicit drug in her thirty-plus years of living.

"I don't want any trouble." She stuffed the bill into the woman's dirty hands. But instead of accepting the money and moving on, the girl became even more irate.

"You think you're something, don't you, you bitch! Dressed all fine and shit. But I got something for your ass."

But Belinda was already running down the avenue, away from the woman, back toward the casino off Lake Ferguson. She was terrified. She hadn't seen a gun or knife, but that didn't mean that the woman didn't have one. She had heard stories of crack addicts who sold furniture and appliances right out from their parents' homes, stole any type of clothing from stores and sold them. *Boosting*, she remembered, was what this little enterprise was called. This woman probably robbed people with some kind of weapon to get the money for her drugs.

Belinda ran for several minutes, never looking back. She finally dared to stop and look back, but there was no one following her. She looked around her. She was still on Washington but near a dark alley, and that frightened her anew because there were so few people about. She turned back up the avenue, breathing a sigh of relief when she saw a police car parked across the street. The officer had to be nearby. She felt a little better, a little safer.

At that moment, she heard a soft sound to her right. A kitten? An injured dog? If it were an injured animal, she was not going in the alley, and if it were a person, she could summon the police. She peered into the darkness. After a few seconds, her eyes adjusted to the darkness. She was shocked to see a little boy standing before a stack of wooden crates.

"Hello? Little boy, are you all right in there? Who's in there with you?" When he didn't answer, Belinda looked around, saw that there was no one about. The boy did appear to be alone in the dark!

She took a step toward him, and he backed away, his hands going up in a defensive gesture. She stooped down, still walking toward him. "It's OK, I won't hurt you. Are you lost?" Then, she heard the sound again, not from the boy. She turned in the direction of the sound and saw a little girl. Belinda looked at the toddler. She looked about two, no more than three years old, and the boy a little bigger, a little taller. Both were dirty.

"Hello, are you by yourselves? Where're your parents, your mommy and daddy?"

The boy said nothing, but he pulled at the little girl, who took a hesitant step backward and then turned to face Belinda. "Baby sheep."

Belinda looked at her. "What?"

The girl walked over to a bundle of what appeared to be rags and touched what was lying on the crate that the boy was so obviously guarding. Belinda tiptoed over to the bundle, her heart like a jackhammer in her chest, and moved the rags around, exposing a baby's face; it looked about six months old.

Of course, Belinda had no reference point. Younger than a year and older than a newborn. It smelled of spoiled milk and dirty diapers.

But more than that, Belinda could see that this baby was not *sheep* as the girl had said for sleep but, in fact, was dead. These children, dirty and smelly, too, alone in an alley with a dead baby!

Belinda looked at the police cruiser. There was still no one inside. *Where was the officer?*

She grabbed the children's hands and started running, tears of sheer terror running down her face. She ran for blocks, her grip on those tiny hands like a vise. Her only thought was to get them out of the alley, away from the dead baby. When she finally stopped running, she was very close to where she'd parked her car. She was breathing hard, as if she'd run a marathon. The children were breathing hard, too, but neither was crying.

"Get in, get in the car!" she screamed at the children, pushing them into the backseat of her car with shaking hands. Once all were inside, she locked the doors and sat at the wheel, shaking like a leaf on a tree. "I'm OK. It's OK." She turned back and stared at the children. "You're OK."

She started the engine and found that she still had the power to drive, to react to traffic. She drove around for about fifteen minutes, trying to think. Finally, she pulled into a hotel on Highway 82 and did the only thing that made sense to her. She checked in for overnight and went to her room with two double beds, where she sat the children on one of the beds and examined them. They were slim but not scrawny; she saw that in the alley. They were filthy and smelled of urine, the sickly sweet smell of baby waste and sweat, their once-styled hair now matted to their heads. The boy had a fade that was overgrowing with spikes of hair around his round head. The girl's hair had been in puffy plaits that were mostly undone. She checked their hair and bodies for lice and anything else but found none. She still had not had the presence of mind to call Angelo, her mother, or 911.

"What are your names?"

The boy pointed to his skinny chest. "Maph-phew," he lisped and indicated the girl with a finger. "She's Sasha."

"Are you sister and brother?"

"Yes." Belinda noticed his accent; she definitely didn't place him as a southerner. Possibly from Chicago or New York, she wasn't sure.

"How old are you?"

"Five. Sasha's three." The girl proudly held up three grubby fingers, beaming at her older brother.

Belinda sat for a long moment, trying to think of what to do.

Finally, the little boy—his demeanor was like that of an old man and not a boy—took the decision out of her hands. "Can we have some food to take back to our baby Adrian?"

Now Belinda looked at Angelo. "I just ran and ran. I was so scared. I didn't know what would happen to them, honey. You saw their bodies! Those horrible scars on Matthew's back. She—*someone* obviously abused them! She must've left them to get drugs and to do God knows what else. They couldn't even tell me when they'd eaten last. I was so scared that I didn't check to see what the baby was, a boy or a girl. All I could think was to get them out of there."

Angelo took his hand from the steering wheel and squeezed her hand reassuringly. "Oh, baby, I'm so sorry. I wish I could have been with you. I should have been there for you."

Belinda shook her head. "There was nothing you could have done. The baby was already dead. And I couldn't leave them there."

"Yeah, you're right. So you think the woman who bumped into you—and the way you described her, she sounds like a crackhead—was that woman in the paper, Trudy. They called her name that first night at home, remember? She was their mother."

Belinda nodded. "She talked the same way Matthew does and…And now that I think about it, Sasha does look like her. I think she was their mother. She probably didn't come back to that alley for days!"

Angelo made a guttural sound of disgust. Belinda knew of his cousins from down in Mississippi, sisters who had turned to the drug years ago. One had almost died, and the other had disappeared into the crowds of New York.

"They cried and cried that night, asking about the baby, but they didn't ask about her, about Trudy. I called you, and when I didn't get you, I called Mama, just to tell her I was in Greenville to do some shopping. I didn't know how to tell her what I did, what I found."

"She must have family, somewhere." He sounded relieved; Belinda supposed he'd entertained all sorts of thoughts and decided that she hadn't done anything morally wrong. She wondered if he would have done the same thing.

"Maybe." She was surprised to discover that, even with her terror having dwindled down to simple fear and frustration, she had thoroughly enjoyed their time taking care of the two children. And she had seen Angelo at the park. His attitude toward them was close to paternal.

Here, let me tie your shoelace, Matthew. Did that mean dog scare you, Sasha? No, kids, don't run; take my hand, both of you.

"Honey, let's think for a moment. You discovered a corpse and didn't report it to the proper authorities. You kidnapped two innocent children. On top of that, you crossed state lines with them. What you did was a crime, a felony. I didn't do anything, so I aided and abetted you; that's gotta be some serious jail time for me, too. Baby, we could go to jail, for a long time!"

"She didn't care about them. *That's* the crime. She probably would have given them away if she could have." She looked back at the children, but they were engrossed still in the entertainment Angelo had loaded into the two tablets he'd given them when they were placed in the car seats.

He lowered his voice. "Well, Belinda, she *didn't.* You took them, and we can't just *keep* them. Thank God, Mr. Sweeney said he could meet us there by five or so." He roughly rubbed his forehead, looking intently at her. She knew he was deeply affected by all this, for he had called her Belinda. Since they started dating, he had never called her by her Christian name.

She held her breath as his eyes softened from love for her. "I think I know why you did it."

Belinda laughed but there was no humor in the sound. "You do? I wish you'd tell me." She had panicked; she freely admitted that. But why hadn't she acted rationally? Called 911? Gone to the police station? Simply left the kids as she found them? She had no ready answer.

Would she have any when the authorities questioned her?

Angelo again reached across the console, took her hand, and squeezed. "Baby, all the while you were running, scared and confused, in the back of your mind, you had to be thinking it."

"What?" She breathed in his scent, the familiar maleness of him. She sat up, looked at him, the truth already in her eyes.

"You were thinking, *Angelo and I can have these babies. We can take care of them.*" He reached up, stroked her cheek. "*We can't make babies, and here they are.*"

Chapter 21

"Is your car outside?" The policeman, dressed in his black uniform with the triangular-shaped Greenville Police Department emblem on his shirt and badge, stood up from the small table where Belinda, Angelo, Mr. Sweeney, and another officer were all sitting. The entire ordeal of coming to the station, meeting their lawyer there, and confessing mostly the most obvious fact—they had brought the children to the station because they believed them to be related to the dead woman Trudy mentioned in the article—had taken less than an hour.

A social worker from the Department of Family and Children's Services had come and taken the children away.

"We'll be just down the hall while you all straighten this out." She was a middle-aged, plump black woman who looked more like a granny than a government employee. Still, Sasha cried, and Matthew sniffled as they were led away. Angelo thought sadly that both were terrified of the unknown once again. He felt his throat tighten as the children's voices got softer and softer the farther they were taken away.

Now everyone was standing. The policeman who had asked to see the car led the way, his arms out from his sides, a habit that must have been born because of his carrying a sidearm.

Angelo pointed out Belinda's Camry, not exactly sure what was next. Mr. Sweeney had cautioned them about making any confession. "Let them talk to you. Volunteer nothing."

"Open it, please." The request sounded more like an order. Angelo depressed the button on the remote door opener, and the lights blinked on as the doors unlocked with the familiar click.

The officer looked in the front seat, giving it the most perfunctory of glances. Then, he opened the back doors, leaned in, and poked, prodded. He straightened and beckoned his superior over, who looked in also, poked, prodded some more. They whispered to each other and glanced back at Angelo and Belinda.

Angelo moved swiftly to his wife's side. Now he knew what the officers were discussing. This would not go well, he thought dejectedly.

"Your car's pretty clean."

Belinda almost answered the men as if the statement were a compliment. Angelo stopped her with a squeeze to her side.

"And those car seats look like they're spank brand-new."

"My clients are law-abiding citizens," Mr. Sweeney said convincingly, ironically. After all, until yesterday, both were. "They know children must be properly secured at all times in a moving vehicle."

"That's the point we're making. In your statement, ma'am,"—he was a white man, youngish, but Angelo could tell that he had a problem giving either of them the respect of titles like *ma'am* and *sir*—"you said you were terrified, that you ran with the children, that you got in your car (I assume this nice Camry) and drove around for a while." His smile was friendly and open. Angelo knew he was laying a trap for them. "That you looked for an officer..."

Belinda answered when Mr. Sweeney nodded his consent that she could.

"I did. All that's true." Her voice rose at the last word, a sure indication she was nervous and not liking where this was going either.

"But you bought car seats."

Mr. Sweeney gave her a look, and Belinda remained silent.

"They're new," the officer insisted. "The only way this makes any sense—and you have to agree that all we're tryin' to get to is the truth—is that somewhere or sometime, the panic and terror you *said* you were feelin' had to leave for you to go out and buy two pretty nice car seats, get them properly installed, and drive them to your home in Memphis."

"My clients did not say they drove to or from Memphis with those kids, just that the car seats were purchased here in the city."

"Then, where were you, Mr. Higginbotham, while all this drama was going on?" This from the district attorney, who had called earlier to say he would be a few minutes late. He was over an hour late and had joined them without much fanfare in the open, crowded parking lot.

Had she mentioned the hotel? No, he was sure she had not. He spoke the truth but left room for open interpretation. "Waiting for her. And the seats were purchased using my credit card." This was also true, but it had been in her possession until they crossed the state line heading here.

"So, if we check those Walmart videos, we'll find both of you with those kids?"

"I did say I was waiting on her. I didn't enter the store." Another truth with open interpretation.

"You're from Indianola, Mrs. Higginbotham?" This question from the other officer, a young, black girl with thick extensions that hung almost to her waist. Angelo thought she could have been pretty, but the makeup must have been at the limit allowed by the department, as were her nails. Out of uniform, he might have easily mistaken her for a pole dancer.

It was in her statement, Angelo wanted to say, but she answered once more. "Yes, visiting my mother—she's recovering from an operation. We're going to drive over after this."

If we're not in jail, thought Angelo.

"Let's go back inside," suggested Mr. Sweeney, even though it should have been at least the DA who said this, but no one countered his words, and they all trooped back into the rather plain, two-story building on Main Street.

They all returned to the same interrogation room (though this was not what either officer called it) and sat back around the table.

"Are my clients free to go?" Mr. Sweeney addressed the DA.

"If they took those kids to Memphis, hell no; kidnapping is a felony."

"My client said she was in Greenville shopping. She bought everything here. What evidence do you have that she and her husband did anything but make those two kids as comfortable and safe as possible, then took the correct action and brought them in to the proper authorities?"

"Are they?"

Mr. Sweeney looked evenly at his counterpart in this weird tale. "Are who what?"

"The children—are they safe?"

It was then that, if Angelo could have, he would have kissed the overly made-up girl for her endorsement.

"Y'ask me, those children were perfectly cared for. My cousin used to work for the FCS. Nu-unh, if them—if *those* children—are part of what that crackhead we found dead was, what this couple did was an act of God. An act of God!" She raised her hand and voice dramatically.

"Could you bring them in, please, Darnika?" The DA gave her a simpering look, as if he was saying that, of course, the likes of *her* would find this so.

"Officer O'Neal," she corrected, before swishing from the room and closing the door with a snap. Yes, he could kiss her.

Chapter 22

MATTHEW DIDN'T KNOW why they were in this building that smelled funny, like cleaning stuff and a dirty bathroom. Sometimes he smelled it at Shay's house. *Shay*. Did he know where they were? And where was Trudy and their baby Adrian? Because he was scared, he even missed Trudy now. And Angelo and Belinda? They had been so nice to him and Sasha, even though he could tell that Belinda was scared at first. He was surprised that adults could be scared of anything.

Now he and Sasha were being taken back down the dark and scary hall to the room where they had left Angelo and Belinda. The woman who was with them asked him a few questions, waiting on his answers like he was a big boy. And he *was*, but he was scared, and all he really wanted was to go home. He was surprised again that he didn't mean the place back in Chicago (his memory of the small place was fading after so many months) or Old Miss Carrolton's old house, not even Shay's warm house with the big television and plenty of food. He meant the place he'd spent the night last night, even though he'd shared the bed with Sasha. He meant Belinda and Angelo's house.

The door was opened for them, and the woman gently pushed them inside. Angelo and Belinda were sitting at the table again, and there was another white man he couldn't remember seeing before. Had he and Sasha done something wrong? His granny—Fat Boy's granny—had told him not to trust white men, especially if they wore a suit. Well, the doctor wore suits, and he trusted him. Maybe his granny was wrong about the doctor. But he knew she was right about *this* white man in the suit. He would have to protect Sasha from him.

"Are you kids all right?"

Matthew looked at the woman with the braids and scooted closer to Sasha, who was snuffling and sniffling again like a baby. He wanted to be mad at her, but he knew he couldn't. "Yes," he mumbled, peeking at Angelo and Belinda. Both were smiling at him, and he could see in their eyes that they were not mad at him or Sasha. So why were they here?

"Do you know Mr. and Mrs. Higginbotham?"

He saw that Angelo was about to say something, but the white man in the suit stopped him with a snap. "Do not answer for him."

Matthew shook his head.

"Where did you spend the night last night, you and your sister?"

The nice lady had asked the same thing. Why was this so important?

"In a bed with my sister, Sasha." When she heard her name, Sasha stopped whimpering long enough to look at her brother. Matthew puffed his chest out. Fat Boy and Trudy had always told him to protect his little sister.

"Do you know where? Were you in Memphis or Greenville?"

Matthew thought carefully. He had never heard of this Memphis, and he knew a little about Greenville, so he said what he knew, the same thing he'd told the nice lady who'd given him and Sasha some crackers and milk.

"I was in Greenville. Sasha too."

"With these people?" The man pointed, and Matthew nodded silently.

The black man in the suit smiled at him like Matthew had won a prize.

"I think this proves what my clients have said all along. We agree that Mrs. Higginbotham panicked and that she committed a misdemeanor by not reporting the location of a"—he looked at Matthew and then at Sasha—"deceased body. There is no evidence the children were taken across state lines, and the boy just said himself that they spent the night in Greenville.

"Further, it is obvious that they were well taken care of. You've been in contact with the Higginbothams' colleagues and superiors. All say they are exemplary, responsible employees. This"—the black man in the suit said, moving his hands toward him and Sasha, back to Belinda and Angelo—"was an unfortunate case of simple panic; true, bad judgment, but I see no reason even to pay a fine. There should be no arrest, no jail time, probation, or anything, because no conscious criminal act was committed."

"Ignorance of the law is no excuse, *counselor*; you should know that."

The white man in the suit was mean, Matthew decided.

The white man in the suit gave him a friendly look. "I heard you hurt your back—got burned pretty bad?" He looked at Matthew like he knew what it meant to be burned like that. "How'd it happen?"

Matthew knew the man had tricked him by acting all friendly. Someone had told him what the white man had done to him. What if he came for him now, for thinking he told? What if that was why their baby Adrian was gone, why Trudy hadn't come, or Shay? What if he'd sicced those mean dogs he said he had on them?

His lips trembled, and the tears were a flood. "That white man put a cigarette on me. He said he'd kill me and feed me to his dogs! Please don't tell him I told! Don't let him hurt our baby Adrian!"

The nice woman patted his shoulder until he finally caught his breath on a hiccupping gulp. He opened his eyes to see the white man in the suit stacking papers and looking mad but not like he was mad at him. Just mad.

"Thank you. You're a brave boy, and I promise he won't hurt you." He looked at the black man in the suit. "Now, we have to…"

The man kept talking, and Matthew lost a lot of the words, but he started to understand that there was something going on about Trudy and that their baby Adrian might be lost or something. Was he with Trudy? With Shay?

After a while, the white man in the suit said he and Sasha would have to go with the lady and that Belinda and Angelo were free to go.

"Are we going to Shay's house?"

The nice woman looked at the two people in the black uniforms.

"You have a place?" The white man in the uniform asked the woman this.

"Yes, they'll be fine. It might help if we could get their family involved, and the sooner the better."

She took Matthew's hand in hers. Sasha had fallen asleep sometime during all the back-and-forth between the men in the suits. The woman picked her up and held her in her arms.

"I understand you all went through her phone and found some names to call?"

"Just take care of them, please," the woman with the long braids said. Matthew thought she was trying to be nice because the white men weren't being nice.

Then, he and Sasha were being taken away again. He thought he heard Angelo and Belinda calling after them, but he wasn't sure. Sasha woke up and started crying. He didn't want to, but he was crying, too.

He wished he could have told Angelo how good those waffles were and that he liked the pajamas Belinda had bought for them. He wished a lot of things that night.

Chapter 23

TRUMAN JENKINS PLACED the receiver back into its cradle with a heavy hand. The receiver bumped around before settling into its correct position. He had told himself that this phone call would come; he'd told himself this for weeks, even though there was a small voice at the back of his head screaming, *No, this would never happen.*

His daughter was dead. That's what the police from that town she was in months ago had said: found dead, with the baby dead, too. Drug overdose, the coroner had ruled. They'd found a small but deadly stash of drugs and that damned pipe. She must have literally smoked herself to death. Not just crack in her system, those drugs in that little plastic bag they'd found were a powerful mixture of crack, heroin, cocaine, and stuff he'd only heard of on television. What was she doing with that deadly combination? True, he could not deny that she smoked crack, but until that phone call, he would have staked his life on it that she barely touched liquor and smoked marijuana just to do something purely social and casual. Up her nose, in her veins? Hell no! The girl could barely swallow aspirins as a kid, and she cried from shots until—well, she never got over her fear of needles, so until she died, he thought miserably. Crack was her drug of choice.

Like she couldn't die from that, Truman, the voice asked him once more.

But not just her, the baby was gone, too, the one he had just met the one time a few months ago. Such a handsome baby, too. He and Fat Boy's grandmother were going to see to it that Adrian's namesake was raised safe. He had no idea how they were going to see to that, but that was their entire conversation on their drive back to Chicago from Mississippi: get the kids, keep them safe, get Trudy into rehab. Or, Lord forgive him, just get the kids back, keep them safe. They hadn't come up with a workable plan, and now it didn't really matter.

He would have to tell his boy that his older sister was dead. Would he be able to take it? His children weren't overly close now, thanks mostly to that pipe taking her from them, but once, they had fiercely loved each other. He knew that his son still deeply loved and cared for his sister.

Truman sat in his favorite chair, a recliner his wife had bought for him on their sixth wedding anniversary. He knew she had actually gotten it secondhand from Goodwill, but it was in great shape then. Over the years, it had been molded to fit his body perfectly. When his wife had died from the cancer, this was the only place he could fall asleep—*pass out from drinking*, that voice said coldly. *Whatever*, he countered silently. He could not sleep in their bed for three years.

He had not been a drinking man before Odessa died. A beer, a few whiskeys—that was it. If he got that glow that loosened up his admittedly staid and proper demeanor, he quit. He liked to be in control, he told his buddies. Then, Odessa was gone, and the drinks kept coming. The fact that he managed to keep his job as a tax accountant at a minority-owned firm was mostly because he didn't show up for work drunk or tipsy, but starting from Friday after work to Sunday and any holiday/off day, he was drunk before noon. Plus, he had a mind for complex calculations, tax laws, and such. He was an asset to the company, and both his employers and fellow employees knew this. Even in this economy, he was fairly certain he could keep this job.

He supposed he could have described himself as a functional alcoholic, which he considered to be an oxymoron. He tried to keep his drinking hidden from his kids, but they were smart. Trudy had never been sympathetic enough to overlook it, and his son dismissed him as weak by the time he was fifteen, with no regret.

At one point in those dark years, he thought he would simply drink himself into oblivion. But then Trudy got pregnant at seventeen with Matthew. The baby boy renewed his love of life, but he continued drinking. Then little Sasha. Still, the drinking continued until seven months ago.

He was not a devoutly religious man, but he believed in a higher power that he chose to call God. So what happened to him could only be called a miracle. Seven months ago, he awoke one Saturday morning. Although he had no problem getting smashed alone, some days he liked to hang out with a few men, play chess, dominoes, cards, or even checkers, and drink a few beers, a lot of whiskey. That morning, he joined them at their hangout, took up a can of beer, and sat around the small table, ready to shoot the breeze and tell a few lies as he dealt the cards. He poured half of it, put the can down, and told his friend he could have the rest. He took one sip of the cold beer and lost his taste for alcohol.

There was no clap of thunder, no lightning bolts in the eastern sky, no vision from on high. He simply did not want a drink. Did not need a drink. He had been stone-cold sober ever since. He did not try to understand what had happened. There was no aversion therapy. He could be around a sober person as easily as he could be around a sloppy drunk person and feel the same.

Though he did not believe in signs and wonders, he realized now that for this moment—telling his son that his sister and nephew were gone, telling his neighbor and dear friend that the mother of her great-grandchildren was dead, the baby boy they had cuddled and kissed and loved so back there in Mississippi was no longer alive—he had to be sober, clearheaded.

He sighed deeply, looking around his living room. His eyes fell, as always, on the far wall, over the giant screen television and his so-called music and entertainment system. It was a combination CD player, turntable, and radio with medium-size speakers. There were a dozen straw hats arranged artfully along the wall. Flowers and brightly colored ribbons decorated the brims. A set of woman hats—his wife's hats. She had never been into those huge affairs women wore to church or the small dainty things that were becoming the rave now. She wore these to the store for shopping, to a party on someone's lawn, while "gardening"—she planted any seed she could find, and every year, he would tease her that the birds were waiting on her to feed them. Hardly anything ever grew but she planted yearly. He loved her for her tenacity. She wore them when the chemo ripped her beautiful curls off her head.

He would never get rid of them.

"Odessa, our baby girl's gone." As clear as if she were cuddled next to him, he heard her voice. *I know.*

"Baby, I failed you. I tried, but losing you...It was so damned hard, so lonely without you. It's my fault." He felt her hand on his cheek. He was not drunk. He was not crazy. He knew what he felt, and, somehow, he accepted this insanity. *No, lovey-dovey, it's not. But you can help her still. Make the right decisions.*

Lovey-dovey—her pet name for him from the day they met as teens. He stood, went to the sink in his bathroom, and washed the tears from his eyes. In time, his strength would be needed to do the right thing.

One thing he had to do now was go across the street to tell Dolly. Her given name was Dorothy, but he'd never addressed her as such. He felt his cheeks heat. Trudy had teased them back in Mississippi about getting together. He had known his neighbor for over a dozen years. He knew her common-law husband, had even tried to comfort her when the old fool had gotten himself sent to Chester. She had seen the row of hats and, when he explained, said she understood. He hoped she did.

He wanted her understanding because Odessa would always be his first love, but if it didn't beat all, he was crazy about this woman who was a full two decades older than him! He was a normal man with, he thought, normal needs in *that* department. Every few years, after Odessa died, he found his way into some woman's bed. The time might last from a good screw to a few good screws. He wasn't looking for much more than that—a way to dull the ache in his groin. (The one in his heart he never would nor wanted to lose.)

But once back in Chicago, he invited Dolly to dinner; later, to a movie; and then, lunch at his place, prepared by his own two hands. Before long, they were eating weekend meals together, reading the newspaper to each other, and worrying over their grandchildren and his son, who had moved to another section of the city and was living with his girlfriend and her brother and his girlfriend, who all attended Chicago State.

Within a month of returning to Chicago, Truman and Dolly's friendship had taken that natural course, and he had stumbled and bumbled his way into her bed and made love to her. She was in her midsixties, but there was nothing he could really tell about her that was different from a woman his age or even younger. Curvaceous yet fit, she looked terrific fully clothed or lying naked in bed, her belly a pillow for his wooly head and her breasts gems for him to savor.

Plus, her being older meant she *knew* things, things that he didn't know older women would know. She knew a lot and didn't mind letting him know it or teaching him a few things. He was an avid pupil.

He had always liked her, held her in esteem, and respected her. When her—he supposed he had always thought of Joe Mack as her husband—husband had been there, they'd been on friendly terms, and that'd been about it. Their relationship had been based on Fat Boy and Trudy's involvement with each other, their children together, more so than anything.

Now Joe Mack was gone, and he was there. He had developed deep feelings for her that he hadn't felt in years. He was pleased when she'd whispered in his ear that she loved him, too, and that she would have to let her old man, Joe Mack Ricketts, go. He wouldn't be eligible for parole for fifteen years. By then, he really would be her old man. But she would not be an old lady; she would be a fine wine.

He walked briskly across the street and knocked on her door. He didn't think he could call her to give her this news. She opened the door promptly. She had a book in her hand and a finger stuck between the pages to mark her place.

Her face lit up at the sight of him, a tall, slim man wearing a thick sweater against the cold and well-worn jeans and sneakers.

"*True-man*, come on in, come on in!" Though his name was Truman, she had chosen to call him this, breaking the name into two words. He liked that. He liked it a lot.

"Dolly." He hugged her to him, kissed her cheek and then her lips, quickly. "I interrupted your reading; I'm sorry." He indicated the book she was still holding.

"Oh, yeah, *Walk in Bethel*—it's her debut novel. Great read. She won some international prize in general fiction a couple of years ago for it, and again just a few months ago."

"OK," he said politely; he then took the book, examined the front and back covers. "Nice design, pretty woman."

"Yes, I understand she does all her cover designs! I'm reading this one first, but I have her other three. I read she just completed her fifth one. She's really good." She took the book back and placed it on a small table by the front door.

"Guess I'll read them when you finish." He had always been a reader and had taught by example his children to be readers also. His son still read but mostly articles related to his job and his studies, forensic accounting. He doubted Trudy read anymore. He corrected himself. She didn't read anymore. She would not read anything ever again.

He gently pushed Dolly onto the sofa, placed his arm around her. "I got some bad news for you, baby doll."

Dolly took in a deep breath. He could feel her shrink back, as if the news would be a physical blow that she would have to prepare herself for.

"Is it the grands?" Both had been reluctant to leave them behind in Mississippi, but Trudy had convinced them that she was clean (she had been) and that she had a job. Now, though he so wanted to believe in his daughter, he doubted that.

"Yeah, but not just them…Trudy's gone, baby. I got the call this morning. Police said it was probably—it was a drug overdose." He started crying before he knew it, the tears practically jumping from his eyes. He hadn't wanted to tell her this news so baldly, but he had no idea how to build up to this, to soften the blow.

Dolly cried also, but softly and quietly. Instead of his comforting her, she was comforting him. Just a few months ago, she had been the one crying over the loss of a child, and he was the comforter. True, Fat Boy was her grandchild, but she had raised him, being more of a mother than his own had ever been. He never knew their roles would be reversed so soon.

"True-man, where are the kids?"

More bad news. He took a steadying breath, but he still choked when he rasped, "Adrian's gone. The police said it might have been exposure. Matthew and Sasha are in foster care, or whatever they call it in Mississippi when they turn the children over to the state." The nice policewoman who had told him this assured him the children were fine, but since the children had family, they should consider coming down and declaring themselves their guardians.

Dolly made a keening sound as she cried in her grief for her great-grandchild. Her tears broke Truman's heart. He held her as they rocked back and forth on her couch in their shared grief and losses. Just as he had lost a daughter, he felt that, when Fat Boy had been killed, he'd lost a son. Her pain was no different.

Eventually, their tears subsided, and they slowly returned to the here and now. He stood to take his leave—they had made plans for dinner at Norman's Bistro, then a short drive up to Oakwood Beach, just to relax in each other's arms and look at the city. That was before the phone call.

Now Dolly held him tenderly. Sometimes he knew she couldn't help herself—treating him like a son. And sometimes, needing a mother's touch, understanding, he let her. "Come on."

"Dolly—"

"Shh-shh. We've got to make plans to get down there, but not right now. Later, True-man."

Her body was his temple. He knelt at her throne, worshiping the treasures she freely offered. He supposed he was what some would call "the other man," and he was cuckolding her common-law husband. But he knew, too, that since Joe Mack had been locked up, there had been no other man in her life, and there was no such thing as conjugal visits in Illinois. Both were lonely. But it was not only loneliness that brought them together. As he entered her, his mouth clamped on a rock-hard nipple; he knew that what kept them sane, whole, and hopeful was the love they shared. Perhaps it had been there all along, underneath that surface of calm water. The eruption of that love rocked them both, spent and sated, and they slept until evening, entwined in her bed.

Chapter 24

TRUDY PARKED THE truck on a side street and got out. Her fingerprints were all over it, and she had taken the man's drug stash. They knew her in this washed-out river town. But maybe no one knew of her and Chris Slack's relationship. Even Shay was not aware of the white man's comings and goings at his place when he was out doing his own business.

She opened the back door and told Matthew and Sasha to get out. She took Adrian from the boy's arms. He smelled like shit. She would have to change him, feed him. Feed all of them. Well, money might not be a problem if she sold this stash. She recognized some of the pills, was sure one of the packets was hashish; another contained coke, and yet another one she could only guess at. A couple of rocks, probably those had been for her for the fucking she'd given him before she bashed in his head with that hammer. (She had driven off with the hammer tight in her hand in the truck and dumped it somewhere along the way to the doctor's little hunting shack.)

She had parked by that familiar crack house up near the river and would sell what she could, smoke the rest, and get some much-needed food and supplies.

She wished the doctor had...what? She almost thought *helped her*. But wasn't he her enemy? At times, he presented himself like the racist she thought him to be. Other times, especially with her children, he was almost...What was that word? Avuncular. But he'd *killed* a man. Well, she amended, the man had brutally raped and beaten her. But the doctor had allowed that to happen, almost as if this were the reason for killing him. But he'd told her he'd explained to the police that he'd beaten the man off her, that the Asian man and the black man must have fought after the attack on her was over, while he was trying to help her and the kids, and had killed each other. Hadn't they tested both of them, him and Trudy, both in the hospital, for gunshot residue? And found none? If they bought that, she thought, they were a stupid lot of police officers!

That was over and done with. But because it had happened at his house, Shay had been implicated; the doctor had cleared his name since he'd sworn that Shay had not been there. Now he would be in trouble all over again if they found the white man dead in his house. How would he explain that, especially since he probably had no idea the man had come by in his absence?

She told herself it didn't matter. She would sell the drugs, hole up for a night in a hotel, feed and bathe her children, and leave the next day for Chicago. It was time to face the facts. Fat Boy was dead. She missed her family, his grandmother. She made no grandiose, sweeping promises of getting clean. Crack was with her, and she was with it to stay. Her children had adjusted—they *had*, she told herself—and if they had, then her father and granny would have to accept it, too. Besides, she was a *social* smoker—at most, ten, twelve times a day. Hell, back home, she knew older people who smoked for days, eating and drinking almost nothing. She was not like them, not at all. Her habit cost her almost no money, what with Shay and the white man supplying her with it. Besides, how many crack addicts had real jobs, were responsible? True, she had no job, but she had skills other than cocksucking and fucking for cash. Her father had made sure she was well read, could dress and speak well when called upon to do so. Maybe she could be a receptionist or a salesperson at one of the stores in the more elite neighborhoods. Start college like she and Fat Boy had discussed. Yes, sell this dope, get the kids ready for travel tomorrow. She felt…excited at the new road she was taking.

China wasn't at the house to take care of the kids while she did her business with the man. She managed to find a towel for Adrian to replace the one the man had jerry-rigged into a diaper back at the hunting shack. Her ability to improvise, to be a problem solver—weren't those talents most employers looked for? Yes, she would do well!

When she asked one of the men in the darkened room about China, he'd told her that she had been picked up for soliciting. Trudy laughed at that. More than likely, she would be out in a week or less. She would make bail or be released based on some oversight. Trudy and Shay had decided that the Greenville police force had more to worry about than a once-pretty woman selling her body for a few dollars.

Like what she was going to do now: sell most of this dope for a lot of cash.

"LD here?" She asked for the owner of the house, the man who did most of the cash and face-to-face transactions. Had he been caught up in China's dramas?

"He here," said a skinny young man with a short row of missing teeth. She unconsciously ran her tongue over her full set of teeth, realizing this was a rare commodity in her world of drugs. The man directed her to a room with enough light to see LD sitting at a table with a girl grinding against him. He was fully clothed, Trudy could see, but the girl was doing some serious humping.

He gazed at her with a slack look on his face. "Hey, long time no see, as they say. You come to get some of LD's special treats?" He pushed the girl away, and Trudy saw with surprise that she could have been a younger version of China. Maybe she was. The girl had to be a relative—same almond-shaped eyes, thick, coarse hair hanging straight down her narrow back. Maybe her sister had taken over China's duties. Trudy mentally shook her head at LD's loyalty. Of course, he had none to anyone but himself.

"Actually, I came to sell—the best." She had taken out samples of all the drugs for herself, along with the two rocks she'd found. The rest should still fetch a pretty penny. She handed over the bag for his inspection. Which was the worst mistake she could have made.

In a flash, there was a blinding light that went to immediate black. It took her three full seconds to realize she had been struck against the head with his fist.

"Bitch, you think I'm crazy? You stroll your crack ass in *my* house of business with other people's shit? For all I know, you could be UC, working for the po-po! Raymond!" A short, beefy man appeared in the doorway, as if by magic. "Get her out of here 'fore I kill her. And those children she brings around here, too. Like this is a goddamn day-care center or something."

Trudy was still trying to clear her head. He bought from others; she knew he did. But she was alone and no match for the muscle he employed.

"Can I at least have my shit back? It's *mine*, LD." How was he to know she'd effectively stolen it?

The man started laughing as if she had told a really funny joke. There was genuine humor in his eyes.

"Baby girl, you best leave now before I do something more than just teach you a lesson in…uh, business etiquette." He looked at the short man. "Raymond, see her out of here, please." He pulled the China doppelgänger back onto his lap. But this time, Trudy heard the distinctive sound of his fly being unzipped.

Trudy found herself deposited on the front porch with nothing to show for her efforts. Her children were sitting on a small padded bench, eyes red with crying and terror. Trudy had all of fifty dollars and some loose change. She would have to find them shelter and food before dark, and the river was already reflecting the rays of a setting sun in the warm autumn sky.

They walked in the darkening streets until she came to a corner store. There, she bought diapers, milk, bread, and some prepackaged bologna. They did not sell bottles for the baby, but the woman who ran the store recognized her from weeks ago at LD's place, went to the back, and brought her own daughter's bottle back.

"You gonna need some baby wipes to clean him up. May as well take a box." She handed the lot to Trudy, took cash only for the items she rang up. "Now, after you change him, you best leave before somebody come lookin' for you."

Trudy supposed she had the look of a fugitive from the law, or at least the look of someone on the run. Trudy quietly thanked the woman, headed to the small bathroom, and made short shrift of changing Adrian. Matthew had stopped crying. She could tell he was simply cried out. Sasha was still sniffling, but her voice was like a kitten's meow. Adrian hadn't cried in hours. If she had time to be concerned, she would have thought that odd. She looked into his eyes and saw an old man staring back at her. Of all the things that had happened today, this was the most frightening thing she had seen.

She soon found a small alley off Washington and stopped there to fix the sandwiches and let them take turns drinking the milk from the carton. She had already filled a bottle with the cold milk. Adrian gobbled down the bottle and cried for more. Her own milk had dried up fast, but it would have done him no good anyway, tainted as her breasts were with crack. The sandwiches were quickly eaten, too, and Matthew and Sasha looked at her with round eyes.

What was that line in the book she had read as a child from her father's paperback collection? *Please, sir, I want some more.* Or something like that. Charles Dickens's *Oliver Twist.* Her father had refused to let her see the movie. *You never know what the director meant, but you always know what the* author *intended, in every word.*

She had nothing more to give them now; she would have to save the rest of the bread and meat until the morning and find milk for the baby. So she wrapped them up in the blanket the woman had stuffed into one of the bags, cocoon style, and in minutes they all three fell into an exhausted slumber. That was when she took out the packet and smoked one of the rocks, using up the last of her matches. She still couldn't believe how she'd lost a fortune in the white man's stash. But LD was a ruthless pusher, a trait she had admired when she'd first met him months ago.

The rock instantly awakened her to her full senses. She paced the alley, her heart hammering in her chest. The high wore off, and she fell into a deep sleep. She awoke a few hours later to the sound of a baby crying. Just for an instant, she wondered whose baby it was.

She awoke fully, with one thing on her mind: smoke the second and last rock. But food had to be the second thought, as her other children stirred awake.

She fed them the bologna and bread. There was no milk or water to wash it down, but at least they had something to eat. There was no breeze, but the morning was still cool. She managed to tear the blanket—it was double ply—by simply unpeeling one layer from the other.

"OK, I'm going to go find some more milk and wipes for the baby, Matthew. You watch over them, OK?" She stood quickly, took up the baby, and wrapped him up in the other half of the blanket and placed him on a small crate. He gurgled sleepily and yawned, closed his eyes. She placed the rest of the blanket around Matthew's shoulders and huddled Sasha next to him.

"Don't go anywhere; you understand me?" Mathew nodded mutely. She smiled encouragingly and told them her plans. "We're going to see Poppa and Granny soon, I promise." When was the last time she'd made them a promise and kept it?

She straightened her shirt. She liked it, but it barely protected her from the chill of the morning. At least it was long-sleeved.

"We're going home?" This tentative question was from Sasha, who seldom spoke these days. Why hadn't Trudy noticed this behavioral change? The little girl had been a regular babbling brook before, but this silence had to be in part due to the white man's abuse and their current situation, rendering the girl almost voiceless. *And your damn pipe sure as hell hasn't helped*, she heard a voice say.

"Just as soon as I get back," she swore, ignoring that voice. She took two steps and then rushed back into the alley. She wasn't sure why she did this, but she did it—she hugged the little boy and girl and kissed the baby on his smooth cheek.

"It's going to be fine, you all. We'll see Poppa and Granny by tomorrow night."

Sasha was sucking her thumb hungrily, and Trudy once more reminded them that she would return with milk and more food.

Turning right up Washington Avenue, she went in search of a lighter. Lighters lasted longer than matches.

Chapter 25

HERE WAS A surprise for Shay: his little house in the country was as quiet as the grave. There was no baby crying, no television blasting some cartoon or a *Will & Grace* rerun, no childish arguments about whose turn it was to change the channel or play with some toy he'd told Trudy he had pilfered for Matthew and Sasha.

He went to his bedroom, the one he shared now, again, with Trudy. The bed was made up but disheveled, as if—*No,* he thought, *no.* As if someone or some *ones* had slept atop the covers. Or fucked atop them.

Damn, Trudy! He knew she had done some things in the past. He believed that doctor she mentioned every once in a while might have had a time or two with her. Then, there were those two men the police had questioned him about earlier. Now he knew that someone else had been in *his* bed with her!

He stepped closer to the bed in the small room. What was that on the wooden floor? Blood? A small puddle, some splatter toward the bottom of two walls that formed the corner the bed was tucked into. He bent down, looked closer. He was not an expert in forensics, but he quaked at his conclusion. This was someone's blood in his house that was not there five days ago when he was there with Trudy. Of course, it could be anyone's blood. Maybe Matthew or Sasha had nicked themselves on something, or it could even be menstrual blood from Trudy. But he doubted either one of these possibilities.

In a panic, he ran from one small room to the other small room, calling out *Trudy, Matthew, Sasha!* Only a weird echo bouncing off his walls greeted him.

He went back outside to where he'd parked the Mercedes. Were those tire tracks in the soft dirt and through the tall grass? Again, no forensics expert was he, but the width of the tracks and the depth of the dirt compression suggested a vehicle heavier, bigger than his car. A truck? He knew only one person who owned a truck and knew where he lived and frequented his house: Chris Slack.

The tracks showed a deeper depression at one point than the rest of the track, as if he'd sped off in the truck. *Well, if Chris was gone, where were Trudy and the kids?*

Shay pondered this question as he walked around the house, still searching and in hopes of finding them more than anything else, when he came upon a sight that almost, literally, scared the shit out of him.

Christian Slack was slumped on the back stairs, as if he had lost his footing and fallen face first onto the steps or had been knocked there by a heavy blow. There was a huge indentation on his left temple, with blood still slowly oozing from the gaping wound and sluggishly trickling down his cheek to his chin.

Shay crouched next to the man. He saw he was still breathing. Labored breaths, a lot of blood, but he was still alive!

He crowded next to the man, "Chris, man, what happened? Who did this to you?" In finding the man, he forgot to ask after his tenants. The man looked as near death as he could.

Then, in a flash, he got it. Trudy had done this to him. Couldn't have been anyone else. As far as Shay knew, the man was a lone wolf. Came and left on his motorbike or in his truck. As far as Shay knew, the man did not even have a woman, at least, none he'd ever thought to bring here.

It had to be Trudy, and the silly girl had stolen the man's F-150!

But say what you would about her habit, her relinquishing her motherly duties over to him, she would never do such a brutal act unless she had a damn good reason. The only reason she had to defend anything was saving her damn pipe. *Oh, my God*, he thought, *or her children*!

He turned the man over, in his haste, to see the extent of the damage. He ignored the training he'd received years ago about head wounds and moving the body. The man's fly was undone, his penis a shrunken lump of flesh poking through the opening. He didn't examine this discovery too closely, but it seemed Chris had gone commando.

He still smelled of sex. *With Trudy, goddammit. Who else?*

But Trudy wouldn't attack him for that. *He* would.

Shay had seen how Chris ogled her, coveting what he was getting either freely and willingly or in exchange for a few rocks of cocaine. Obviously, Chris had made his way in while Shay was away.

But her disloyalty to him or his surprising anger over her being with another man were now irrelevant. He was literally staring at her infidelity, bleeding on his back porch. Chris had fucked her. Probably wasn't the first time, but judging by the man's injury, undoubtedly, the last time.

He leaned closer to the injured man, shook him until he groaned to alertness. Although he already knew the answer, he asked anyway. "Chris, who did this?"

"That bitch."

Shay needed to hear the name. "Who?"

The man tried to adjust himself to a sitting position and groaned painfully at his fruitless efforts. "Trudy." Shay got his answer.

He cautioned the man. "No, better lie still, dude. That's quite a dent on your head." It was all Shay could do not to vomit. Blood, he could take, to a degree, not oozing gobs of it and flesh showing from the wound. *And was that bone*?

"Why'd Trudy do this?" He kept his face blank. The man tried to focus on Shay.

"Gonna kill her." The man's eyes rolled back in his head.

Shay shook him roughly. "Why? What'd you do to her?" He'd done something—of that Shay was sure.

The man coughed, but thankfully there was no blood spewing between his rubbery lips. "Was just gonna use my finger. Couldn't've hurt her."

"Finger? What?" Trudy did not hide her opinion well that she thought Shay was not a deep thinker. But here, even she would have been proud of his epiphanic power of deduction. "Sasha? You were—" He remembered Matthew. The boy had been terrified lately, refusing to let Shay help him in the bath, not speaking, wetting himself. Shit. This slug had done something to him *and* Sasha.

He said what he wished he could send into the void, that he wished was utter rot, but he had to know, had to hear the man say it. "You were going to use your finger with Sasha?"

Chris Slack held up his right index finger. Idly, Shay noticed that the cuticle around the nail bed was ragged, as if he had been doing rough work. Although

Shay balked to Trudy about men having manicures, he thought Chris's paws could use some maintenance.

The man chuckled painfully. "See, like this, jus' wiggle it around there. Tight as a drum, I bet." His finger slowly rotated and flipped up and down.

Shay knew the man was scum. That hadn't meant a lot to him before, one way or another. After all, he himself sold drugs, had told Trudy and Slack of committing a few more crimes and misdemeanors. But to abuse children, children he almost saw as his *own*, he could not allow that, no.

He wasn't a murderer. But he was a man who had his own beliefs of what was right and what was wrong. Selling drugs to adults who had money to pay for them was within his definition of "right." Selling to children of any age or race who had or did not have money was "wrong." Screwing any number of willing and interested women, whether he paid or not, was also within his realm of "rightness." Touching a child with any thought beyond simply touching them with kindness and caring smacked of the worst "wrong."

He wasn't a murderer. But he was a man. He raised his foot and kicked the man in the side as hard as he could. He didn't feel or hear any bones crack. Not satisfied, he walked to the other side and repeated the gesture, putting all of his emotions into it. The man yelped pathetically and lost consciousness.

Shay turned smartly around and walked to his car. As he settled behind the wheel, he took out his cell phone and was about to press 911. These phones had GPS, so he knew he would have to have his story right. He could not leave and then pretend he was returning for the first time. They may be able to figure that out. He dialed using his throwaway, and immediately there was a response.

"What's your emergency?"

"This guy I know is at my place, badly hurt. I found him outside my house. It looks like someone tried to kill him. I see a head wound, but I don't want to move him."

"What's your name?"

Shay told her.

"Can you apply CPR?"

"Oh, he's breathing on his own. Just hurry."

"Could you give me the address where the victim is?"

Shay told the woman where his little house was located.

"Are there any weapons involved?"

"No, I think he was beaten with an object of some sort, maybe a wrench."

"Are there other people hurt?"

"No, well, I don't know. When I got here, he was already hurt, and he was alone."

"Someone will be there soon, sir. Do you want to stay on the line?"

Shay didn't think so. He hung up, went to the back porch, and sat next to the man. He also knew not to strike the man again. Fresh bruises might make him a suspect.

He took out his other cell phone that he reserved for certain people and customers. Trudy was one. He texted her a simple message.

I got you.

Then, because he felt this was a necessary action to take, he walked to the edge of the nearby creek, barely a stream, but deep and muddy enough. First, he stomped the device as best he could, shattering its face and exposing its electronic guts; then he threw the destroyed phone as high and as far as he could. He had a fairly good arm. The phone landed in the middle of the bayou, rippled the dirty water, and disappeared from view.

I got you.

He settled back and watched the man struggle to breathe. Maybe he had cracked a rib. He took out a pack of gum, took two slices out, and started chewing. He examined his nails. Maybe he'd get that manicure, after all.

Chapter 26

BUCK WALKED UP to the police station. He had gotten a call from the sheriff's office that he was needed there for questioning. He had been assured that this was routine in an ongoing investigation.

"Can you make it, Doctor, around six?"

Buck thought hard. He had heard nothing on his radar. He was not implicated in any questionable behavior. Barry would have told him something.

"I'll have to rearrange a couple of appointments." More like a date, but he didn't have time to think of that and what it might mean to him.

"That would be great, Doctor. Six it is?"

The caller had not waited for an answer. Buck made the phone call, apologized to the person on the other end.

"No problem."

"Believe it or not, it was the sheriff's office." He was now practically squeaky clean. His dealings with Barry were of a strictly social nature. If he had to deal with a lawyer or anyone from the penal system, he directed all the calls to a friend up in Tutwiler. Let him worry over that.

Now he sprinted up the few steps into the building and went in search of someone in charge. Eventually, he was directed to a room where other people had already gathered. He scanned the room. Sheriff Gaston wasn't among them. A police officer, a black couple he didn't know, and a young man whom he immediately knew to be that girl's—that Trudy's—friend Shay. He'd never formally met the man, but he'd seen pictures of him on her cell phone many times. Come to think of it, that couple looked vaguely familiar, too.

"Dr. Bowden," the policeman said and moved smartly across the room, his hand outstretched, "so glad you could come and on time, too. Please, sit down; join us."

Buck sat, tucking his tie in as he did. He knew then that whatever he was here for, it had all the world to do with Trudy. Had she said something about their relationship, what he'd done? If so, where was she? And if she had said something, surely, he would be under arrest, not just here for questions.

"Let me introduce everyone." This from the second police officer who joined them with several cups of coffee in Styrofoam cups on a tray; a pleasant-faced, heavy-hipped black woman, with braid extensions practically to her waist, smiled vaguely at the small crowd.

"Dr. Bowden was Miss Jenkins's doctor when she first got—when she was arrested for drug possession and intent to sell. He found her a special program that would help rehabilitate her with no jail time." The woman officer gave him a grateful smile, and he lifted his lips in the semblance of a smile. He still wanted to know why he was here exactly.

"Dr. Bowden, this is Ms. Dorothy Ricketts and Mr. Truman Jenkins. Mr. Jenkins is the…the dead woman's father. And Miz Ricketts is…" The woman frowned, as if trying to figure out the dynamics herself.

"I was Trudy's grandmother. Her babies called us Granny and Poppa," the attractive older woman said firmly.

Buck almost choked on his tongue. Dead woman? Trudy was dead?

He held up a long hand with tapering fingers: a surgeon's hands, a musician's hand. "Wait, are you saying that Tru—Miss Jenkins is dead? How? When?" He was unaware of how high his voice had risen in disbelief.

"Her body was found three days ago along with a baby that we suspect was her baby."

"It was her baby," the man said with finality. His voice shook, and Buck realized he was under great emotional stress. The baby was his grandson.

"I'm sorry for your loss." Buck took a cup of coffee, sipped gingerly. Hot and strong, it tasted terrible, but he drank it for something to do as he gathered his thoughts and processed this information.

Trudy dead, the baby dead. Where were the kids?

He looked at the two officers, made and held eye contact with the black girl. "She had three kids."

Before the policewoman could respond, the woman who claimed to be the children's grandmother spoke again, her voice just as firm as the man's. "We're here to get them and take them back with us."

Buck sipped the coffee again, nodded, because he had nothing to add to that. He looked at the police officers. "What did you have to ask me?"

The male officer settled himself on a chair, his long legs curling under him as he sat. "When was the last time you saw her?"

Buck looked at the young man, who was looking at him very intently. Buck knew then he would have to be very careful in his answers, not to bring any suspicion on himself. But he'd had nothing to do with her sad death.

"A week ago. She came to my hunting shack with her kids in a truck that—" He looked at the man and woman. "My friend in law checked the truck. It wasn't registered to her. She might have stolen it." He took a steadying breath, tried to alleviate their heartbreak. "The kids were fine, hungry but…fine," he added brightly, as if this tidbit of information was of some import. "We—my friends and I—fed them and changed Adrian's diaper. She didn't stay. I gave her some money to help with the kids."

The female officer adjusted her braids, asked the question Buck prayed would not be asked. "If you weren't her doctor—that is, if she wasn't your patient—why would she look for you?"

"She wasn't looking for me, miss—officer. She was on the run." He looked at the young man, this Shay, once more, and spoke almost harshly directly to him. "I figured she was in trouble, and she wanted to hide out there, but my friends and I were there already." His deep voice was a sneer. "Obviously, she had no one whom she could trust or *depend* on down here." He cast Shay a look meant to melt his bones. *Obviously,* you *weren't doing such a great job*, he thought. A blind man could see the words stamped on his face as he sized Shay up and down.

"We recovered the truck. It was abandoned near a house we know is where crack and other drugs are sold, where other *activities* occur. Shay told us it belonged to a Christian Slack." The female officer looked with longing at Shay.

Buck nodded his bald head. "Yes, my friend said that was his name. He said this Slack fellow had done time out East."

"Well, Slack is in a coma and might not recover. We think he sustained those injuries at her hand." The male officer looked at an iPad lying before him, the screen bright with activity as his fingers flew over it.

"Then, he was doing something to those kids. I'd bet my life on that."

The man and woman reached over and grasped each other's hands tightly, as if this statement reaffirmed the existence of the girl they once knew and loved, a girl who would protect what she loved from harm at any cost.

Again, the female officer looked at Shay, who had said nothing. "Yes, we got that from Shay. He said he believed this Slack man abused the boy and was going to or may have…touched the little girl."

The woman burst into tears, and the man looked as if he wanted to murder someone. Buck felt he could understand their rage and hurt. He had three children himself, and even though they were essentially adults, he still felt extremely protective of them, which was why—he tried to convince himself—he'd done the things he'd done.

"When she—when your daughter—came out to my place, the boy had burns on his back. They were pretty fresh. I don't think your—Trudy—knew that when she came out there. No, I don't think she knew." He glared at Shay and glanced at the couple, his eyes showing his feelings for their pain.

He looked politely at the white policeman. "Do you have any more questions for me?" Buck made his voice calm, even solicitous. He couldn't wait to leave.

"How long had she been back on drugs, do you think?"

Buck looked at the officer and then at Shay. Good money could not have prevented him from saying, "I would say you should ask *him* that question. The money I paid her for the few errands she did for me could not have been enough to support a habit *and* feed those children."

"I'm not under arrest, *Doctor*."

The look in this Shay's eyes told Buck that he knew exactly what "errands" Trudy did for him.

Buck's hackles were raised at the insolence in the man's voice, that damning and condemning look on his face. But he didn't want to engage in a pissing contest with him. For one thing, he would probably lose.

"Well, I don't know anything about this Slack guy. When she left me—left me and my friends—she was fine, and her kids were fine. I believe she was back on drugs, but I have no power in that area. I couldn't arrest her."

"You could have let us know." Even the white male officer seemed angry that Buck had let the girl go.

"Unless you didn't want her to talk about those *errands* she did for you?" Shay glared at Buck, and he felt his face grow hot with rage and even contrition.

Buck threw up his hands in exasperation. "Ask me anything; give me a lie-detector test. Hell, I took her to the hospital, so she could deliver that baby boy. I saved her from being brutally raped by a guy who ended up dead, on *your* property." He pointed an accusing, trembling finger at Shay. *Careful, Buck*, he heard himself whisper in warning. He breathed out.

"Yes, I thought she was back on drugs. No, I don't know this Slack guy. I hadn't seen her in weeks before she showed up looking like she'd been caught in a windmill. We fed her and those kids of hers, and she left. End of my story." He settled back in his seat and trained his glacier-blue eyes on the couple. "Your daughter was intelligent, but she made a lot of bad choices. Maybe the program I put her in could have worked if she was determined to stay clean. She just wasn't." He gave a small, pitiable smile, even glanced over at Shay. His words, he realized with some surprise, were from the heart.

He surreptitiously glanced at the clock on the wall. How long would this take? He still wanted to make that appointment. He did *not* use the word *date*.

"Where are Matthew and Sasha?" He looked at the officers.

The woman answered. "We placed them with the state until we could notify her family." She looked at the couple, and Buck and Shay looked at them also.

"We got here late last evening. We still haven't seen them yet, but we plan to leave with them, going back to Chicago, as soon as we can." The man spoke quite determinedly and with clear diction. Buck could tell he was an educated man, even though he was being eaten alive with grief. Hadn't Trudy said once that the father of her three kids was like a son to him and that he was dead also? Three deaths in less than a year. Yes, he could see how that could tear at a man's soul.

"Officer, could you bring the children in, please?" The male officer looked hopefully at his colleague.

The woman sashayed from the room, her eyes once more taking in Shay.

No one spoke, and in a couple of minutes, there was a small explosion at the door as the children erupted into the room. Matthew threw himself at the couple, who were standing with their arms outstretched. The little boy literally took a flying leap into the man's chest.

But it was the girl who caused everyone to tear up, even the stalwart male officer. She hung there, suspended in disbelief and indecision, eyes streaming. There was Buck, whom she recognized and liked but who was not always kind to Trudy. Buck watched as she considered Shay, who was probably always kind to Trudy, Matthew, and her, even, probably, when they were all being bad. He watched silently as her eyes went to the older couple, to Poppa and Granny, safe harbors in this storm she and her brother were often caught up in.

She blubbered and whimpered until the female officer took her in her arms and handed her over to the couple. The little girl nestled into their shoulders as they stood in close embrace, holding the boy and girl between them.

Buck cleared his throat after a few seconds, and this small sound seemed to break the spell they were all under. "I'm sorry for your loss," he said once more. He stood close to the couple, stroked the children's heads with real affection, and then turned to the police officers. "Am I free to go?" Surely, if there was some suspicion in his earlier actions, now would be the time to apprise him of his rights?

A thought came to him and Shay at the same time, for they spoke together.

"How did they get here?"

"Who found them?"

Officer Drake Grimes adjusted the gun in his holster at his waist. "That's a story that is worth telling." So he and Officer Darnika O'Neal told it, not needing to embellish a single, fantastical detail.

When they came to the conclusion, the woman was once more crying, and the man was sniffling back tears.

The white men in the room shook their heads in disbelief. But Officer Grimes had already made some peace with the way black people thought and about this situation in particular. Not Buck.

"But she kidnapped them. They could have been—" He threw up his hands, his head shaking from side to side. How could they believe that this couple had done a good thing?

"Our babies are alive because of them." The man was stroking the woman's back. Seeing this gesture of obvious deep feelings for each other, Buck remembered something else Trudy had said and what he had in his own records. Her mother was dead. Yet this woman had said the children were her grandchildren. *What exactly was their relationship?* he wondered.

"And let's be honest, because they really were doing the best they thought they could do at the time, no charges were filed against them. Not even a fine. And I guess I have to agree with Darnika—Officer O'Neal. Those people saved these here children's lives." Drake Grimes shrugged, as if to say to Buck: *Look, they have their own ways. Let's leave it at that.*

Mr. Jenkins looked at Darnika. "I don't suppose you could tell me where they are, where they live, so we can thank them?"

Buck's eyes widened in surprise. Surely, this was not protocol—encouraging communication with the kidnappers and their victims?

Darnika shook her head, and the serpentine braids swayed back and forth. "No, sir, just know that they only wanted to help." She smiled at them, but Buck saw something pass between them. He was a doctor and, despite his past, a damn fine one. So he could read people when even they could not tell him their problems. The look said, *Don't worry. As soon as I can, I'll tell you all about them.*

The children were settled against the couple, and Buck was told that he and Shay were both free to go. He shook everyone's hands, going around the room, smiling at the children and gently stroking a shoulder or curly-topped head and even giving Shay a firm handshake. It seemed this chapter in his life was finally over.

He left the room with Officer Grimes, leaving behind Darnika, Shay, the children, and their grandparents. He wanted to tell Grimes that he should go back into that room, as he was sure his fellow officer was breaking all kinds of procedures and policies, but he said nothing of the sort. He was not like Pilate, but he had removed from his life, if not washed his hands of, all this drama.

He settled behind the wheel of his car, a sleek, silver-toned Jaguar that he had found displayed on a site out in Texas. The man who sold him the car was an expert in refurbishing and selling cars, specializing in classic and vintage vehicles. The thirty-year-old car ran like a dream. True, he had to drive down to Jackson or up to Memphis to get service or parts, but he didn't mind. Because of the superb condition of the automobile, this was the first extravagance he'd indulged in in years despite his profitable activities.

Meeting the man who sold him the car also further cemented this change in Buck's life. Stanley Driscoll was a stand-up sort of guy, as honest as the day was long and a true straight shooter. He was married to a woman who had five kids already. They had twin teens, a handsome boy who resembled Stanley and a pretty girl Stanley assured him resembled his beautiful wife, Connie. The two men were similar in age. Buck figured he was a few years older than Stanley, but they bonded over the passion both had for anything motorized. Buck was by no means an ace mechanic, but he enjoyed the occasional tinkering under the hood of his car.

Buck soon learned that Stanley was a man satisfied with his life. He had his health, his children (even claiming the other five, even though Connie had been widowed only months when Stanley met her), and his livelihood. And above all else, Connie.

Buck had his children's love and his career. But he wanted more, and what he had with Trudy and those other women earlier did not meet his emotional needs. He accepted that what he wanted was what Stanley clearly had. He wanted a complete life that included a woman to come home to, to love, to be loved by, and one to call his own.

He drove off, joining the night traffic as he headed toward his home. But he would pass it to stop at a house just two doors down from his own gray, two-story wood-frame house. The house he turned the nose of the XJ6 into was at the end of a short driveway. The house was large and, to Buck, rather unimaginative in its boxy design: a multicolored brick home with several gables, hedges galore, and the requisite magnolia and dogwood trees in the front yard.

It wasn't to his liking, but that was all right. He had no plans to live in it. He got out of his car, adjusted his suit of clothing, and wiped the toe of his leather loafers against the back cuffs of his slacks, to give the shoes the shine they'd had earlier that day. He'd wanted to stop at his home to freshen up, maybe even change his shirt and underwear, but his time at the police station had prevented that luxury. Or his getting flowers.

The door opened and he smiled, his entire being lighting up. His heart was full but light. He was fifty, soon to be fifty-one, past middle age but not too old for love, he realized, as he embraced the tall, olive-toned woman.

He had given up figuring out his emotions. The saying *the heart wants what the heart wants* must have been true. Had anyone told him he would fall for a woman in science, he wouldn't have been shocked. He was in medicine, after all. But had he been told that this woman would be a native of the island Asian nation Sri Lanka who, with her parents, had emigrated to England, and that she would settle in the United States after receiving both her medical degree and a PhD in virology from the medical school in Birmingham, Alabama, and then specialize in infectious diseases, he would have been stupefied. But that was what he did do.

Her name was Dr. Marina Rupasinghe. She was forty-three and had recently moved from Jackson, where she practiced medicine and taught at the medical school, to the Delta to work in private practice.

He chuckled at his thoughts. Lion's share. Her surname actually meant the *beautiful lion*. Well, she was a beautiful lioness—that was certain—and she had a lion's share of good looks: dark, luminous eyes, black hair, white teeth in a dusky-colored oval face. She wore her hair short, and the mass of dark curls were cut to fit her outgoing, outspoken personality. She had full lips, and her nose, though well shaped, had flaring nostrils. At times, though he never said this, she reminded him of Negro women he'd seen or known over the years. He wasn't sure if this comparison would be a compliment or an insult to her, so he never spoke his thoughts out loud.

They had communicated both professionally and personally to the point that he found himself looking forward to her e-mails or brief phone calls. It wasn't until she asked about life in the river town of Greenville that he had ever thought something could develop between them.

There were East Indians here in the Delta; some were doctors or nurses, and others were businesspeople. They were quiet, kept to themselves, even though they tended to live where the white people lived. So he was used to seeing them, if not overtly interacting with them. But she pointedly reminded him that she was *not* Indian; she was Sri Lankan with British citizenship and permanent-resident status in the United States.

He accepted this difference just as he had accepted that the few Africans with American citizenship he had met had said they were truly African Americans, whereas the blacks he grew up with, worked with, befriended, were simply Americans of African descent.

Tomatoes, to-mahtoes, he thought.

He kissed Marina slowly, enjoying the softness of her lips against his. He imagined them to be pillows to rest his own mouth on, to soothe him.

"Long day, my dear, with the coppers?" Her accent always came as a pleasant shock to him, hearing the clipped English accent overlaid with the singsong of her parents' speech pattern.

"The police?" He liked her British slang, but he still found himself translating back into American, as she called the English he spoke. He tipped his head to the side, shrugged. "Just questions about this poor girl's death—she was a patient of mine, an addict who overdosed." He slipped his hands around her waist and held her close. They had plans of going across the River to Arkansas for a quiet meal, but the closest restaurant with the atmosphere—and cuisine—both wanted was over two hours away. Before his visit to the police station, they would have made that drive there and back. Not now.

"Where's Mark?" He was her sixteen-year-old son by her deceased husband. How she had become a widow was still unclear to him. Her husband had been killed around the same time as Lakshman Kadirgamar's assassination, but Buck was not sure if their deaths were related. He didn't want to know.

"Upstairs studying. I made dinner—a lamb dish I think you'll love."

He kissed her once more and followed her into her well-appointed dining room. The kitchen flowed off the room by a large open area that connected the two rooms. She had set the table with sparkling wineglasses, shining silverware, and floral-patterned plates and bowls.

He wondered about Mark. He was a great kid, at that gawky age of legs and hair. He was at the top of his class because when Marina said study, the kid actually went to his room and studied.

Buck wasn't sure what Mark thought of Marina and him dating. (Were they dating, he countered, not sure if the kiss was the answer to that question or not. It was, after all, their first nonplatonic kiss-kiss, hug-hug that everyone did these days.) The kid could barely remember his father, and there did not seem to be any overt idolization of a dead man who may or may not have died honorably and nobly during a period of the country's history when not many people were dying nobly or honorably. Marina was a direct person, treating Mark in some ways like an adult roommate and at other times like the teenaged son he was.

His own daughter had surprised him by returning home for a month from her internship appointment. She was out with friends, but they had plans on spending time together the rest of the weekend. He had already told her about Marina, and she was curious to know who this woman was who had at long last captured her father's attention. He didn't correct her, for she and her brothers believed that he'd had brief affairs over the years, none of which lasted long enough to warrant his introducing them to his children. They would never know of his former, illicit activities with those female prison inmates.

He settled at the table, sniffed the air for the many, slightly unfamiliar aromas: lamb, not a typical meat in the Delta, even though he knew of people in the country who had raised a few goats at one time. She had explained earlier that she had the cuts of meat flown in on dry ice from some butcher in Saint Louis. She had assured Buck that the meat was halal, and he figured it had something to do with being kosher. More or less the same, she had laughingly told him. But since she was neither Jewish nor Muslim, saying *halal* or *kosher*, for her, simply meant the meat would taste the best when prepared. Sampling the spicy lamb dish, he couldn't argue the point.

"Tell me more about the girl."

(He heard *gehl*.)

"She was a mother, also, you said?"

He sipped the wine, looked at her, wondered how much he should tell her.

Before she could press him more, he turned the tables by asking her about her research on the Zika virus, her reason for relocating from Jackson to the Delta. Although she was in private practice, she also monitored exposure and treatment to the Mississippi "hummingbirds," as both she and Buck called the black swarm of mosquitoes that hung over the bayous and creeks.

But how long could this topic be sustained? Everyone, she sighed, had solutions that went from the sublime to the ridiculous.

"Bloody tiring week it's been." Her voice reflected the week she'd had.

He smiled at her "coarse" language. How could these be swear words? *Bloody* and *bollocks*? But he liked sitting next to her while she talked.

He asked questions, kept the conversation going by giving his opinions. This was his land, and he was a doctor also. But eventually, her silence told him he had to talk about the events of the day, about his trip to the police station, about the dead girl.

He wanted very much to make love to her eventually. He had no idea whether he was getting close to that opportunity. If they became lovers (*when*, he corrected himself), he wanted as much of a clean slate as possible.

"She moved here from Chicago."

He began the story with the lamb and steamed veggies, and over dessert, he told her about helping with the delivery of the baby who eventually died of exposure. During coffee, he backtracked to putting Trudy in a program that failed miserably when the woman he'd known all his life, who was their caretaker, died of a heart attack. When he finished his story, as much as he could safely relate to her, it was dawn, and they were curled beside each other on her long sofa. Of course, it did not take all night to tell the girl's story, but there was Marina's own opinions, her own worries and concerns as a mother. By the time both had come to a mutual conclusion of their long talk, he could hear Mark walking around upstairs, and the TV weatherman was saying there was a surprising development off the coast of Africa that could become a tropical storm this late in the season. Though there was no promise of more between them, the fact that they had essentially spent the night together was not lost on either one of them.

At breakfast, Mark asked Buck if he could tell him more about the cell cycle and how drugs were used to treat cancer by interfering with certain steps. Marina had already frankly informed Mark that she and Buck had talked all night. She had even said, much to Buck's chagrin, that that was *all* they had done, actually saying, *No hanky-panky.*

She listened intently to Buck's answers as she scrambled eggs and made toast. (She did not apologize to Buck for not having bacon; they did not eat pork.) Buck made a few mistakes, and she corrected him without apology, and he accepted this correction without rancor. The thought came to him unbidden: had she been black or white *American*, he might have argued his case. But she was *foreign* and therefore different enough to be looked upon as acceptably *superior* in her intellect: exotic in both mind and body.

A look passed between them over the mango and peach nectar—a common drink in Colombo, she informed him. He had honestly thought she meant Columbus, Mississippi, or Ohio. When she laughed at this, he thought how nice the sound was. That look between them spoke volumes.

When he left to go to his house to shower and dress for work, she stood in the doorway, her mascara slightly smudged (she'd cried over some part of Trudy's sad tale) and kissed him with Mark looking on, drinking the nectar.

"I'll see you tonight, Henry." There was the slightest breath she took as she said *'enry*. But the promise was clear. He would bring his toothbrush and change of underwear—and those flowers, an armful of them, exotic and beautiful, like her.

Chapter 27

TRUDY SAT ON the little rickety chair, a piece of discarded junk, in the alley, horrifyingly, terrifyingly alert. She had mixed the contents of the leftover stash of drugs she'd managed to keep from LD and his goons into a coarse powder and smoked the lot. The high petrified her. She could feel her cells breathe in and out, could feel her liver awakening to the job of trying to detoxify those toxins flowing in her blood, her brain, her lungs, even her bones. More than crack, she knew. Maybe this was what a speedball was. Chris's cocktail of drugs could have included heroin, cocaine, even meth. She didn't know, and, looking around the empty space where her children *should* have been, she didn't care.

Maybe—floating above herself, into herself—this was what heaven was all about. Crashing and rising again and again, this endless cycle of ecstasy and the abyss: maybe this was what hell was about.

Yes, *hell*, because her children were *gone*. She had left Matthew...Her brain was slipping. Yes, she had left that boy there to watch over...watch over...There was a baby lying on the crate. His face was serene in its sleep. But this baby was not in slumber. He was cold and so very cold and so...This baby was dead. Where was...There was another child. Her child...Her fingers moved like snakes, and her hair turned to marigolds, and she smelled of licorice, and she heard the scraggly little plant beneath her feet push its way free from the soil.

My babies are gone. Someone took my babies. I—

She felt her heart in her ears, could see it before her eyes.

Oh, that lovely smell again—what is it? Mama, I'm home. Daddy doesn't like to race against me because he says I cheat, but I'm just faster. Look how long my legs are. She was a giraffe in the Serengeti, and she was looking down at this tiny bundle, and she was looking for

Matthew and Sasha—yes, my babies!—and they were eaten alive by the wolf she saw lurking in the dark. But the wolf became a beautiful brown Asian woman who said she had not eaten her babies. She had sold them to her. Didn't she remember?

She settled her wings against her chest and sank to her haunches in the black sand. She watched the tide of the lake that was a river that was a sea that was an ocean that became a planet of water, and then there was Fat Boy pulling her up, asking her what was she doing sitting down on such a beautiful day.

"Come on. Let's go to the park." Then, he noticed the baby, and then she noticed the baby as their son together, and she cried in his arms, happy to present such a perfect baby to the love of her life.

"This is your baby, Fat Boy."

And she was being kissed and kissed and kissed again. "He looks like me, doesn't he? Hey, little man, little Matthew." Trudy stroked Fat Boy's beautiful face. Somewhere in a memory, a thought, maybe a dream, she had been told his handsome face had been disfigured. People lied all the time, she thought, letting him pick up the baby, hold it against his chest, and coo at the baby, who smiled back, showing those toothless gums and causing her and Fat Boy to laugh and laugh. She stood close to Fat Boy. There was something she needed to say, something that was important that she must tell him, but the memory wouldn't form.

"Where are we going, baby?" She leaned into Fat Boy. He smelled of sun and flowers. He was sun and flowers. He'd said they would go to the park, but where was the park in this place?

She watched Fat Boy wrap the baby tenderly in his arms. There was that memory again that she could not grasp, of people, of events, of…

Fat Boy held his arm out to her, and she was fitted against him like she belonged there, had been carved to fit his curves and ridges.

"I figured to the park then home." He kissed the soft spot on the baby's head.

"Yeah…Maybe we should call him Adrian, after you." That sounded right, despite his having named the boy Matthew.

Fat Boy laughed indulgently at her, and she felt her skin glow, heat with love for him and the baby in his arms.

"We can call him whatever makes you happy, girl. I just want you to be happy. Let's go."

And they walked into the welcoming park.

Chapter 28

Dolly Ricketts directed Truman Jenkins through the dark streets of Memphis. It was late, but the people had assured Dolly and Truman they would stay up until they arrived at the house in Midtown on North Evergreen.

Just as Buck had thought, Officer Darnika O'Neal had indeed spilled all she knew of the Higginbothams and encouraged Dolly and Truman to call upon the couple to thank them for saving both Matthew and Sasha.

"We're here," Truman told her unnecessarily, as he got out of his car, a clean 2005 Chrysler 300, and opened her door. Dolly knew he had bought the car because the design was reminiscent of the E Class Mercedes Benz, the car he was partial to but could never afford.

They began undoing the children from the car seats. (The Greenville police had kept the car seats when they'd let the couple go; Dolly had agreed with the rationale of Darnika: they may as well take them since they would need them anyway.) The front door to the charming two-story house opened with a flood of light, and two people ran down the short walk to the curb.

Dolly could only make out the happiness in their voices. Their words were lost amid the chattering of the children.

The man reined in his catapulting gait and stopped before Dolly. She noted his looks—handsome but more *common*-looking than gorgeous, movie-star material. He had what her mother would have called a good face, an honest face.

"Good evening! I'm Angelo, Angelo Higginbotham, and this is my wife, Belinda." Dolly's hand was wrenched from her side and pumped several times. She almost fell forward from his forceful greeting.

"I'm Dorothy Ricketts, and this is Truman Jenkins." She had never married her Joe Mack, but she had taken his name as soon as their first baby was born over forty years ago.

She watched Truman shake hands with the man and his wife, who was as pretty as he was good-looking, but she had a certain…staidness about her. No, not that. Dolly thought she had it: cautious reserve. *She's scared*, Dolly thought in some surprise.

The children were made much of, and the children responded just as they had at the police station with Dolly and Truman. To Dolly, little Matthew looked stunned that he was reunited with the people who had saved him. Sasha was dancing from her to Truman and then to the Higginbothams.

"Come on in, please." The woman led the way into their living room. Dolly looked around curiously. Very nice but not overly decorated. Antique pieces that probably belonged to some long-dead relative blended in with modern pieces that looked durable if not overly expensive.

"You have a nice home," Truman said, looking about also.

"We like it. Sit, please." They looked at Truman and Dolly expectantly.

Dolly realized that, although they were happy the children were there, they wondered why. After all, they had kidnapped them. *No,* saved *them*, Dolly corrected herself, remembering Officer O'Neal's assertion.

"We just wanted to thank you for what you did." Truman sat very close to Dolly, held her hand in his. She stroked his knee and watched the other couple as the light of understanding appeared on their faces.

"Oh." The woman, Belinda, looked suitably surprised. "How long are you going to be here?" She let Sasha climb into her lap, and the girl looked content to be there, just as content as she had been with Dolly earlier.

"We're headed back to Chicago, but since it's late, we'll find a hotel to crash in." Truman looked at Dolly decisively, and she smiled that smile that told him she agreed.

"No." The man, Angelo, shook his head. "You all can stay here tonight, head off first thing tomorrow morning. I doubt it'll mean a lot to these munchkins what time you get in."

"We're not munchkins. We're children!" Matthew screwed up his face. Dolly could see her Adrian in those eyes of his.

They all laughed, and this made Matthew clown a little. Dolly's heart swelled as the boy tried his hand at little jokes and dance steps that looked more like he was barely keeping his balance on the hardwood floor. Sasha got into the act and was busily twisting her little body from side to side, with no rhythm whatsoever. Were they going to be all right, after all? So much had happened, things Dolly was sure they could not articulate, which she and Truman would more than likely never know. But it was as he had said to her on the drive up from Greenville. Children were strong and resilient.

"Have you arranged the—" Belinda looked briefly at the children and then pointedly at Dolly, and Dolly understood. The funerals: for Trudy, for the baby Adrian. True-man had arranged the bodies to be shipped to Chicago, to the same funeral home that had handled Fat Boy's remains. The papers that released the bodies into their custody had been numerous and tedious, but they had completed them all as part of their last duties as family members to the deceased.

The funeral would be in a week. Dolly spoke these details quietly to Belinda while True-man and the children trouped into the family room with Angelo to catch the last minutes of a Grizzlies game.

"I think I met your daughter, Trudy? She…I gave her some money."

Dolly breathed out, shook her head. "For drugs." It wasn't a question. The pain made her feel hollow. To know that Trudy, a girl she had practically raised, was walking the streets, begging for money to buy drugs while her babies were left to fend for themselves, to *die*, was just shameful. And painful.

"You and your husband—Angelo?—you don't have children?" The house was large, and from what she could see of the neighborhood as they drove up, it was located in a quiet, dignified area of the city. It spoke of old money or at least old families with deep roots connecting the families to one another. It had to have a good school system, safe parks, a place where children could flourish, grow to their full potential, without fear of the gun or needle—or pipe.

A look passed through Belinda's eyes, but it was so fleeting, Dolly thought she had imagined it, not a look of sadness or anger for her asking what might be an intrusive question, Just…the look said, *Let's talk about something else.*

So she did. "True-man and I aren't the kids' grandparents. I'm their great-grandmother, and he's their grandfather." She explained about her and Fat Boy being the dead girl and her father's neighbors for several years.

"But you seem—" Color rose in the young woman's cheeks. She had noticed Dolly and Truman's behavior toward each other: neighbors maybe but lovers definitely.

But Dolly was tired, and they had offered her and True-man and the kids a bed for the night. "It's a long story but, so far, a pretty good one!" Both women laughed and were still laughing when the men and children returned to the living room.

Dolly scooped up Sasha while Matthew hung between the men, pretending to be as tall as they were. She noticed the way Belinda's arms hung emptily in the air.

"You sure you don't mind us…?" Truman looked at Dolly and then at their hosts for the night. Their generosity was unexpected and, considering the circumstances that led to their meeting, incredible.

Angelo had moved to his wife's side, his arm loosely around her waist. Dolly knew they were making sure not to interfere with her and Truman's roles as the children's legal guardians.

"Nah, glad to do it. That's a long drive ahead of you."

Dolly reached out and took Angelo's hand. He did not remind her of her children, nor did his wife, but she still felt an odd kinship with him—with her.

"Can you show us where we can put them down?" She nodded her stylishly coiffed head toward the nodding children. Matthew was practically asleep on his feet, and Sasha was already knocked out, her head lolling against Dolly's shoulder.

They were led upstairs, and Dolly was surprised to see that they were led to a room that looked as if it could have been the master bedroom itself but obviously wasn't. Belinda directed their attention to the en suite bathroom. Dolly kept her house back in Chicago as clean and neat as a pin and well decorated, but this place made her efforts seem futile.

She sat on the queen-size bed gingerly. With its floral-patterned comforter and many pillows, the bed felt warm and welcoming.

"I guess we better put those two between us, True-man."

The Higginbothams were still in the room. Truman was standing self-consciously by the bed. Dolly knew that they knew by now that she and Truman weren't married, but they were too polite to say anything. Besides, she and Truman were too old to worry about their feelings. They would sleep together.

"We have a room—another room, that is—the kids c-could use."

Both Dolly and Truman jerked their head to the tone of Angelo's voice, not nervous but *something*. Dolly's heart told her to trust these people, but maybe they had secrets. All families did.

"The room's right next to this one," Belinda offered quickly, as if reading Dolly's thoughts. "The bathroom's just across the hall. But you're probably gonna want them with you."

Dolly almost said, *No, I want to be with True-man tonight, alone*, but she did not. The children were their responsibility now. Would be for a very long time.

"Well, they're asleep. Probably gonna sleep through the night…Show us?" She stepped close to Truman, Sasha still in her arms, and managed to slip one hand into his back pocket, a habit she had that he liked.

This room was smaller but just as well decorated. It was obviously a guest room for some relative's child. The twin bed had bright colors on the comforter, and the walls had paintings and posters of some popular Disney characters. Even the little lampshade by the bed was gaily colored. There was a small table with a pair of miniature chairs pushed up against it.

Had they lost a child? Children? The room was welcoming, but it possessed, to Dolly, a shrine-like appearance.

She turned back the covers and laid Sasha down, fully dressed. She removed the girl's shoes and socks, the thick sweater someone in Greenville must have given her. Truman did the same for Matthew. Neither child stirred.

The four adults left the room, leaving the door ajar. "Just in case they wake up scared," Angelo said.

Dolly nodded her agreement, and she and Truman bade them good night and went into their room. Neither had brought pajamas or sleepwear in with them. It was late, and Dolly would not ask Truman to go to the car to get their bags. One night in their undies would be all right.

Truman closed the door quietly, came to her.

"They're good people." He removed his shirt and sweater, kicked off his shoes and stepped out of his slacks. He carefully placed the clothing and shoes on a chair. He would have to wear them tomorrow. In shorts and a T-shirt, he sank onto the bed, sighed in contentment at its comfort.

While he had been undressing, Dolly had also been divesting herself of her standard long-distance traveling outfit: a tracksuit, T-shirt, and gym shoes. She removed her bra, and her full breasts swung free. She put the T-shirt back on and stood before Truman with her T-shirt and panties on.

"They're like what we used to call Buppies back in the eighties." She sat on the bed also. Truman said nothing, and she understood. He was too kind to say that thirty years ago, he was a kid in his teens. She was the one who was an adult, living with Joe Mack, raising their four kids, gainfully employed. Still, even that knowledge did not make her regret her decision to love this younger man.

"When we were watching the game, I got the impression that they want kids, but he never said why they don't have any." Truman draped his arm around her, leaned against her.

Dolly nodded, cozied up to him. "Same here. Like maybe their babies died or something. That little room was carefully decorated, like they wanted to preserve it for their child or children."

"But they're not dangerous; I'd stake my life on that."

Dolly agreed as she reached for the lump of hardened flesh in his crotch. She could feel his racing pulse through the cotton, through his erection. Maybe they shouldn't make love. After all, there was some protocol to follow, wasn't there? Strange bed, guests in a house. Not married?

True-man groaned deep in his throat, and she cast those thoughts aside. As he settled on his knees before her opened thighs, she leaned over with a small grunt and hit the wall switch, plunging the room into darkness.

Something pulled her from her sleep a few hours later. It was True-man, standing at the slightly open doorway. A weak shaft of light from the hallway illuminated his handsome profile. She padded to the door, naked and cool. She peeped around his shoulder to see what had his attention. The Higginbothams were standing in the hallway. Angelo was behind Belinda, holding her in close embrace. Both were rubbing her belly; then his hands crept up to her breasts, down to her crotch. They stared at the door to the children's room. Then, without a word, they walked back to their room, her head on his shoulder, and closed the door.

True-man looked down at Dolly. "Wonder what that was about?"

Dolly shook her head in silence. She wondered also but had no clue. The way the man was touching his wife was not exactly sexual or sensual. It seemed to Dolly as if he were searching for something on her person. When he could not locate it, he stopped his search, and they went back to their room. Most strange.

She picked up her watch from the bedside table, pressed a button, and the face lit up: 4:05. Her friend Samantha back in Chicago had a Movado watch that she took pleasure in telling Dolly cost over $1,500. Dolly's Timex cost less than seventy bucks. And she proudly informed her bragging friend that, in the dark, she could always check the time. *Could her Movado do that?*

She climbed back in the bed, True-man warm and close to her.

After several seconds, he spoke softly in her ear. "Baby, are you thinking what I'm thinking?"

She pretended that he was thinking of making love again, and she made him ready. But, honestly, when he whispered his thoughts, she really was thinking the same thing. She kissed him deeply as he stroked her breasts in the darkened room. The decision was made.

Chapter 29

SHAY HAD A secret. In fact, he had several. The first one was that he was adopted. Not a bad secret, just one that he had not shared with anyone he'd met while staying in Mississippi. Not with Trudy. Not with that slime Christian Slack.

He did not know his birth parents; both were of African descent, he knew this simply by looking in the mirror. But more than that, he had no clue. Nor, he told himself, did he care to know more.

His adoptive parents loved him, had raised him in an exclusive Highland Park neighborhood on the lake, imparted values in him that they themselves had been raised with—honesty, respect, a strong work ethic. That was part of his secret.

He had no clue about so-called ghetto life in Chicago. Even though Trudy had not been raised in tough, gang-riddled areas, he knew she knew more about "street life" than he did. His use of slang, his claim to that life, had been learned from videos, movies, and books. When he could literally send a text to his parents to buy him the Mercedes he was driving and they wired money into his account, he knew he could not *talk the talk* and *walk the walk* that Trudy did.

He had also spent no time in jail; nor had he stolen from stores, as he'd led both Trudy and that scumbag Slack to believe. True, he did sell dope here, but more to say that he had experienced the life of a black young man, though he knew most young black men were *not*, in fact, dope dealers. He had gathered all his experiences into a folder that he would use in his dissertation, changing the names to protect the "innocent."

Another secret: he was a PhD candidate with a combined concentration in anthropology and neuroscience at the University of Illinois in Chicago. His studies centered on the development and continued presence of drug cultures in small southern towns and the effect long-term drug use had on cognitive reasoning and neuronal development. Although part of his research would be in controlled laboratory settings using rats as an animal model, he had a component that best served him "in the field."

He'd chosen southern towns because he had presented the premise that some drugs were used as a way to escape the lack of opportunities that seemed to define the South, whereas others were used *because* there were opportunities. If his hypothesis proved null, he would devote a chapter or two in his thesis on how the South was perceived by people of other regions and cultures in the United States. So there would be the requisite socioeconomic factors to consider. Would the use of drugs fall strictly along those demarcations? Rich people into coke or heroin, maybe meth, and the poorer population into pot, crack, and alcohol? Would that demarcation include rich blacks falling on the same side as rich whites, or was this more about money and not race? He had quickly learned that the Asians in the southern states were either very low in population or they essentially were not drug users, their numbers being insignificant, as compared to the whites and blacks. He would do an entire chapter on that curious aspect of his research, providing theories on this conundrum.

He had been to Tennessee, the Carolinas, and northern Florida. His last stop had been Greenville, Mississippi, when he had met the ill-fated Trudy and her children.

He hadn't anticipated that wrinkle—developing genuine feelings for people who would end up as *subjects* in his dissertation, but he had. He had cried real tears when he'd learned that both Trudy and Adrian were dead. He couldn't save her—not that he'd tried overly hard. She was addicted to crack, and this much he knew—rich or poor, adopted or not, drug addiction was real, and the unfortunate addicts almost beyond redemption. But for a few months, he'd made her and those kids happy; he knew that. Though he was by all accounts an enabler for the girl, he preferred, rather, to think of himself as her *facilitator*. Had he not been there, surely she would have turned to prostitution, or worse, even though he could not think of anything worse than selling your body. *Oh, yes, you can: selling those kids*, a voice whispered in his mind. He knew then that he could not use his experience with Trudy and her kids, Slack, or that damn doctor in his dissertation. He had crossed too many lines, the ethics one being the most blurred.

Now he was ready to return to the university after his yearlong field research in which he had been, in those other states, those other towns, an observer only, simply collecting data by discreet interviews and not so discreet questionnaires and surveys. He had sold the Mercedes, pocketed a portion that would take care of his airfare back to Chicago. The rest he had sent as a check to the address Mr. Jenkins had provided for him. *To help with the funeral and the kids*, he'd said back in that police station in Greenville.

He adjusted his seat on the airplane. As always, since he was a child with his parents, he had traveled first-class. No need to break that tradition now. He touched his head and felt the ghostly weight of his dreads. He had cut them off yesterday. He now sported a low cut that, with his glasses instead of contacts, his neat slacks, wool sweater, and leather loafers, made him almost unrecognizable. He had removed all the rings and studs from his piercings. Certainly the ticket in his name made him out to be William Sire (pronounced *see-re*) Gallagher, the surnames of his Norwegian father and his Irish father, not the guy called Shay.

That was the biggest secret, he supposed. He was adopted, not by a loving black, heterosexual couple who had trouble conceiving or who took him in because of family connections. No, his parents were two fifty-three-year-old Europeans who had, as two young homosexual men, met in England thirty years ago, became a couple, and emigrated to the States. They had decided, twenty-five years ago, that they wanted a baby. And there he was, an abandoned black baby in foster care.

That his childhood was idyllic might have been an overstatement. But he was raised in the bosom of two loving men, who doted on him and each other, who made sure he was raised in a neighborhood and attended schools that were diverse and free-thinking enough that two white men raising a black boy was not so unusual or noteworthy. And since he knew nothing of his origins, he had accepted them as his only parents. Though they had always maintained that he should be proud of being black, he had not considered this racial pride until he was seventeen, nearly nine years ago. After all, he was fluent in Norwegian and could mimic his Irish father's brogue to perfection. He'd had to *learn* black slang and so-called vernacular. Even the most basic of the cultural mores seemingly common in American blacks were not part of his upbringing.

True, he did smoke pot, but most people did, regardless of race—even President Obama had admitted to it! He wasn't into heavy drugs or dangerous shit. Leave that to the slime Chris Slack. Here, he chuckled humorlessly. The man was still in a coma, but the doctors down in Jackson, where he was transferred from Greenville, were hopeful. He could not care less.

His name had been cleared of any involvement with anything that had happened with Slack's injuries. He still wondered about that doctor, though. He had no proof, but he believed the man *knew* something, was into *something.* No, not about Trudy's death—that was an overdose.

But what about the two dead men on his property? He knew Trudy was doing something shady for the man. But she was cleared of any involvement also, because of the doctor's testimony. She never admitted to doing anything other than *doing the BJ for pay*, as she said. And she claimed she stopped when they met and hooked up. But he was convinced he was still seeing her, not just the BJ but *screwing* her.

He sighed heavily. Well, whatever had happened between them, with those men, it was over, and he was out of there, on his way back to his true life.

A girl had settled beside him. He was so deep in his thoughts, he had no idea how long she had been sitting beside him in the wide aisle seat or if she had spoken to him or not. He glanced at her. Though she was now sitting, he could tell she was statuesque—maybe five feet ten, like Trudy had been. He openly stared at her: blond, blue eyes, very nice figure. Growing up in the rich and white Chicago suburbs, he had dated his fair share of white girls.

He extended his hand. "Bill Gallagher. But people call me Shay." (He'd made the name up after reading a book in which most of the black men had odd-sounding nicknames that defied explanation.)

The girl—she looked about his age, maybe a few years younger—took his hand and gave it a quick squeeze, not exactly a shake but firm enough that he knew she had no problem interacting with strangers. Or strange black men.

"Sylvia Bowden. People call *me* Sylvie." She laughed, and he found himself responding to her humor.

"On your way to Chicago? Is that your home?" They were on a direct flight to the Windy City from Memphis International Airport. Maybe she had a connecting flight, but to where? If to the west, Chicago would not be the connecting city. If to the east, it would more than likely be Atlanta.

"Yes…And you, Shay, is it?" She maintained eye contact with him, and he appreciated this. Though he detected a pretty strong southern accent, it wasn't that southern belle accent he'd heard the few months he'd been in the river town. Like saying *rot* for *right* and *greenvuhl* for *Greenville*, while the blacks he met said *green veal*, two separate syllables.

"Oh, yes, I'm in grad school there, and my parents live there—in Highland Park. I've been doing research for a year, and I'm going back to get all the facts together, present them to my committee." He wondered if he looked as boring as he sounded, but she was nodding, her blond brows drawn together in interest.

"You're in grad school?"

He could see her surprise, and it rankled him that she was surprised. As if blacks couldn't get their PhDs?

"Yeah," he said flatly and turned his face from hers.

"I want to get *my* PhD—in ethnobotany. Or maybe do medicine. I spent the last three months in Moengo, Suriname, and learned so much about how they use medical plants to cure—oh, from warts to weight gain!" She laughed, and he jerked his head back around.

She was looking at him, her blue eyes gleaming. "Yeah," she continued, as if his previous dismissive gesture had not happened, "there are, like, two hundred or so plants there used by the indigenous people. My research was to assay fifty of them—plants, my choosing—and identify as many of the active ingredients in them as I could." She sighed and peeped at him. "People don't know that most of the medicines we use today got their start as natural products in plants, bacteria, and *sponges*!" She laughed again, as if this were really funny.

Suriname, he thought. What he knew was that this was a small country in South America, with a lot of people there who had their roots in Africa and spoke—was it Dutch or Portuguese? He decided to ask the girl.

"Well, their official language—lingua franca—is Dutch, but most of them speak…I don't know, some form of creole they call *Sranan*, which, confusingly enough"—here, he watched her laugh heartily—"is also the lingua franca, but I spoke English my whole time down there, and they thought that was so funny because of my southern accent!" She stretched the last two words out, making fun of her own speech pattern. A girl who could laugh at herself—he liked that.

"So, you're a science major?" He almost said *too*, but he stopped himself, not believing this coincidence of meeting a fellow nascent scientist.

"Yes, I'm at Mississippi State, but I'm flying to Chicago to hang out with one of the students I met during my internship."

"A girlfriend?"

He knew that if she gave him a blank look, it would be her *girlfriend*, as in lover. If she looked away with her eyes cast down, it would be a boy she was interested in but not an official *boyfriend*. If just a friend, boy or girl, she would smile, her eyes on his. He had studied people since he was a child himself. There were few emotions he could not decipher just by paying attention to people's faces.

Her eyes shone into his. "Sarah Kimbrough—she attends a university outside Chicago. She's meeting me at the airport and driving us to her home, someplace about an hour from the city, she said. We were in the same lab, and she invited me there for a long weekend. But I wanted to see my dad before I flew there." She ended her little monologue on a breathless lilt.

"Your dad lives in Memphis?" Of course, she could be from almost any part of the state, even from Arkansas or—

"Greenville. That's in—"

"Mississippi," he said happily. "I was just there. In fact, I came up this morning by car." He had hired a friend to drive him up and paid him with the last of his marijuana and forty bucks for gas.

"Small world, Mr. Shay!"

Both were laughing like old friends.

He thought back over her introduction. Greenville…

"Did you say your name was Sylvia—"

Again, she interrupted as he spoke the last name also. "Bowden," they said in unison.

He would stake his life on this. Trudy never said his last name, not even his first name. He was simply "the doctor." But hadn't the officers at the police station called his name? Wasn't it—

"Is your father a doctor there?"

"Where? In Greenville? Yeah, Leland too. He has to drive around sometimes to see patients." She pronounced it almost as the blacks did—*Green vil*, heavier on the first syllable but not as light on the second one. That pleased him for some reason.

She touched his forearm, palm flat on his sleeve. She did not move her hand away once she had his attention. "You know my dad?"

He thought about his answer to that. *Yes, I'm pretty sure he was screwing my friend. I think he had something to do with two men's deaths at my house. I'm sure they were big-time drug dealers. Maybe your old man was in on it, too.*

He couldn't believe this coincidence. He was sitting beside the daughter of a man who may or may not have been involved in unsavory acts with a black girl the same age as his own daughter, a black girl Shay had cared about.

But he could not be so Medean—he would not destroy the child (this pretty girl) to gain revenge against the father (the doctor). He had accepted that that brief part of his life was just that—a brief part. The children, he understood, would go home to her relatives in Chicago. They would be safe and loved. The doctor—well, the doctor might shit himself if…

"I do not, but I think I met him once a short while ago." He smiled at her. She smiled back. There was no mistaking this look. She was interested in what he had to say. Not just about her father.

"We were both—"

What were we? Choose the safest answer.

"We were witnesses to a crime and were asked to come into the police station to give as much information about it as possible. Did he mention anything to you about…about a crime involving a dead woman and her baby?"

She looked concerned, her mouth turned down at the corners. "Yes, he did, but just that this girl died from drugs and even her baby died from exposure."

He couldn't believe that was all she had been told. But he supposed the doctor, like almost any father, wanted to protect his children, especially his daughter, from the harsh realities of life. And, in this case, protect her from his very private life. Shay gave an inner grunt of disgust—protect himself. *Asshole.*

"A little boy named Adrian."

She didn't miss this. "You knew her. She was your friend."

"Yes. And your father was right. She was—she died from a drug overdose." He sighed heavily, stretched his legs. He noticed her hand was back on his sleeve, fluttering above it as she said comforting things.

"I'm sorry…that poor baby. Are you all right now?"

He thought seriously about the question. He was going back to the life he knew. He did not know the life Trudy had lived. He was at best a peripheral participant in it. Would he have met her if not for his own research? He doubted it. He was glad he had met her. Loved her. But he knew, even if she had lived (and how he wished she had!), he would have moved on. He would have had to move on. His interactions with the tragic girl told him he was not enough for her to give up her habit. If her children weren't enough, he knew he never would be.

"I think I'll be OK."

He gave his seatmate in first class a bright smile. The flight attendant had poured each a glass of white wine (both had been carded, and both had laughed at that) and left a small fruit-and-cheese basket between them to share.

They clinked the glasses together.

"You didn't say what part of Illinois your friend lives in…Sylvie."

As they winged over the hills of Missouri, they shared their stories of classwork and classmates, professors and exams. When he, in explaining some tricky part of his qualifying exam, had laid his hand on her knee, she did not pull away.

As the captain was telling the passengers about the Gateway Arch in Saint Louis, she whipped out her cell phone and showed him pictures from her summer in Suriname. The girl she was visiting was Caucasian, but he saw there were two people who were obviously black and a third person, a scrawny boy, who could have been Latino or mixed. In all the photos, Sylvia (he would call her Sylvia) was smiling or laughing, not the fake *say cheese* smile but one that reached her bright-blue eyes.

She showed him a photo of the doctor. (Yes, that was him, all right.) The picture must have been taken over ten years ago. Though balding, he had thick blond hair around the crown of his head. He was surrounded by two boys and a girl. When Shay looked closer, he saw that it was the girl beside him. The boys were her brothers, she said in mock complaint.

He noticed there was no mother in any photos. (She showed him about a dozen, commenting on each one, as if he would know about the people in them.) Nor did she mention one. Was the good doctor a widower?

"You lost your mom?" He wondered if he should have asked. Perhaps the pain was still there, beneath the calmness and happiness of her exterior.

She made a sound at the back of her throat. "Well, let's say she lost *us*. My dad raised us." She gave him a look that said not to push this anymore. He didn't.

When the flight attendant offered them another glass of wine, both refused, but he asked for more strawberries and teased the girl by feeding a berry to her, bit by bit.

He would see her soon, he promised as they touched down at O'Hare. She said she hoped so and boldly asked for his cell phone. He handed it over, curious as to her actions. Once he unlocked it, she pecked through the prompts until she got to contacts. She typed in her name, cell number, and e-mail address.

"Now you have no excuse *not* to see me, Shay."

At baggage claim, he helped her with her one bag. The girl was there to pick her up, and he was hiring a limousine to take him home. Introductions were made. The girl gave him a polite but uninterested look.

"Enjoy your stay," he said to Sylvia, not sure if their little flirtation on the plane could endure the light of reality.

"I will, I will," she crowed delightedly, smiling at her friend. As he prepared to walk away, his sleeve was caught, and he looked to see Sylvia next to him; the girl, Sarah, was standing off to the side.

"I'll call you tonight," he said, not sure he would or not.

He felt his hand squeezed.

"And I shall answer," she quipped, causing him to laugh.

He watched her sail off with her friend. Yes, he liked that girl. And he knew he would be calling her that very night.

Chapter 30

(Two Years Later)

JEREMY PARKERSON HAD been Belinda's gynecologist since she moved to Memphis, so well over ten years. His diplomas and certificates bore testimony to his good standing in the medical community and the love his patients had for him. Belinda was no exception.

She liked him for his professionalism. He could look her in the eye and explain that the itching she had was a mild case of a yeast infection and recommend an over-the-counter remedy that should work wonders, after having peered, poked, and prodded as deeply into her as Angelo had. Thank God she enjoyed her husband's touch over this clinical probing.

He sat now looking intently into her eyes, his brown gaze soulful and caring. She thought that he could tell a woman anything—cancer, no baby, an anomaly that would leave her crippled—and she would be able to take it, leave his office peacefully with that life-altering knowledge, because of those eyes.

His look now told her in no uncertain terms that he had news that would not be good.

"How long have you been bleeding this heavily, Belinda?" He snapped off the latex gloves—she was not allergic—and flipped them into a nearby garbage can labeled *Hazardous Waste.*

Idly, she thought that her secretions—her *humoral exudates*—were hazardous, dangerous. *This is menstrual blood, a simple indication that, of course, I'm not pregnant.*

That was why she was here, because of the bleeding—for him to tell her… *something.*

"It's not cancer, is it, Dr. Parkerson?" Belinda's back stiffened, ready to hear this. Yes, ovarian, uterine, cervical—a woman's cancer, one that could rob her of her *womanness*.

The doctor looked confused for a moment. He shook his head slightly.

"What? No." Then he gave her his smile that made women either fall in love with him or at least regret that he knew intimate details about their private parts and had no interest in them beyond these four walls.

"No cancer, Belinda. Numerous fibroids."

Those words hit Belinda like a kick to her abdomen. She thought back over the last—how many months? Five? Six? God, maybe longer? Yes, her periods had intensified in their flow. Not bad, she thought. Same number of days. Same pattern. Just that heavy days now meant *really* heavy days. She was here because her period had gone off two weeks ago and had come back on over the weekend. That had never happened before.

Her periods never bothered her; unlike Geetha, the little Indian woman who worked in the same office of the Department of Education branch in Memphis, she had not had to go home, lie down. Or like Gabriella, whose personality split from being a nice, calm woman into a screaming banshee. Belinda never had cramps or mood swings. Lately, just heavier flow. Now, to be told she had fibroids. But the doctor had said no cancer. That was a relief.

During her pelvic exam, the blood had flowed so freely that Dr. Parkerson had remarked that it was as if someone had actually stabbed her.

"What are we going to do?" she cried, more surprised than scared.

The doctor sat back in his chair, steepled his fingers, looked at his patient over them. "There are a few options: none of them particularly problematic."

He produced some brochures, handed them over to her. When she went to open one, he covered her hand with his own, stopping her actions.

"Take them home, read them over, and we can make another appointment to discuss the best treatment for you. Some are invasive, some not so much. Others are more drastic—and more permanent—than others."

This last part disturbed Belinda.

"Dr. Parkerson, are you talking about a hysterectomy?" She knew women who had fibroids. Some older women had had their uterus removed, gone into early menopause, younger friends who had had the tumors removed by surgery. They invariably grew back, some had argued. There were still others who had had the uterine fibroid embolization procedure. That seemed the best option. Why read the brochures? She was going to choose that route. She told her gynecologist.

"Then, we can talk about dates and times—when to start, Belinda." He smiled a little. "Are you sure you don't want to talk this over with Angelo?"

She spread her hands. "He would agree with this; I know it."

"And you do want children?" he said, considering, his brows furrowing.

Belinda waited. Another shoe was about to drop. She was sure of it.

"Even with the procedure, you may have difficulty getting pregnant"—he sighed—"and carrying the baby full term. Not all the time. Just laying it all on the line for you."

Belinda gathered her purse, an expensive frippery she had seen in a little shop off Union in Midtown and couldn't resist—leather, trimmed in gold-colored metal, money not well spent, but she felt like treating herself these days.

"I...I probably won't be getting pregnant anytime soon." She had adjusted to Angelo's sterility. And now, with the new development in their lives, she was thinking that he was also adjusting.

She mentioned that new development, which he knew about. Dr. Parkerson watched television; he listened to the radio; he read the papers. The Higginbothams' new *development* was all over the media.

"How's that going, anyway, Belinda? I read the article in the paper yesterday." Dr. Parkerson had stood also, but he had his hand on the door; he was not ready to let her leave yet, Belinda could tell.

She smiled, and her happiness, despite the news he had just delivered, bubbled over. She thought once more how much she and Angelo's lives had changed in the last two years.

Angelo had earned his master's, had received a very nice increase in pay. More responsibility but also more freedom in his job. Her work was steady, and the pay, always when working with the government, was great. But that was not the new development—at least, not the one that made her want to sing. And since she could not sing a lick, that was happiness, indeed!

The article Dr. Parkerson referred to was in a small newspaper with a small readership but obviously large enough to catch the doctor's eyes.

Kidnappers Set to Adopt Children!

The title of the article was designed to shock, she knew. Angelo had threatened to sue, but the editor had assured them they would be shown in the best possible light. Somehow, the paper had got hold of the paperwork from two years ago down in Greenville. Even though there had been no charges pressed against them, someone from the Greenville Police Department had talked to the press—maybe that female cop. What was her name? Darnika O'Neal—she had said that Belinda and Angelo had rescued the children from an alley and that the DA had wanted at the time to file kidnapping charges against them. Though she had been clear in her statements that no such charges were brought against the couple—*a couple of heroes*, she intoned to the press—the newspaper had chosen to go with the title.

That was six months ago.

Now the paper reported on a monthly basis the progress of the case that, to her and Angelo, wasn't a case at all.

Dolly and Truman Jenkins (*Yes, we got married!* Dolly had screamed over the phone to Belinda and Angelo, who was listening on the extension) had relocated to Memphis, quite near Belinda and Angelo. They loved the city, she said. Besides, she was from the South, she gurgled. Coming home.

Truman got a job as a senior accountant with a small firm downtown, and Dolly worked as a home health-care nurse for *old, rich people*. "In that Germantown you guys have. I got the training from all those years in the hospital," she told the Higginbothams.

Before long, the Jenkinses were regular visitors at the Higginbothams' home. The visits eventually turned into allowing the kids to spend the occasional weekend. Then, one day, over coffee, Dolly spoke quite frankly to them.

"I was talking to True-man, and he and I think—we agree…" She looked at her husband, and he nodded, squeezing her hand. "We would like to know if you would like to adopt Matthew and Sasha."

Belinda and Angela had stared at the couple, convinced they had heard quite wrong.

"What?"

"Adopt. I'm not getting any younger, and they love you."

If she were looking for some agreement in her statement about her getting older, there was none. Though in her sixties, she had the look and energy of a woman almost half her age. And her husband, much younger, they had discovered, loved her and was blind to any hint of aging in her. So that argument was weak as water.

"But you're their guardians. Legally." Angelo refilled their glasses with tea.

Truman loved this man's tea. In fact, Angelo could cook like a chef when he put his mind to it!

The children were in the room that even the Higginbothams had started calling the *children's room* playing a coloring game. Matthew had turned into a handsome boy, and Sasha was a beauty.

"We'd still be right here, but as grandparents. You both know as well as Dolly and I do that they would have no problem calling you Mama and Daddy. They never called anyone that before." Every once in a while, Truman looked like a grieving father.

"Yeah, but—" Angelo looked as if he had been hit by a lightning bolt.

"If you're thinking about that time back in Greenville, don't worry. We know you were doing the right thing."

So the next day, Angelo called Mr. Sweeney, who, just as surprised at this suggestion, said he would look into it.

"It can take time, and it could get complicated," he warned.

Only, there were no real complications, just time.

The adoption became something of a cause célèbre. There were the naysayers who argued that the Jenkinses were being railroaded into giving up the children due to their ages. That was utter rot, and Truman had no problem firing off on them in a public forum; the local radio stations ate it up. The supporters thought the Jenkinses were being totally unselfish in their love for the children and that the Higginbothams were equally unselfish by opening up their home and their hearts to the siblings.

The right-wingers did their best to color Fat Boy and Trudy as "dangerous and abusive drug addicts who willingly and with forethought did abandon their children." This time, Truman and Dolly did sue, getting Mr. Sweeney to represent their case of defamation of character and libel.

Even Belinda's mother weighed in by telling her daughter and son-in-law that sometimes God closed a door just to open a window. Angelo ignored that platitude and accepted that he was looking forward to being what he thought he would be forever denied: the opportunity to be a father. Belinda's mother thought they should put the announcement in the newspaper, like a birth or an engagement.

"Ma," wailed Belinda, "there is no need for us to do anything. The media are all over this. All we wanted was to help."

Her mother had kissed her on the forehead, like when Belinda was a little girl. "Baby, you did. And now look how that one act has turned out!"

Belinda said, yes, wasn't that something. Then, her mother handed her the newspaper. Belinda expected to see another terribly written article about the adoption, but instead it was the society section.

"Who's getting married this time, Ma?" Her mother followed births, weddings, and funerals. *From the cradle to the grave*, Belinda thought.

"A boy I used to know—he's younger than me, but I knew him when we lived out in the country."

She handed the paper to Belinda. The engagement photo showed a tall white man: bald, handsome, and smiling. He looked fit and happy. His name was Henry Bowden. Next to him was a dark woman who on first glance looked black. Her name was Marina Rupasinghe. Belinda wondered what kind of name that was. She was tall and beautiful.

"Says here he's a doctor—that both are."

Her mother nodded, studied the photo. "Buck—we called him Buck. They say he was doing a little shady stuff for a while. You know how people talk. But I never believed it of him. Buck was one of the nicest boys back then."

Belinda was only mildly interested. "Like what?"

Her mother shooed the gossip away with a wave of her hand. "Drugs—not using them, getting people to sell them. I don't believe it. There was even talk about his having something to do with those two babies you and Angelo are adopting."

Belinda perked up. "What?"

"Yeah, something about him knowing that girl who died. Those are her babies, you know."

"Trudy—her name was Trudy. He knew her?" Belinda thought back over the last two years. Had his name ever come up? She recalled Shay's name, Fat Boy's, too, but no one else. The children had never mentioned him, and neither had the Jenkinses.

"Hmph, like I said, people gossip. I saw Buck last year over in Greenville, same as always, friendly like he was when he was a little red-necked boy on the farm. No, I don't believe he was doing anything of the sort, and I never will."

"So you're going to the wedding, Ma?" Belinda was in the mood to tease her mother now. The doctor would not figure into the adoption process, good or bad.

"Sassy miss! I could if I wanted. Buck is like that. But I think I'll go to his daughter's wedding instead." She whipped the page around, and Belinda was once more staring at a photo of an engaged couple. The girl was blond, quite pretty, but not overly beautiful. There was a resemblance to the doctor in the smile and the eyes. The groom was literally tall, not so dark, and handsome—a black man. Though the South was changing and interracial couples were on the rise without much commentary, it could still be a surprise to see.

The groom-to-be was named William Sire (which she read as *sire* and wondered about that odd middle name) Gallagher. Her name was Sylvia Bowden. He hailed from Chicago, and she had graduated from Mississippi State University with a degree in biochemistry with a concentration in plant pathology. The brief article said that he was going to work in the private sector with some large pharmaceutical company, and she would be entering graduate school in Illinois. The date of the wedding as well as the location was the same as her father's.

"A double wedding? So you *are* going!"

Her mother laughed at the joke she had played on her daughter. "Buck keeps in contact with a lot of the folks from the place. His best *men* are some boys who were his best *friends* back then: Jimmy and Jason Something-or-Other." She looked at the picture critically. "That's a handsome boy, isn't it?" Belinda laughed with her mother and agreed that this William Sire Gallagher was indeed very handsome.

And within a day, she had forgotten all about the doctor, his daughter, or the fact that her mother was attending their weddings.

Now Belinda walked out of Dr. Parkerson's office and into the arms of Angelo. He greeted the doctor quietly. She knew that he was worried about the excess bleeding, but she eased his mind by whispering that there was no cancer, his biggest concern. She would explain about the fibroids later.

She felt him tremble in relief as he held her to him. She did not think he would do more than hug her or maybe give her a peck on the cheek. She was pleasantly surprised when he held her close and kissed her quite thoroughly, to the utter delight of a very pregnant young lady and a manly-looking woman who was holding her hand tightly.

To Belinda, Angelo seemed oblivious to this unconventional couple; he had eyes only for her. Her face heated with a rush of feelings for him.

He shook hands with the gynecologist. "Doctor."

"Angelo." The doctor spoke in a friendly manner, but he stood there, frankly looking them over. "Whenever you all decide, you know I'm here."

Angelo smiled but said nothing. He cupped Belinda's elbow, ready to escort her out of the outer room.

The doctor walked to the door that led into the hallway and stood there, watching them walk away. Belinda knew he watched them until they left the building. She gave Angelo the brochures, let him peruse them.

"He gave you the options, right?" He started the car. Though she was quite capable of driving herself, he had insisted on taking her, staying in the waiting room, and taking her home.

"Yes, babe, I'm going with UFE. We have to decide on a date to get started. He said getting pregnant could be difficult."

Angelo said nothing about the irony of that statement. The doctor didn't know. Then, a smile crept across his face, starting with his mouth, going into his cheeks, and stopping in his beautiful eyes.

"Well, we'll deal with that." He slipped a CD into the CD player, and the refrain of a blues song filled the air.

Both started laughing. This was their war song, the song that brought them together, that brought the children into their lives, the song that would keep them there. But unlike the song, they had not lost everything; their system was a winning one. Still, Little Milton sang out, appealing to anyone in hearing distance, "Casino Blues." They would not have the blues all the time. Their blues were, in fact, over and done with.

"Let's go pick up our children!" And they were off into the Memphis sun.

Epilogue

(Fifteen Years later)

He had been born here, not too far from this spot. He had once lived in this cold, windy city that was home to award-winning actors, sports teams, and musicians. This city could be called a renaissance city, he supposed. It boasted everything the visitor would want. He sighed, and the heat of his breath condensed the water molecules he exhaled, making his breath look like steam. He knew this factoid because, according to his grandmother, he had science in his genes, from his father. He didn't know about that.

Just like he didn't recall his time here. There were flashes of him with his grandfather, his granny. He was small; his grandfather was talking, sometimes smiling. His granny with a treat. A cookie? Maybe.

There were other flashes—a young man with a smiling face and his eyes. That was his father. He was sure of that. Sometimes, he could hear the young man's voice, addressing him directly. *Matthew, you are one smart boy! Babe, can you believe it? He's actually reading this book!* The pride and love he heard in his mind from this man were unmistakable.

Matthew reckoned the *baby* this man—his father—addressed was his mother. A pretty face floated into his mind's eye: thick dark hair, an Afro with long, tight curls all over her oval face. She was smiling proudly at this announcement. *Of course, he's smart; he's* my *Matthew!* He sometimes wondered if he imagined her response just because of the love he heard in it. Or the tight hugs he received—from both. Did he remember these truly, or did he simply *want* them to be real?

He remembered the pretty, oval face changing, growing hard and sad, vacant and lost—empty, no words sometimes. He remembered the pipe, the hunger that came with it, the pain.

He gazed down at the four headstones. He read them as he chose to, not in order of death, maybe in order of life. His father first (*BELOVED SON AND FATHER*, the block letters read, etched into the white marble), Adrian Ricketts. He shook his head. He was only a few years shy of his own father's age when he died. Then he moved over, skipping a headstone. OUR BABY ADRIAN. He remembered him clearly, his baby brother, Adrian. He even recalled that he seldom thought of him as just Adrian or baby. He was usually *our baby Adrian*, as if he *belonged* to them. And in a way, he did. He had. He'd lived only a few months. He recalled his toothless grin when he was tickled, his gaping mouth when he cried for food (again, the young man sighed), which had been often back then, back before, back before their baby Adrian went to sleep that cold night and never woke up.

Back before…He took a step back to the tombstone he'd skipped. TRUDESSA JENKINS. Just a year older than he was now. He wondered why she—his mother—was buried next to his father, next to Fat Boy, as if they were husband and wife. He supposed in a way they were. He had it on good authority that, even though there were *extenuating* circumstances, his parents had loved each other. Once. Fiercely.

He adjusted his coat about his broad shoulders. He was taller by an inch than Fat Boy, his grandmother said, broader in the shoulders, too. But just as handsome, she asserted. To know that he resembled his father made him…happy, he supposed, especially since he barely remembered him.

The snow fell like white shadows before his eyes, landing on his lashes, his skin, where it melted immediately, cooling his skin. It had been snowing all day long. He lifted his feet, and the boots he wore were sunk in the white stuff. He gave a small smile. In Memphis, the place he called home, it snowed rarely, and when it did, the city simply wasn't prepared: accidents, skids, closings. And this was for only a few *inches*. Here, in this place, a few *feet* of snow and the people still milled about, going to work, to school, riding buses and driving cars. The South was nothing like this place of smoldering heat in the summer and freezing cold in the winter. Had he liked it when he was a child?

He was told of stories when he and his younger sister, Sasha, would cry to play in the snow, to have snowballs thrown at them, both laughing madly as the frozen spheres of ice made contact with their well-protected little bodies. Though the memory was more imaginary than real, he so wanted to believe he did remember it. Happy times.

Five years ago, he had been given his father's music collection. Of course, it was worthless. And unexpected. Even now, with so many artists crossing over, gathering followers of practically every cultural and racial background, his father's taste in music was still astonishing. Matthew had never heard of most of them. And all were either old or dead or dead and old. Country and western: when he'd listened in surprised awe, being assured by both his granny and his poppa that the artists were indeed his father's favorites, he'd had to laugh. He'd laughed until tears came to his eyes, and he told himself he'd laughed until he'd cried over this ironic twist.

But, no, he'd cried because he'd had a memory, a real one, of his father dancing his mother around their cramped apartment (he remembered how small their place was!), singing some song. Lord, the tears had not stopped. Lyle Lovett! The words, those words…something about the man's "baby" not tolerating stuff from him, how he stayed out late and came home to not only a cold shoulder but no food, no wine. Some things just weren't to be tolerated: like using crack, like neglecting your three children until death was an inevitable result, until you died yourself.

He *remembered.* The look on that couple's faces, his parents' faces, was love, was unmistakable.

The memory and the tears were cathartic for him. He knew now he had loved his parents; he knew this fact without being told by his grandparents, without taking the memory from a photo or two. He knew they loved him, *his father and his mother.*

He went to the last of the four marble blocks—his grandmother. Again, the simple epitaph: ODESSA JENKINS, BELOVED WIFE AND MOTHER. His pops talked of her a lot, even though he was happily married to his second wife. (Could a relationship get any stranger? His maternal grandfather marrying his paternal great-grandmother!) She had been a great wife and mother, his pops had said. His uncle, Trudy's younger brother, remembered her and agreed on that. Sometimes, his pops said, he could see her in Sasha. Had even seen Trudy in Odessa.

He addressed the four tombstones as if the people buried beneath them in the frozen ground could hear him. He stood directly before his grandmother's.

"Pops said you loved to garden, that nothing ever grew"—here, he chuckled at his grandfather's laughter—"but you never gave up. He said he loved that about you. He said you used that same spirit to live as long as you did with that cancer, said you fought it off like you fought to grow those seeds and plants. I'm gonna do my best to have that same fighting spirit, Grandma."

He moved to Fat Boy. He could say only one thing that told his entire feelings.

"I just wish they would have taken the cash and left." He wiped his eyes, stinging from the numbing cold and from his grief. He knew what his father's "business" was what had led to his untimely and tragic death. He found it ironic, he supposed, that he had, since he was a teenager, smoked the very drug that had been his father's livelihood. He knew, too, that his parents worried. Would he graduate to a worse drug? Would he end up like Adrian, his father? He dabbed at his eyes again. He would die an old man, he vowed, maybe a bit mellow, a bit serene, but he would die having never tried any other drug, illicit or otherwise. He owed that much to his father. His parents.

He reached down, touched Adrian's marker, said nothing audible, but the breath in the air marked his words: "Our baby Adrian."

He stood before Trudy, his mother. His shoulders heaved as he remembered how he'd watched over her, watched out for her, watched her, and worried over her: how he had wished that she would leave them and never come back, how he'd worried that she'd leave them and never come back.

Then, one day, she didn't come back. All his worrying: too much of a burden for a five-year-old to carry. He touched the cold stone once more.

"Trudy, I can stop worrying now. I stopped worrying. And nothing bad happened, not to me, not to Sasha. I did what you and Fat Boy told me to do: I took care of her." But he couldn't take care of her or their baby Adrian. But he did not say this, feeling that if he put the words on the freezing wind, he would be disloyal to the woman who had once been a very good mother. He turned slowly from the graves, heading toward the vehicle that had brought them to this place.

As he walked, he waved to the pretty young lady standing off to the side.

She came forward, walking slowly, not just because of the snowdrifts but because she had balked at coming here. *Healing*, her parents had said. *Cathartic*, her grandfather had said, always sounding like a retired English professor instead of an accountant nearing retirement age. *They're your* folks, said her feisty granny, never one to mince her words.

She was twenty, a sophisticated junior in college down in Tennessee (at least, *she* preferred to think of herself as sophisticated). She thought coming all the way up to Chicago to visit dead people she did not know or remember was just plain silly. And she did not recall any of them—certainly not her grandmother, dead long before she was even thought of. But she also had no memory of the man they called Fat Boy, her father. Poppa had said she was crazy about him, loved being carried around on his shoulders. She read the brief, unimaginative (to her) epitaphs. She sighed, drew her coat about her shoulders tighter. It never snowed this heavily back home, and, if it did, *sane* people were not outside, walking around, and certainly not in some cemetery! She shivered, more out of indignation now than the freezing cold.

She stared at the tombstones: Trudessa and Adrian. She wished she could remember the baby. There were pictures of all four people all over her grandparents' home back in Memphis. Her grandfather was always saying how much she resembled her mother, his daughter, Trudy.

She could remember saying the word *Trudy* as a kid, but, other than when Matthew mentioned her name, she did not remember *her*. She had tried over the years to bring forth a memory of the pretty girl, but nothing ever came forward.

Her earliest memory was of her and her brother running, running, running. Was there someone with them, running also? She always thought, *Yes*, but whom? In that memory, there was a feeling of terror. How old was she? She had a flash. Three, her small fingers held up for *whom* to see? She drew a blank.

Her next clear memory was when she and her brother settled into bed with their parents, Angelo and Belinda Higginbotham, standing over them, smiling and wishing them a good night. She was five; she knew that because Matthew was in second grade, and he brought home his books to show her the stories in them. She was in kindergarten then, but his books were always more exciting, and who liked coloring or doing silly finger-painting? Some of his books had just *words*. Those were her favorites. She could use her own imagination to decide how long the girl's hair was or how dark her skin was.

She adjusted the wool hat over her thick hair. *That's your daddy's hair!* Who said that? Her grandfather often said something like that but not exactly those words. Granny? Maybe, but was that her voice? She was eighty-three, as feisty and fit as ever, but, even with age, her voice had not changed. That was not her voice.

Slowly, as if her head were on a motorized column, she drew her eyes to the marker again. TRUDESSA. Could it—

But she was so young when her birth mother had died; she recalled nothing about—

Running again, crying. Hair flying, someone laughing, a deep, robust laughter that—

Being caught up in arms, squirming, still crying. *She never likes her hair combed.*

The laughter, patient, amused. *Yeah, 'cause it's* thick, *just like yours!*

She touched her hair, removed the cap. It *was* thick, and she *did* hate having it combed. Her friend Janada at school always teased her. *Girl, when I first saw that hair of yours, I thought it was a brown helmet on your head!*

Being—

Was it Mama, Belinda, talking to Dad, Angelo? But—

She smiled, the tears of memory mixing with the tears of cold. Not her mother or her father.

But that's precisely who it was: her mother Trudy combing her hair and her hating it, her father Adrian laughing and telling her to just wait awhile and she would be a pretty girl. *Didn't she want to be a pretty girl like her mommy?* A memory of her settling in arms, warm and comfortable. Love? Unmistakably yes. She was loved by these people she had thought she could not remember.

Her grandmother was right. She needed this, needed to know that *somewhere, sometime*, she had been loved by her birth parents, to know that she'd loved them. *Once upon a time.* Like the beginning of so many of the books she'd read from her childhood.

She turned to the two couples standing near the car that had brought them here. Her great-grandmother was held in a firm embrace by her grandfather. He was in his early sixties now, handsome, funny. Her granny, smart, beautiful even now, and damn strong. Poppa was dedicated to her, even though he pointed out things his first wife, her grandmother, loved. Granny's common-law husband had died last year in prison. *His grave is somewhere around here*, she thought.

Her own grandfather had been paroled three months earlier, Granny's son and therefore Fat Boy's—*Adrian Senior's*—father. They would visit him later in the housing the city provided for…for men like *him*, she thought, instantly ashamed of the fact that she was ashamed of her grandfather.

She walked toward them, her eyes now on her parents.

Belinda smiled at her approaching daughter. It was funny. She never thought of her as once belonging to anyone else, only to her and Angelo—the same for Matthew. She and Angelo never got pregnant themselves. In fact, five years ago, she decided—the UFE procedure had been successful but not in preventing the growth of new tumors—simply to have the hysterectomy. Now they had no chance ever of getting pregnant. But had there ever been?

It had been fifteen years since they adopted the two children, fifteen years since the newspapers and televisions jumped on their private bandwagon. But it was a lifetime to Belinda.

She would never say this adoption was the easiest thing she and Angelo had ever done. The children's teenage years were a nightmare to them. As if overnight, the helpful, playful Sasha became a screeching, crying shrew. Matthew became a silent monolith around the house, oftentimes not deigning to speak to anyone or acknowledge their presence. Her and Angelo's questions and requests were met with grunts and eye rolling, as if whatever they said to the teens was the silliest, stupidest, most moronic idea to be conceived by a human.

Belinda often sought understanding in her mother's kitchen down in Mississippi or Dolly's living room five minutes east of them. She listened to her friends and coworkers. *Do you drink? Don't worry, you will,* they all asserted. But, of course, she did not.

Her mother would laugh and shake her head. "You can't remember being the same way?"

"Most certainly not," Belinda responded, indignant at such a suggestion.

"Well, you were." Her mother patted her on the shoulder and forgot all about it.

Would she have adopted them if she had known raising them would be so hard, so demanding of her time and patience? She never gave that thought a second one. Yes, without a doubt!

Then, just when Belinda decided that she and Angelo might be happier living in their cars to avoid the teeth sucking, the pursed lips, and the raised brows, the behavior stopped. That was three years ago. Sasha suddenly needed her opinion on her clothes, her hairstyle (*natural, yes, always*, they decided), friends. And boys.

Belinda was no fool. If her daughter expressed an interest in a boy, any boy, she listened, *really* listened to what the girl was *not* saying. Then, she would talk about a fictitious cousin.

I was talking to Susie last night, and her boyfriend told her he wasn't feeling *her going back to school for nursing.* Her daughter was adamant that any man who didn't support his girlfriend's career aspirations wasn't worth it.

She should get rid of him; kick him to the curb!

Belinda's ploy had worked. The boys who wondered at Sasha's study habits or desire to go into research were made short shrift of.

The same cousin met men who threatened her with bodily harm, slept around, borrowed huge sums of money with no intention of paying her back, used drugs to the point of self-destruction, or lost job after job, or left in a huff over the smallest self-perceived infraction. The girl spoke vehemently and passionately on the hapless woman's love life and her choices in male companionship.

Of course, Belinda never confessed about the nonexistent cousin, and the girl never forgot her own words. Belinda had met her daughter's latest unlikely lothario, a lanky, bespectacled engineering major who had the driest sense of humor Belinda had ever known. She adored him but was smart enough not to let Sasha know. Contrariness was not heritable, but they both had a lot of it between them.

Matthew liked hanging with his father, at football or basketball games, mostly, but it was there that they bonded the most. Though he grazed his mother's cheek instead of bestowing an actual kiss upon it, he did so with regularity and without any prompting from her. Oddly, they bonded over laundry, folding towels or sorting underwear. He would tell her snippets of his life, leaving her to fill in the gaps, which she was happy to do.

Her bosom swelled with pride, with love. Sometimes, she was jolted into reality—these were not her birth children, but did that really matter? When Sasha was that devoted child or the screaming teen, or now, the young lady on the threshold of womanhood, she never said the words that would have left Belinda curled up in a corner, desolate and bereft: *You're not my mother*.

Belinda leaned against Angelo, a soft smile on her face. Angelo rubbed her shoulders and back. He thought of removing the gloves from his hand to make skin-to-skin contact with her, but damn, it was cold! Despite the weather, he'd wanted to make this trip. He felt they should be commemorating something, but what? An anniversary? No, more some type of memoriam.

Through Dolly and Truman, he had gotten to know Fat Boy and Trudy—before the drugs destroyed their lives. Fat Boy lost his in an attempt to save Trudy's. They'd loved each other, he was told by the Jenkinses, and he believed this.

Fat Boy and Trudy's love for each other was shown in those two children that through a miracle became theirs. He recalled those years of exasperation he shared with Belinda raising tweens and teens. His patience and her practicality were the best combination to raise two headstrong kids.

He wouldn't say they were perfect. No good parent would.

He had discovered that Matthew smoked pot, had started at eighteen, and had lost his virginity at nineteen. Though he objected, his only advice had been to use that condom (infertility was not genetic, he told himself, forgetting, as always, that it didn't matter if it was or not—these were not his biological children) and not to graduate to any other drug or smoke it in public. Eventually, he assured his son, even Tennessee would have to see the sense in decriminalizing this herb. But he found it funny, telling his buddies Tyson and Dave that his son had smoked before he poked.

Sasha gave her friendship and trust too soon. By the time she was thirteen, she realized that a friend was not one who received always. Sometimes they were supposed to give. Through her many bewildered tears, she had to learn that life lesson the hard way.

He and Belinda had even adopted that age-old practice, without knowing they had, of owning the children preferentially.

Your son took the car when he was expressly told not to.

My daughter got all A's!

Your daughter/son is driving me crazy!

He sighed in contentment as everyone settled into the SUV he'd rented to drive around the frozen city. He would not miss it when they returned to the relative warmth of Memphis. But he would take back with him a little more than the snow and ice. He would carry across those state lines, much like Belinda had so long ago, memories and love. But this time, there would be no hysteria or panic. This time, they would all make the trek together, willingly, lovingly. He cranked the engine, turned the heat up.

He let Matthew dictate the music they would listen to. He grinned at the choice the youth made. He recognized the trembling timbre of the long-haired Texan's voice. He didn't know the song, but he knew it was country and western. *Where had he picked up a taste in that?* he wondered, lifting an eyebrow at Belinda.

She grinned, too, and he was struck by how she resembled the young woman he'd met over twenty years ago and, had he been able to look across the ridge into the future, would have known how to respond to her question, "What's happening in your life?"

He would have answered her, enigmatic, "You are, and it's going to be a great one—just wait and see!"

He picked up the refrain of the song and sang along with the man and his son.

They all sang about the winding road, how they all had arrived here, in their own promised land.

The Birth of *Casino Blues*

In actual fact, *Casino Blues* began and ended for several years as a short story that I was lucky enough to get published in an anthology by Ana Monnar called *For Your Eyes Only*. The people who read the short story liked it, even gave very good comments about it, and I thought, *Well, that's that.* Then, my niece wondered, *What happened next?* That ubiquitous question was one that I had always given to *great* literature. Was my short story not complete? Was it worthy of that question?

So, on the advice of my (now *favorite*) niece, I revisited the story of a woman who kidnaps two abandoned children, seemingly (at the time of the short story) to have her and her stupefied husband raise them together. As I revisited these people, I got to know the mother of those children better, their father, and even a little about their extended family. I took great pleasure in developing these characters into flesh-and-blood people whom you may meet on the street, speak to, but never know their true story.

The birthing process was difficult, as any real mother will tell you, but once the child is born (in this case, my fifth novel), the pain fades to a distant memory, replaced by joy and love.

I'm grateful for the people who read the manuscript and gave me the encouragement to pursue its story to the end. I'm grateful to AM, KB, and TC. You all know who you are. I think without your input, I would still be wondering how to tell Trudy's story, how to make Fat Boy real.

I look forward to others getting to know the characters. They may anger you, sadden you. But that's what real people you know do, do they not?

Discussion Questions

1. This is Stiffin's fifth novel. Have you read any of her previous titles?
2. Were you engaged in *Casino Blues*; did it take you time to get into the story?
3. Describe a few main characters. Did they seem real to you, in either their actions or dialogue?
4. What are the dynamics of a couple of your favorite characters? Did they evolve for the better?
5. The plot had a few twists and turns; were you surprised by them? Was the plot formulaic or predictable at all?
6. Stiffin used some interesting ploys: she had one of the characters (Dolly) read Stiffin's own novel (debut novel, *Walk in Bethel*), and she made Stanley Driscoll (*A Winter Friend*) a "real" character who interacted with Buck. Have you seen similar techniques in other novels?
7. Dr. Henry "Buck" Bowden literally got away with murder. What are your thoughts on this?
8. Stiffin said *Casino Blues* was a short story that developed into a novel. Did the novel read as a continuous story or interlocking short stories?
9. Were there certain passages that resonated with you? Why?
10. Were the characters' actions the result of their own choices, or did destiny play a hand?
11. Does the setting figure in as a character? Knowing that the locales are real, does that make them real to you, like the bistro where Belinda and Angelo first meet or Betty's Place in Indianola?
12. Is the ending satisfying to you? Uplifting, pessimistic?
13. Why do you think Stiffin wrote this novel?
14. If you could ask the author one question, what would it be?

Other Titles by Rose Mary Stiffin, PhD

Walk in Bethel
Winner in International Competition in General Fiction, 2015 and 2017

Reflections

Groovin' on the Half Shell

A Winter Friend

All titles available as e-books and paperbacks from Amazon.com or CreateSpace. Visit rosestiffin.com.

To book Stiffin to speak about her novels or her work, please contact her at rose.stiffin@yahoo.com.

50778905R10148

Made in the USA
Columbia, SC
16 February 2019